COMMAND THE MORNING

By Pearl S. Buck

FRIEND TO FRIEND [with Carlos P. Romulo]

MY SEVERAL WORLDS

THE CHILD WHO NEVER GREW

AMERICAN ARGUMENT   HOW IT HAPPENS

TALK ABOUT RUSSIA   TELL THE PEOPLE

WHAT AMERICA MEANS TO ME   AMERICAN UNITY AND ASIA

OF MEN AND WOMEN   FIGHTING ANGEL

THE EXILE

*

THE CHINESE NOVEL

[NOBEL PRIZE LECTURE]

*

LETTER FROM PEKING

IMPERIAL WOMAN   THE HIDDEN FLOWER

GOD'S MEN   COME, MY BELOVED   PEONY

FAR AND NEAR   PAVILION OF WOMEN

KINFOLK

PORTRAIT OF A MARRIAGE

THE PROMISE   DRAGON SEED

TODAY AND FOREVER

OTHER GODS   THE PATRIOT

THIS PROUD HEART

A HOUSE DIVIDED   THE MOTHER

THE FIRST WIFE AND OTHER STORIES

SONS   THE GOOD EARTH

EAST WIND: WEST WIND

*

VOICES IN THE HOUSE

BRIGHT PROCESSION   THE TOWNSMAN

THE ANGRY WIFE   THE LONG LOVE

*

ALL MEN ARE BROTHERS

[SHUI HU CHÜAN]

TRANSLATED FROM THE CHINESE

*

CHRISTMAS MINIATURE

MY SEVERAL WORLDS [Abridged for Younger Readers]

THE BEECH TREE

JOHNNY JACK AND HIS BEGINNINGS   ONE BRIGHT DAY

THE BIG WAVE

YU LAN: FLYING BOY OF CHINA   THE DRAGON FISH

THE WATER-BUFFALO CHILDREN

THE CHINESE CHILDREN NEXT DOOR   STORIES FOR LITTLE CHILDREN

COMMAND THE MORNING

A NOVEL BY

PEARL S. BUCK

THE JOHN DAY COMPANY, NEW YORK

To

TAD DANIELEWSKI

who joins me in appreciation and gratitude to the many scientists who so generously shared with us their time and their experience

Then the Lord answered Job out of the whirlwind,
And said;

Gird up now thy loins like a man,
For I will demand of thee,
And answer thou me.

Where wast thou when I laid the foundations
of the earth?
Declare, if thou hast understanding.
Who hast laid the measures thereof,
If thou knowest?
Or who hath stretched the line upon it?
Whereupon are the foundations thereof fastened?
Or who laid the cornerstone thereof?
When the morning stars sang together
And all the sons of God shouted for joy?
Or who shut up the sea with doors when it brake forth,
As if it had issued from the womb?
When I made the cloud the garment thereof,
And the thick darkness a swaddling band for it,
And set bars and doors,
And said,
Hitherto shalt thou come but no further,
And here shall thy proud waves be stayed?

Hast thou commanded the morning? . . .

—The Book of Job: 38;12

I

THE YEAR WAS 1940. In September of 1939 England had declared war against Germany but it was spring again, and Americans were still safe.

Yes, Burton Hall was thinking, we are still safe. It was spring even in California, where the signs of new green and first flowering were always less obvious than in his own small garden in the suburbs of Chicago, which he had left only two days ago, to come here by plane. The plane had been a cause for argument with his wife, Mollie.

"If you're determined to die," she had grumbled, "I wish you'd choose a way that wouldn't leave you in pieces. I want something to bury and make a monument to, anyway."

He had grinned. "Monument! You haven't seen the half of what I'll be doing if we get into this war."

He had planted a loud kiss on her plump cheek and had whirled away to the airport in his old convertible.

Now, forty-eight hours later, he was lunching at the Faculty Club in Berkeley with William Thompson, a fellow scientist. He continued his conversation.

11

"I told Mollie three months ago that we might be in the war by this April. Thank God I'm wrong. I hope I'll always be as thankful when I'm wrong."

Across the table the noonday sun shone through Thompson's big thin ears until they looked like pink butterflies on either side of his pale and narrow face.

"Did you ever see pink butterflies?" Burton Hall asked with irrelevance.

Thompson looked startled. "Butterflies?"

"Pink ones."

Thompson considered seriously, knife and fork poised above his chopped beef. "I never saw them pink."

"I haven't, either," Burton Hall said abruptly. He sawed his way through a slice of thick red roast beef. "Now to go back to what we were talking about—"

They were talking about the war catching fire in Europe and Asia. They were talking about their fellow scientists, escaping from Germany and Poland, Austria and Hungary, to shelter first in France and then in England, and now flocking into the United States, bringing their fearful stories.

"Think we can keep out of it?" Thompson inquired. He finished the last bits of meat on his plate and put his knife and fork side by side, neatly and exactly.

"We can't escape," Burton Hall said. He was a big man, tall and lean, heavy-boned, red-haired, bold in profile, his green eyes set deep under bushy red brows.

"I suppose not." Thompson's high listless voice betrayed no concern beyond weariness. In the same mild manner he continued. "The Nazis are already working on atomic energy. They have the theory of separating uranium 235. That might mean that they intend to make an atomic bomb, though Fermi doesn't think they can. . . ."

Burton Hall scanned the menu, searching for apple pie. "Fermi's hunches!"

12

"His hunches are about one hundred per cent right," Thompson argued.

"About is too much of a chance to take," Burton Hall said. He turned to the waiter. "Apple pie. Make it à la mode. With cheese—"

"I don't see how you can tolerate such concoctions," Thompson said.

"Because I'm a horse," Burton Hall retorted. That high thin voice of Thompson's had the whine of a mosquito. Damn the fellow. He hadn't come here to talk about hypothetical weapons—and knew instantly that he was lying to himself. He had come here in fear and resolution with exactly that purpose, because Thompson was a top scientist and had made a cyclotron whose beams could smash the nucleus of an atom and the most important thing in the world just now was the atom, a minute particle so small that the eye of man could not see it except as a faint sparkle upon a photographic screen. Desire for apple pie faded from him. He leaned forward, his face close to Thompson's surprised and spectacled eyes.

"Are you ready to spend the next year with me getting this damned thing made?"

"If I have to," Thompson said. "Although I'd like to get my cyclotron experiments finished and some sort of conclusion arrived at in time for the big international conference next autumn."

Burton Hall pushed aside the plate of apple pie the waiter set before him. "There's a lot of things we'd like to do that aren't going to get done—not now, anyway. I'm collecting scientists, nothing but the best, raking them in from every corner in industry and universities. My next man after you is Stephen Coast. Know him?"

"Young, isn't he?" Thompson said cautiously.

13

"They've got to be young for this job," Burton Hall said. "Young and daring."

"Aren't you going to eat your apple pie?" Thompson asked.

"No—I'm suddenly not hungry—and I'm supposed to cut out desserts, anyway."

Thompson did not reply. He was counting change, coin by coin, and Burton Hall waited, his green eyes staring bleakly across the crowded room. Eating and drinking in comfort, all these fellows, each of them snug in his little place in the university without a thought of what was ahead! He would call Stephen Coast today. It would be late afternoon in Chicago, late on a Saturday afternoon. Then he would indulge himself. His private secret reason for coming to California was to travel to a certain remote mountain upon whose flattened top stood a giant telescope. There, his human eyes multiplied a million times in power, he would gaze into the mirrored reflection of stars invisible until now, and galaxies fifty thousand light years away from where he stood. As some men turned to God for strength to stay them in times of terror, as others turned to strong drink or lust for women to escape their own horrors, he turned to the stars and the expanding universe.

"Well," he said abruptly. "If there's nothing more to be said, can I count on you, Tommy?"

"If worst comes to worst, Burt."

"It'll come, I'm afraid."

"I hope not."

They shook hands and he climbed into his rented car and headed toward the mountain range beyond the horizon.

* * *

The night was clear. His car climbed the rough road with surprising ease and he rounded the last high shoulder of the

14

mountain, rumbled along the graveled road of the forest and came out at last on the top. There in the faint light of the new moon he saw the immense silvery dome of the largest telescope in the world. Tens of years of the labor of hundreds of men had gone into its building and in the labor several men had died.

If he came this time next year again, and he had come every year since the ground was broken and the bedrock blasted for its foundation, the work would be finished. Unless his country was at war!

He parked his car outside the tall fence of woven wire, showed his pass at the gate and walked into the main entrance. Its simplicity suited his taste. Patterson was waiting for him, Reuben Patterson, the astrophysicist in charge, a Vermonter, thin and sandy and spare of speech.

"Hello, Rube," he said. He paused to look around. "Say, I like this better every year—big and plain, and those hidden lights, red and green, eh? And that curving staircase and everything quiet—rubber floors, I see."

"Introduction to space," Reuben said.

He led the way and Burton Hall followed across the wide foyer and into a small side door. He paused again to gaze into the machinery of the giant telescope. Immense steel beams stretched high above his head and upon four huge piers of concrete the telescope itself was braced and girded and braced again, upon one pier the enormous steel ball-and-socket joint and upon the others the three oil jacks for precise levels. Beyond the vast hall for the machinery necessary to operate this monstrous eye devised by man, were rooms for the astronomers, for sleeping, for eating, for rest and work, each perfectly designed for its purpose. Burton Hall's restless glance comprehended every detail, approved the air conditioning, the furnaces, the hundreds of circuits made of fine copper wires braided by hand as he well knew

15

and years in doing, the machines mounted on pedestals of rubber and springs lest the slightest vibration jar from complete accuracy the single purpose of the whole. Above all was the telescope itself, sheltered under the huge silver dome towering to the sky, and pointing its tubular eye upward to the stars.

In almost total silence Burton Hall now spent the next three hours under the high silver dome. He came out as he had before, a humbled and inspired man. To know how stars are born, how great they grow, how long they live within their firmament, this was his passion and why had he not clung to it?

He turned to Reuben. "Why did I ever get mixed up in cosmic rays? From this"—his long arm swept the circle of the dome—"to the nucleus of an atom, a thing so small I can never hope to see it, is a far, far cry."

Reuben did not smile. "The line is direct from atom to star. You can't miss your way, Burt."

The two men gripped hands and Burton Hall swung down the moonlit road. Eastward against a darker sky he could see the first glitter of snow upon the mountains of the San Bernardino range. Wonderful beauty of Earth and why was it not enough for the restless spirit of man? Why, he inquired of his own soul, must he too pursue the endless knowledge beyond? The cosmic hunger to know! Swerving too close to the perilous cliffs of the narrow and winding road, he drove in unconscious recklessness while he pondered the mystery. There was no escape from the pursuit. When man ceased to want to know, he regressed to savagery. He returned to beast. There was no alternative, the stars or the jungle. . . . And suddenly he remembered that he had forgotten to call Stephen Coast.

*   *   *

A beam of dying sunlight crept across the floor and Stephen Coast sighed. The afternoon was ending, the calm of a Saturday afternoon, and he alone in it. Helen, his wife, was at a bridge party next door. The house was quiet and the hours had passed like minutes here in his basement laboratory. He had nothing to show for his work except a feeding bowl for Scrap, his cocker spaniel. Still, it was what he had planned to do this afternoon, he had done it, and he was satisfied. A stainless-steel dish, set into a sealed container, and in the container an electric coil attached to a battery chamber, meant that Scrap's food would not freeze at night.

One of these days, maybe next week, he would wire the mat in the kennel for the old dog. Helen did not allow dogs in the house and such was the power of her decisive nature that Scrap, always sensitive, could not be persuaded to enter even the kitchen door. Shivering and afraid, he besought his master Stephen not to lead him into temptation.

Six o'clock! Good God—Helen had said that at five o'clock he was please to turn on the oven so that the roast would be done at seven! He washed his hands in haste and leaped up the narrow steps to the kitchen. At the same moment she entered the back door. He stopped, smitten by guilt, and she laughed.

"You forgot to turn on the roast."

"How did you know?"

"Your face always tells me."

She kissed him briefly and turned on the oven.

"I'm sorry, Helen."

"We'll just have dinner an hour later." She took off her hat, a small affair of crimson ribbon, very smart with her black suit, and fluffed her curly dark hair. "What did you do this afternoon—your book?"

For the last five years he had been measuring cosmic rays, those beams of heat invading the earth's atmosphere. He

17

had climbed Himalayan mountains to stand shivering and half frozen in snow, he had descended into the hot depths of mines in the coal regions of Wales to discover their penetration and from his findings it was his task now to weld a book. The book, they agreed, was to be transmuted into that precious material, money, to build the house Helen wanted. He had promised he would reform, that he would not use more money to pay for yet another journey, next time to the equator, to discover what the swelling of the globe at that circle might mean. First the house—

He lifted the lid from a blue porcelain jar which contained cookies. Helen snatched the lid from him and replaced it firmly.

"That's cheating—just because you forgot the roast!"

He yielded, as he did in all small matters.

"You didn't even work on your cosmic ray equations," she announced.

"Is my face that much of a tattletale?" he moaned.

"So what did you do?" she demanded.

"I made that warming bowl for Scrap," he confessed.

"Stephen! All afternoon! For a dog! You promised you'd begin your book today."

"I'm utterly unreliable," he admitted.

She threw him a shrewd glance, her eyes very blue. "And you don't intend to change."

He reflected. "No, I suppose I don't. I haven't time for it."

She laughed her sudden bright laughter, and running to him, she embraced him violently. "You are so adorably honest—and so utterly hateful!"

He endured the embrace with patience. Then, facing her reproachful eyes, he bent from his height and kissed her cheek but so lightly that she seized him by the shoulders and shook him as hard as she could. He was a big man, though spare, and she was a small slender woman, and he was amused and immovable.

"Do you know how long it is since you have made love to me?" she inquired fiercely.

He went on guard at once. "It was a week ago."

She lifted black eyebrows at him and pursed her red mouth. "Two weeks! And if I weren't the most patient woman in the world, married to the most abstracted cold-hearted scientist ever born, I'd—I'd—"

He saw that she paused for his question. "Do what?"

"Run away," she said quickly. "Run far away, even though the night is bitterly cold."

"It would be a great waste of time to run after you," he said, considering, "but I suppose I would have to do it."

She burrowed her head into his breast. "I'd come back if you didn't."

"You would," he agreed. "You certainly would. You couldn't bear not to know what I was doing without you. You'd be afraid I was doing too well."

She was laughing again. "Oh, I know you don't need me. But at least you might pretend you do!"

Prudently he did not reply to this and she lifted her face. "Kiss me properly," she commanded.

Years ago when they were freshmen at the same college, she had taught him exactly what she meant by a proper kiss and he now proceeded to the duty. A pleasant duty certainly, and he anticipated the glow that could still creep through his veins. His lips pressed to hers, he measured the increasing warmth and devised in imagination the sort of precision instrument that might chart the rising force of love. In its own secret fashion this too was atomic explosion.

She pulled away. "You're not thinking of me!"

The telephone rang and he turned toward the rescuing instrument. She pushed him aside. "It's for me. I'm expect-

19

ing a call. The Porters want us to come over tonight. I told them I'd have to ask you."

"Meaning what?" he inquired.

"Meaning exactly you know what," she retorted. She bit her lower lip and her eyes dared him.

He accepted their invitation.

"Tell them we can't come. Tell them I have a previous engagement—"

"Oh no—"

"With you—"

"Oh darling—" She snatched the receiver, listening a moment, then handed it to him.

"It's not the Porters. It's God. He wants to talk to you. From California."

He shot her a reproving look and then tuned his ear to hear his superior, the great physicist, Burton Hall.

A loud male voice roared over the wires. "Sorry to call you at this hour, Steve, but it's important."

"Of course."

"If the government asks me to head up a certain project, I want you to come with me."

"Where, sir?"

"I don't know yet. I can't even tell you what it is. But you won't regret coming. It's the biggest job in the world."

"You can't tell me any more than that?"

"No. It's secret, classified."

"Who else will be in it?"

"All the top scientists and with them the best of the younger men, hand-picked. You're the one I want first."

"It's hard to say no to you, sir, but—"

A snort of raucous laughter burst at his ear.

"Make it impossible, Steve, or I'll be compelled to draft you. I won't leave you behind."

20

Stephen Coast hesitated. He had worked under Burton Hall ever since he finished college.

"I must talk with my wife, sir."

Across the room Helen made hideous faces. "Don't say you have to talk with me," she hissed. "It's a fetish with him that you don't talk with any wives except his own!"

He laughed. "Helen says she doesn't want to be talked with."

"Good girl," the voice rasped at his ear. "She'll come along. They always do."

"Always," meant his own wife, Mollie, the mother of his two sons, the eternal mother, kind and interfering, adoring and ever-present. There was no way of getting away from her, Helen had once declared in mortal impatience.

"Maybe he doesn't want to get away from her," Steve had suggested.

Helen had opened her blue eyes wide under black lashes. She had thrown a single lucid word at him. "Stupid!" It was enough. They had fallen into mutual laughter.

"I'd like to hear about it, sir," Steve said now, "if it goes through."

"Good, see you Tuesday morning at the lab."

The receiver clicked at the other end of the wire. He hung up and stood oblivious in thought. In silence Helen waited. She opened the oven door, pulled out the small roast and prodded it with a long iron fork. Then she thrust it inside again and slammed the door.

"Good-bye, my house," she murmured. "Good-bye, my darling new house, the house I'll never have, my home, my castle, my sweet retreat! Good-bye, my white rose arbor—good-bye, my blue garden, larkspur and cornflowers and delphinium. Good-bye to everything—"

He came back from distant places.

21

"Good-bye to nothing. It's there waiting—delayed, I agree, but there. You'll have it all some day."

"When I see it," she retorted. But she was still incorrigibly gay and forgiving and she danced a circle around him, flourishing her full skirts. "We'll have a baby," she sang. "We'll have a little baby to keep me busy. While you play with stars and atoms, I'll play with him."

She stopped by the stove and turned off the gas.

"Is this the time?" He looked at her sobered, but she continued her dance, narrowing the circle until she ended in his arms, her lips upon his.

"Let dinner wait," she murmured.

. . . Two hours later she drew away from him. "It won't happen," she said. "It won't happen this time, either."

She sat upon the edge of the big double bed and pulled on her slippers. The light of a rising moon filtered through the drawn white curtains.

"What makes you say that?" he demanded. "You were perfect. So, I may say, was I."

She shook her head. "Your heart wasn't in it."

He pondered the accusation. "Not true."

She turned on him, a slender naked figure, and seized him by the ears. She bared her teeth, half playfully, and gazed down into the depths of his eyes. "Then your mind wasn't here, and damned if I don't think your mind is your heart and your heart is your mind, and you don't know the difference."

He looked up into the accusing blue eyes and unable to deny the truth he pulled her down again until her mouth was upon his and her dark hair flowed over his face.

*   *   *

22

On Tuesday morning Burton Hall glanced across the desk at Stephen Coast. He put down the paper knife he had been twisting in his fingers while he talked.

"That's all I can tell you, Steve. The rest you'll have to take on faith. It's essential work in a dangerous hour. We'll have to get the method tested somewhere—and then go into production."

"You don't know where or when?"

"Not yet. But it'll be in some lonely Godforsaken spot where there's no human traffic and where we can guard the approaches—and the exits."

"How long before we move?"

"I don't even know that—it depends on how soon we can get Washington to wake up. Just don't dig in anywhere for the moment, that's all. Don't buy a new house."

"No, sir."

He looked down, thoughtful. So he would have to tell Helen.

Burton Hall's voice broke sharply across the thought. "I need your help. That's enough, isn't it? Or have I learned to depend on you too much?"

Stephen Coast did not reply. The pale April sun shone across the large old-fashioned office of the university and fell upon the worn carpet at his feet. He met Burton Hall's eyes, green and intense under the bushy eyebrows.

"These foreign scientists, sir—aren't they inclined to panic? One doesn't blame them after all they've been through abroad, especially the ones from Hungary."

"I suppose you're thinking of Szigny. Yes, he's excitable. I pour skepticism on him but he doesn't weaken. He simply reiterates his usual charges that Americans are children, sleeping like babes, stuffing ourselves with food, playing with balls and making love—especially making love. He insists that our obsession with sex for its own sake makes us stupid—dulls the brain. By the way—I'm having dinner with Thompson tonight. He came back with me. Have you met him?"

"I've heard of him, of course," Stephen said.

Burton took the paper knife again, a narrow scimitar of steel and gold.

"I picked this up in Turkey last year on my way home from Nepal. I wonder if we shall ever have time again to measure cosmic rays in our leisurely fashion? I think not. About Thompson—he's a marvelous fellow. He was a graduate student of mine here twelve years ago—maybe thirteen. A fertile brain—always thinking up new things and making them work. He's nearly finished his cyclotron, by the way, and he expects to do something really great in the treatment of cancer. . . . He'll have ideas today. They flow out of him—it's chain reaction. Hotel Bellamy, seven thirty. A bit of luxury, before we plunge into austerity."

"I'll be there," Stephen said.

He rose to leave but Burton Hall was still remembering, his heavy features suddenly lightened by the intelligent awareness in his eyes, now subdued to tenderness.

"Thompson stopped one day to see me on his way to California—he was already teaching there then, and he showed me the plans he'd drawn for that cyclotron, as he called it. He's not a good draughtsman—I had to use my imagination—the damned thing looked like a toy. A device, of course, depending on the circular path of charged particles in the magnetic field, increasing, you know, until you've reached the necessary kinetic energy for striking the target."

Stephen sat down again. "What does he use for the target?"

"Almost any element," Burton Hall said. He lit his pipe. "That's the beauty of the cyclotron. You can adjust the particle energy to what you want—hundreds of MEV, if you like."

He laughed suddenly. "Did I ever tell you my story about MEV?"

Stephen shook his head.

Burton's eyes shone with mirth and a glint of malevolence. "Mollie—that's my wife, you know—was dusting my desk one day and she kept seeing memoranda about MEV. 'Who's this MEV you're always writing to,' says she. 'I never heard of her before,' says she. 'Sweetheart,' I said—my wife and I are very affectionate, you know—'Sweetheart, she is one million electric volts.' 'Oh,' says she, 'I thought'—well, you know what she was thinking!"

He bellowed his loud laugh and Stephen smiled. Plenty of cause for Burton Hall's wife to be jealous, but what had that to do with MEV?

Burton turned off his laughter abruptly. "Well, the question is whether the cyclotron will be useful in what lies ahead of us. I'll tell you this much, Steve. Anyway, it's useful to the extent of letting us track down the path of single nuclei. We'll know what minimum energy we need to crash a given nucleus. All our work on solar energy is going to help us now. I'll bet you've often wondered what good your cosmic ray stuff would do you in the end."

"You taught me not to ask questions," Stephen retorted. "Pursue knowledge for its own sake, et cetera—"

"That's my text," Burton Hall agreed. "And it's led—or will lead—us to the secret of the sun and life itself. Think of it, Steve, we'd all be dead if it weren't for that secret, the sun long since cold if it weren't for the sacred source of thermonuclear energy. Explosion—that's all it is. We're on the eve of discovering the greatest of all explosions. Hans Bethe—what would we do without the European scientists? They've had generations in which to apply their concentrated brains to concentrated problems, while we've had no time. We've had to make a nation from a wilderness. We

25

musn't disregard these foreigners, Steve. . . . And I must stop preaching. I should have been a preacher. I can't escape my heritage. Did I ever tell you my father was a Methodist circuit rider?"

"You have told me," Stephen said firmly. He got to his feet again. Burton Hall was growing old—old for a scientist, that is. One saw it in these reversals of memory. He must be forty-five, maybe more. The best creative scientists were under thirty and young enough to be daredevils.

"Yes, my dad was a rip-roarin' preacher," Burton Hall said, and tenderness infused his rich voice, "and my mother was a Presbyterian, bless her calm soul. So how can I escape them?"

"You can't," Stephen said at the door. "Good-bye, sir. I'll see you this evening."

How, he inquired within, how would Helen take this new move? Move where, she would ask, and he could not answer the question. Burton Hall would not think it important. Perhaps even he did not know where the move would be. Well, there was no need to call Helen yet. He might find out more tonight. Time enough to talk when he reached home, whenever that was. She ought to be used to waiting by now. He put aside the thought that she was not used to it and never would be. "I have a mortal disease," she had once declared. "It is called impatience of the soul."

He put that thought aside, too, and stepped out into the cool morning air. Rain this afternoon, the radio had prophesied, perhaps April snow. He took a deep breath and quickened his steps. He was glad to be alive and young, and in the laboratory across the marble paved court of the university his work waited for him. Then suddenly he remembered he would not be home for dinner. He took the receiver from the telephone on his desk and dialed.

"Helen?"

"The same," she said, "yesterday, today and forever. And I have a steak for dinner tonight."

"Helen, I have to tell you—"

Gaiety forsook her. "We can't buy the house."

"Not yet, darling, but—"

"What does God want now?"

"Something terribly important—I can't refuse—"

"Oh, of course," she cried, "everything is so important to him."

He let her wail and then spoke.

"Shall I resign from my job?"

He waited for the still small voice he knew so well.

"No, Steve."

"You'll have your house, you know."

"Yes, Steve."

"Do I love you?"

"I—think so."

"Do I?" he demanded.

"Yes."

"Just remember it," he said sternly, and suddenly he remembered. "Oh, and by the way, I shan't be home for dinner. . . . Burton Hall wants me to meet Thompson." He hung up the receiver, oblivious to her reply.

❊   ❊   ❊

The lobby of the hotel was crowded by half past seven, a huge lobby, nevertheless, banked at the left by Oriental screens twelve feet high. In the center a fountain poured out silver streams and above it birds, in an immense cage and tied by invisible threads, fluttered and sang. Stephen looked about and saw no one he recognized. He was incorrigibly punctual and now he was the first. "How much time you waste by being always on time," Helen had com-

27

plained only this morning when she came flying downstairs minutes late as usual. He could not change himself. His father had trained him too well. Grace must be said, though in Quaker silence, before food could be eaten, and three times a day that tall and professional figure waited at the head of the table, gravely patient while the family gathered. Time became immovable and solid, a substance to which one bent one's will.

"When one has work to do—" he had said to Helen this morning while she clattered the dishes on the table.

She had interrupted briskly. "How dare you talk about time?" she demanded. "Don't you believe Einstein? It's all relative."

That was one of her amusing and slightly irritating habits, he reflected now, standing before the fountain and watching the fluttering birds. She acquired the scientific patter and she used it to tease and defy him and succeeded the better because to his secret astonishment he perceived that she understood amazingly well the principles which she professed to disdain, and this not by any application of her darting impatient mind but by flashes and flairs of what could only be called intuition, a word he disliked. He let all this slip from his mind and concentrated on the birds, a bevy of green parakeets and yellow canaries. One of the canaries, a slender male creature, burst into song and inspired half a dozen others to contend in melody and sound. The females, he observed, pretended indifference. They paused on the narrow bars beside the seed cups and picked at their food. Did they hear or care? He pondered on the subtle difference between the sexes. Take aphids, for example, or fruit flies—he was no biologist, but he had talked half idly with Stanton, the head biologist, at dinner one night.

"It may be that the only importance of the male is that he is an instrument of survival," Stanton said.

"Horrid thought," Helen had interjected, but her eyes were bright with curiosity. "Go on, Hal," she had urged.

"I am working with aphids," Stanton said. He was carving the roast delicately and precisely, laying one thin red slice upon another. He had continued to talk in his dry careful manner. "I find that when food is short and there is a question of survival, which means struggle, more males are born. If I increase the food supply and the need for struggle subsides, more females are born."

"Now what does that mean?" Helen had asked.

"You tell me," Stanton had said and laughed.

There was no question of scarcity in this hothouse atmosphere of the hotel lobby. Full seed cups, leaves of crisp lettuce and crumbled hard-boiled egg provided provender for female flourishing. They were still stuffing themselves, indifferent to the urgent singing of the males.

From this microscopic world he was diverted by Burton Hall's big voice.

"There you are, Steve—have you been waiting long? Here's Thompson just in from California—Tommy, you know Steve Coast. Cosmic rays, etc. My best young man. . . . Oh and Steve, I brought along my first assistant, a student in my graduate class, Jane Earl. I've reserved a table."

Burton Hall was already halfway across the lobby. Stephen shook hands with Thompson. Yes, he remembered the small thin figure, his face delicate and wan, his colorless hair a mouse grey and falling. And who was Jane Earl? He had not seen this girl before. She was young, perhaps twenty-two, dark, perhaps beautiful, he was not sure, but certainly very smart in her black dress and small white hat. She was quiet and her voice was clear. He fell into step beside her.

29

"I haven't met you before, have I?" he said.

"I came here from New York less than a month ago," she said. "Nobody's met me."

A nice girl, he decided, composed and not coquettish. He forgot her as soon as they sat down at the table, although she faced him between Burton Hall and Thompson.

"Don't talk until you've decided what to eat," Burton Hall directed. "I always have steak. You'd better all have steak. Right? Four steaks, green salad, coffee. . . . Now then, Thompson, what progress have you made with your atom-smasher? Very fast protons on a beam to you, Jane, plus a magnet, though why I should think there's anything you don't know—a smart girl this, Steve—pity she's a woman. Cyclotron is simply a high-energy particle accelerator, of course. Protons, deuterons, alpha particles, are the projectiles and the target particles are changed into radio-active isotopes. Wonderful—wonderful—"

"There are disadvantages," Thompson said in his thin dry voice. "The isotopes can still be destructive of normal tissue and that means we can't yet study small organisms or cells."

"I prefer to think of the advantages," Burton Hall retorted. "The radiations, penetrating, ionized, can destroy malignant tissue—"

The talk flowed on in the familiar pattern. Jane Earl, Stephen observed, said nothing, a valuable, silent woman, who could be ignored while males argued happily. They withdrew into their own world, men of science, comrades and brothers, closer to one another than to wives and children, their language secret, their minds attuned.

A cigarette girl, half nude, blond, provocative, offered her wares. Burton Hall answered her smile and bought a pack, the others refused. They sat back in silence and watched the night show begin upon the small stage at the end of the dining room. Six girls in silver tights and

30

brassières and wearing tinny smiles went through their paces. Thompson glanced at them and looked away. Stephen drank his coffee slowly, reflecting upon the folly of such amusement when the most exciting pastime in the world was within the four walls of his own laboratory. Burton Hall stared at the girls, his green eyes cynical.

"What it will mean when we really use mass production to pull this energy out of the atom," he mused, "on a large scale, to heat and light the world—"

"Or destroy it," Thompson put in.

"Pessimist always," Burton Hall countered.

"Is that committee in Washington doing anything?" Stephen inquired. He raised his voice against the raucous music of the dancing girls.

"Secret, of course, whatever it's doing," Thompson said, "but we'd have heard of it if there were anything spectacular. I doubt they're taking it seriously. And we ought to, we must, if I'm to believe Szigny."

Burton Hall laughed. "Has he been shouting at you, too? What would we use the energy for? Did he say?"

"We could drive ships with it," Stephen said, "or we could separate uranium 235."

"Drive ships!" Burton Hall echoed with contempt. "All right, Tommy, you tell him."

They were interrupted by applause. The dance was over and the girls were prancing off the stage. Three tumblers took their places.

"We know the Nazis are working hard and they have smart men," Thompson said. "They've made progress in separating the two forms of uranium. And believe me, they're not thinking of using it for peace."

Jane's calm voice broke in. "Should we discuss it here?"

The men stopped their talk abruptly. "Thank you, Jane," Burton Hall said. "Keep reminding us. Let's meet at my

31

house tomorrow night. Thompson goes back to California the next day."

Silence fell. The men ate rapidly and with concentration. Around them the tables filled. Waiters, passing with piled trays, snarled at each other under the cover of determined smiles. Urgency rose like a hot steam in the noisy dining room as the waiting guests crowded about the door. The maître d'hôtel watched with restrained impatience any guest who lingered over coffee and cigarettes.

"Will we ever have time again to be polite and urbane and or even just plain pleasant?" Burton Hall croaked.

"People make an excuse of war even in Europe," Thompson drawled. "My wife was in a department store yesterday and a bunch of clerks were talking together, paying no attention to customers. My wife tapped one on the shoulder. 'Will you wait on me?' she asked. You know my wife—a soft-voiced shy sort of woman. Can't kill a tick on a dog. The girl snaps back at her. 'Madame, don't you know we're going to have a war?' My wife snaps back—first time in her life, I swear. 'Must be so,' says she, 'or they wouldn't have you here.' "

They laughed, swallowed their coffee, and ignoring a Negro blues singer now upon the stage, they pushed their way between the tables and parted in the lobby. Among them only Stephen had a hat and he waited in line to retrieve it. Hat in hand at last, he heard a flutter among the birds and he could not forbear stealing a moment to see what was going on among that minuscule population. He returned to the aviary. A pair of canaries had built a nest in a corner between two branches of an artificial tree. The tiny female was sulking, obviously refusing to sit upon the nest where lay two eggs no larger than the jelly beans children consume by the handfuls. The male, slender and arrogant, was shrieking and scolding, but to no avail. The

32

stubborn female hopped to the seed cup and whisked the seeds furiously right and left. Still scolding, the exasperated male sat himself down on the eggs.

"Poor little man," someone said at Stephen's elbow. He turned, half-startled, and looked into a pair of dark eyes, level with his own. Jane Earl stood beside him, tall and slim and cool.

"It's silly but there's something fascinating about these creatures," he said.

"I love them," she replied. "I could watch them by the hour, and some day I shall."

"I wonder what it is," he mused.

"They live their little private lives so desperately in earnest, in the midst of all this glare and publicity," she said.

She had a lovely voice, he thought, the sort of voice a woman should have—soft, with fluid inflections.

"How come you're a scientist?" he demanded suddenly, forgetting the birds.

She laughed. "I'm just interested. I've always been interested."

"In science?"

"If that's what you want to call the eternal curiosity that drives you," she said.

She smiled and turned away with a wave of her gloved hand. He averted his eyes from her graceful figure. In the cage the female canary had relented. She approached the nest and pecked at her mate. He rose, hopped three inches away and stared at her severely from one eye and the other while she settled herself in calm. Then he fluffed his feathers and burst into triumphant song. Stephen walked away. Who was the victor? He could not decide.

✦ ✦ ✦

. . . The next evening Mollie Hall set a percolator of hot coffee on the table in her living room and two dozen of her best Lenox cups and saucers. Sandwiches and cookies and pink paper napkins—scientists were always hungry—lean and hungry. They wore themselves out from within, she told Burt. They were having a party tonight for Tommy Thompson. They were all coming, all the lab men and their wives —and Jane Earl. Dear Burt, the best husband in the world, but still so handsome that she had to watch him! She went with him everywhere, just to protect him. Oh, she knew her duty. Scientists were so absent-minded. They didn't notice when women made up to them and when they did notice they were so pleased. Burt could be so easily flattered. He believed anything a woman told him, once he noticed her. She went to the stair.

"Burt!"

A bumbling growl replied.

"I'll come up," she called patiently. "I'm sure I put it in the drawers with your other shirts."

He was looking for his favorite blue striped shirt. Oh, what a child he was! What would he ever do without her? Suddenly the doorbell rang and she was flustered. What should she do first?

"Wait a minute, Burt," she shrieked and hurried to the door. One of the foreign scientists, of course, always on time. She opened the door upon the slight grey figure of Ernst Weiner—a German wasn't he, or may be a Hungarian. She could never keep them straight.

"Come in," she said kindly enough. "Burt will be right down."

She took his hat firmly away from him, a battered wreck of a hat, but they had no money, these foreigners, and pushed him toward the living room.

34

"Pour yourself some hot coffee," she told him. "Make yourself at home."

She bustled upstairs and halfway remembered to go slowly. She had gained weight and her doctor had warned her about exertion. But what did doctors know? It was no picnic to be the wife of a man like Burt. He stood now at the top of the stairs, bare to the waist. In all the years they had been married she had not been able to persuade him to wear an undershirt the way he should. Her father would never have gone without an undershirt. As for pajamas— well, she would not think about that. How Burt could sleep indecently naked—

"Who's that downstairs?" he demanded.

"Weiner. He's always too early. Now let me see about that shirt."

He pranced after her into the bedroom as lively as a big dog and she reached expertly into the second drawer and pulled out the shirt. He snatched it away from her.

"I swear it wasn't there a minute ago."

"Oh, Burt," she sighed.

He was pulling it on, not listening. "Look here, Mollie, I want you to get the wives out of the way."

"I know. Don't I always?"

She went about the room picking up his underwear and socks and three soiled handkerchiefs.

"You've been wiping up some sort of ink or acid or something. Look at these handkerchiefs!"

He ignored her. "We have a terribly important conference tonight."

"You're always having them."

"This is something worse."

"War?"

"Don't ask me questions."

"You mean we can't talk again?"

35

"Not for months. Maybe years."

She sank on the nearest chair, her arms full of clothes. "Ever since our honeymoon—twenty-three years ago."

He snorted. "Don't bring that up again. Maybe I'll have you cleared this time. Yeah, that's what I'll do."

He zipped up his trousers and peering into the mirror he combed his stiff red hair into a brush. The doorbell rang again and he clattered downstairs and flung the door open. They were all there, his brothers in science, and he loved them. Behind them were their wives.

"Come in," he shouted. "Come in, fellows. There's coffee and liquor." He joined them as they crowded into the living room, their wives following. Apart from men and women alike Jane Earl walked quietly and alone.

"Girls!" Mollie called from upstairs. "I'll be right down. Help yourselves to coffee and sandwiches. We'll go out into the glass porch."

Helen Coast, following close behind Stephen, murmured into his right ear. "It's exactly like a card party—sounds like it, looks like it. Suburban and safe, wouldn't you say, and instead it's the most explosive spot in the world—all these male brains! Who is that tall dark girl? Do you know her?"

"Jane Earl," Stephen said. "There's Weiner. I want to ask him something."

He left his wife and pulled a hassock to Weiner's side. The grey pallid Hungarian smiled dimly, and put out his right hand, a limp pale instrument, and touched Stephen's hand.

"How strong is your hand," he murmured.

Stephen laughed and drew the hassock closer. "Have you read the report from von Halban, Joliot and Kwarski?"

Weiner nodded. "It is the first step," he whispered, "but not too promising."

He continued and Mollie interrupted.

"All right, girls! Burt is making faces at us. That means get out, women. So we get out—"

She herded them toward the porch. They turned their heads, one after another, to look at Jane Earl. She was seated in a green armchair, the russet brown of her suit in contrast. She smiled at them faintly, almost apologetically.

"Move in, Jane," Burton Hall said. He got up and went to her chair and pushed it into the circle of men. "We can't spare you, you know. Want to take notes while we talk?"

"Of course." She rose from the armchair and seated herself on a straight chair by the table. From her brown calfskin handbag she took pencil and pad and then she slipped her small hat from her head. Her hair glistened a dark bronze in the lamplight and her skin, Stephen suddenly noticed, was cream white. Very nearly a redhead, he thought, but pleasantly not one.

"Well," Burton Hall was bumbling, "what do we actually know about the Germans? Who have they got, in the first place?"

"Hahn," Szigny said in a hoarse voice. "They have Hahn and he is equal to ten of us together."

"I won't accept that," Burton retorted. "Besides, what is Hahn doing? Does anyone know exactly?"

Weiner coughed behind his hand. "Excuse me, I think such things are not important, what one is doing and another is doing. We are in a race, so everybody is doing something to reach the goal. And the goal, what is it? It is fission in chain reaction. In my opinion, we are now about to discover this. If uranium 235 can be separated from uranium 238, which two are like the Siamese twins, then we will have it."

"Agreed." Thompson said. He sat in front of the lamp and the light shone pink through his large thin ears. "The explosive force," he went on, "will be one hundred million

37

times that of TNT. But it's much more complicated, I can assure you, than Fermi thinks it is."

"With a brain like Fermi's all things are simple," Szigny muttered.

Talk had begun, developing inevitably into scientific argument. Their brains battened on argument. The air of concentration thickened. Jane's quiet look, moving from one face to the other, recognized the familiar set of eyes and lips, the intent and listening stare. The search was on. She opened her bag and drew out folded pages and broke across the men's voices.

"I have an advance copy of *Nature,* from London. A friend of mine works in the office there and he sent me the copy of a letter Lise Meitner and Frisch sent to them. Shall I read it?"

"By all means," Burton Hall exclaimed. "The only question is why haven't you read it to us before?"

"It was only just published and I received it in the last mail this afternoon. I had barely time to glance at it."

She smoothed the pages. "They say—'It seems possible that the uranium nucleus has only small stability of form, and may, after neutron capture, divide itself into two nuclei of roughly equal size.' " She looked up and met Stephen's eyes, fixed upon her. "That's fission, isn't it? And they say in the letter that the elements resulting are radioactive—very much so."

Weiner was listening with such intensity that he trembled. His nearsighted water-grey eyes peered at her through thick spectacles. Drops of sweat hung on his temples. He wrung his bony hands.

"I think they will tell this to Bohr." His voice was a whisper. "And Bohr will certainly tell it to Einstein and Fermi and we will all know. But the critical point is the chain reaction, as Dr. Coast—"

38

"Call me Steve, will you?" Stephen put in.

Weiner hesitated, smiled and went on. "There is still no importance unless one explosion sets off another."

Stephen turned to gaze through the window. Spring snow was beginning to fall in large soft flakes in the shadowy reflections of the lamplight. The air was windless and they drifted down like flower petals, the pull of gravity scarcely strong enough to overcome their fragility, so nearly weightless. The talk flowed on, it fired into argument again and suddenly Burton Hall was cursing as he always did in anger or admiration when he was roused. "Tommy, you son of a bitch, will you get it into your thick skull that we don't have enough uranium and we don't have enough heavy water, and God—or the devil—only knows what the Germans are doing with the heavy water in Norway? Why, man, Rusinow in Russia was fooling around years ago with nuclear reaction. And what about Hideki Yukawa's work in Japan? And Nishina's cyclotron? You're not so damned far ahead as you think you are—"

"Burt!" Mollie's voice screamed through the closed glass doors at last. "Aren't you about ready for refreshments? It's getting cold out here in the porch. We want hot coffee. It's nearly twelve o'clock."

"We'll have to let the women in, damn them," Burton Hall groaned. The hours had slipped away. Against the windows the snow was piled high. He nodded violently and leaped across the room and stood with his back to the doors. "You understand, fellows, this is top secret—all of it. We've got to think what to do."

"I should think we ought to notify the government of our fears," Stephen said.

"No doubt of it," Thompson said. "But shouldn't we wait until after the conference? We'll have more to tell because we'll know more."

"Not from the papers that will be read," Burton Hall said.

"But we will have private talk," Weiner suggested. "I will myself talk with certain foreign scientists. I can find out. They will tell me secrets that they want Americans to know."

"After the conference," Burton Hall agreed. Behind his back his wife was tapping on the glass.

"Burt, let us in!"

"Meanwhile," he said sternly, "not a word." With this he opened the door and the women came in. The tense atmosphere dissolved into a fragmentation of voices, words, movement, and the smell of hot coffee.

Driving home an hour later Helen, wrapped in her fur coat, murmured half asleep into the darkness.

"What has that woman got that I haven't got?"

Stephen peered through the night. Spears of white snow darted against the windshield, like flying electrons, he thought, but he was the opposing force, their energy spurious.

"What woman?" he inquired absently.

"If you don't remember I won't remind you," she said and subsided again into sleep.

*   *   *

In the morning he woke early. His mind was fresh and his thoughts followed one upon another as sharply clear as the lines of silver-white snow darting against the windshield of his car at midnight. Hideki Yukawa, that Japanese scientist, who had forced respect from them all, was devising theories of a new component in the atom's nucleus! Meson, he called it, a strange word, sounding half-Japanese. And Wolfgang Pauli, Austrian, had created the word neutrino for those particles which, still unseen and lighter than any others, carried no electric charge. Strange and symbolic that the interchange of minds around the world should find expression in the names they bestowed upon these children of their brains! And the Japanese were no whit behind the Americans, what with Nishina's cyclotron. He must talk with Thompson about that cyclotron. But the British were still closer than any of them to the final secret of energy.

Absent from its shell of flesh, his mind wandered on its solitary way while by habit his body performed its necessary tasks. He brushed his teeth, he took his shower, he shaved and put on the fresh clothes he found laid out for him on a chair, and neatly he tied his tie. Then, decently clean and garbed, he went downstairs into the dining room. From some far distance he smelled coffee and finding his cup full he drank. His glass of orange juice he likewise consumed in oblivion, then a plate of bacon and eggs, toast and another cup of coffee. These his body accepted and absorbed. Fed and warmed, he rose from his chair and pushing it carefully into place, he walked across the room to the hall and found his hat and coat. At this point his mind perceived that he had eaten a meal, a good meal, somewhere. He hesitated, returned to the doorway and looked blankly across the room. Habit worked again, the nice habit of the well-trained child, his mother's voice teaching him. Always thank your hostess—

"Thank you," he said clearly. "Thank you very much. I enjoyed the meal."

He was startled by a peal of laughter, clear and ironic, a mingling of mirth and reproach.

"Stephen—Stephen Coast!"

His mind returned entire. He faced his wife, Helen, with whom he breakfasted daily.

"Do you know where you are?" she demanded.

"Of course," he said.

"Tell me where you are," the skeptical woman insisted. He looked about the room and recognized it. "I'm at home," he said, "where else would I be?"

"Then why," she inquired, "do you stop at your own door and thank me for a meal? Do you remember having seen me before?"

He sighed, he blushed, then laughed. "Will you ever forgive me?"

"Oh Stephen—"

"I don't know why you married me," he muttered.

"I wanted to—terribly."

"Sure?"

"How sure!"

She was in his arms and out again, straightening his tie, parting his hair with her forefinger delicately.

"I hate to leave you," he muttered.

"But you must," she said. "I know that very well." She gave him her brilliant smile for a parting gift.

* * *

In the middle of the sixth row in a conference hall, six months later, Jane Earl sat wedged between two perspiring men. They were Europeans, unaccustomed to the torrid temperature of American furnaces, and their heavy woolen suits gave off the odor of chemicals mingled with human effluvia, their heat intensified by the concentration with which they listened to Burton Hall. He stood upon the platform, huge and impressive, his reddish hair aflame in the lights which streamed down from the ceiling.

"It is probable," he declaimed, "that bombardment with slow neutrons will cause fission to take place in uranium 235. The problem is that U-235 is less than one per cent in

42

any sample of ordinary uranium. We now know, however, thanks to the predictions of Enrico Fermi, that it is likely, in regard to transuranic elements, that the plentiful uranium 238 can also capture slow neutrons. Moreover, in U-238 approximately one atom out of every one hundred and forty is uranium U-235. We know that U-235 will undergo fission with fast neutrons as well as slow neutrons. I need not tell my fellow scientists what this means. Your minds leap ahead of mine. Yes, we may create atomic power from the fission of U-235 with slow neutrons, or create a chain reaction with fast neutrons. This second recourse would result in explosion. The only question now is—can this explosive energy be controlled?"

On her right Jane Earl heard a suppressed cry of agony. The bald-headed man snatched his handkerchief from his pocket and wiped his sweating face. He leaned across her to hiss guttural German to the man on her left.

"Hans, what should we do with these Americans, telling their secrets everywhere?"

The man on her left leaned to answer:

"Perhaps it is already too late."

The acid odor of decaying teeth crept through his ragged beard. She stirred and they glanced at her and drew back hastily.

"Excuse me—"

"Excuse me—"

They bobbed twin apologies and she smiled. "It is quite all right. But I am interested, sirs, in what you have said. Do you really think that there should not be such conferences as we are now having?"

They had found their audience. On either side she heard their breathy arguments, good men she could see, anxious and frightened, their memories still alive with fear.

43

"Certainly there must be no more such conferences. It is very dangerous. I assure you—"

"I assure you, miss, the Germans are working very hard upon atomic weapons. Why else do they neglect Sweden and proceed to Norway? It is Norway that has the heavy water which they need. Ach no, not the French—the French are not important."

"Joliot-Curie has the cyclotron, nevertheless."

"Ah yes, Curie—but they have him."

She listened while Burton Hall finished his paper and MacLeod took his place. She must talk with Burton Hall immediately. She watched him, a restless figure on any platform. She knew him well; sooner or later upon the excuse of a telephone call he had forgotten, or thirst or fatigue, he would leave. In the middle of the third paper advancing a theory for the use of centrifuge in separating uranium isotopes, she saw him rise from his chair and steal from the platform. As quietly she rose from her seat and left the hall. In the lobby she ran down a small stairway and through the basement, a forest of pipes and hot-water tanks, and emerging again she met Burton Hall at the back door.

"Hello," he said, "what are you doing in the cellar?"

"Trying to catch you before you escape. I have something to tell you which may or may not be important."

"Let's go and have a drink."

She followed him into the cool autumn air, modified this day by bright sunshine. Burton Hall drew a deep breath and then another.

"I love my fellow scientists," he announced. "I love them dearly. Brothers under the skin, every one of them, and oh, what dull brothers they can be when they make speeches!"

Jane laughed. "You're poseurs, every one of you, showing off before one another. I don't know why you do it, you're all

44

alike and you know it and you don't deceive anybody, not even yourselves."

He looked down from his height and his green eyes sparkled suddenly with a slightly livid glow. "When are you going to give up?" he demanded.

"What I'd like to tell you—" she began.

He interrupted. "What I'd like to tell you, my tall girl, is that I want to sleep with you."

She heard this unmoved. Whether he was serious, whether this was his notion of persiflage between male and female, were questions she had not tried to answer. She wanted very much to be in love and she was not in love with Burton Hall. She ignored his burning gaze.

"Two foreign scientists sat beside me. They disapproved of you because you were discussing matters which they think should not be discussed now. I feel I ought to tell you so, although you know already what their point of view is."

He lit his pipe as he walked and drew on it fiercely. "Don't you scare men away with such brains as yours?" he demanded.

"Yes," she said coldly, "but not the men I'm interested in."

He took his pipe from his mouth and roared. Startled passers-by stared into that laughing cavern and went on.

"Don't think I'm afraid of you, tall girl," he said. "Now tell me exactly what it is your foreign friends said."

She had him now. She was down to his bedrock and there he was all scientist. No woman in the world could compete with the insatiable fury of the searcher in him, stalking truth wherever it was hidden, universe beyond universe. She knew and revered the range of his mind, uncorrupted by the momentary lusts of the massive body in which he lived.

"The point is this," she began and followed the path of argument. He listened as coolly intent as though she were a man. No, this communication was not even that of men. It

45

was the flowing together of brain cells in a fourth-dimensional space, as silver and gold, pressed together, mingle their solids. Into the interstices between their particles, the spaces infinitely small and microscopically endless, the alien atoms move in margins composed of both elements. So the particles of her brain moved toward his until their thoughts were simultaneous.

"You are right," he said at last. "You are damned right, tall girl. I just haven't taken seriously enough the fact that we're catapulted suddenly into another age. I've got to clam up, even though I'm a scientist, used to pouring all I know into the common reservoir of knowledge. We've all got to clam up—we're enemies, even among ourselves. God, that's a thought—it's horrible!"

But would he be able to clam up? she was thinking. He was trained, as they all were, to think of himself as a link in a chain of searchers, the first of them doubtless some unknown creature who rose on his hind legs and stared at the sky. But the chain was recorded at least twenty-five centuries ago—

"The British fellows have been wiser than we," Burton Hall was saying. "But then we don't have a Lord Cherwell. Smart cookie, that Winnie Churchill! He dragged Cherwell out of his professor's seat in Oxford, as you know. Janie, weren't you sweet on Cherwell once? When you were in Cambridge last year?"

"Don't be silly," she said. "Here's where I stop. I have a luncheon engagement."

"Who with?" he demanded.

"None of your business," she said sweetly and left him abruptly there in the middle of the sidewalk.

She entered the restaurant with a vague pervasion of guilt, the hangover of a childhood in India made rigid by discipline against Indian tendencies to lie, her parents insisting

46

that a lie was one of the seven sins. She had no engagement beyond a hope, which she denied, that Stephen Coast would be there. Once, before she had met him, he had been there. She had come that day with Tomas Freitsch, the German biochemist.

"Do you see that man sitting at the small table?" Tomas asked.

She had looked, had shaken her head. "It is Stephen Coast," Tomas said, "and please do not look at him with such eyes because you will make me jealous. And I do not know what I will do when I am jealous because until now I have not experienced the emotion."

She had smiled and looked away obediently, always wary of such talk from a scientist. They were like children, abstracted in the play which was their work, and yet, diverted, they were capable of a singlehearted pursuit of the diversion, dangerous and intense. And she had never been in love. One couldn't count a childhood crush on a handsome Anglo-Indian science teacher. Yet if she had not met Raman, would she have been a scientist? Unanswerable question!

She seated herself now at the same small table from whence she had first seen Stephen Coast. The hour was barely noon and the place was half empty. He was not here. She pulled off her gloves and glanced at the menu. She was glad he was not here. She had enough to think about now without the complication of a new emotion. Not to be involved! That was the necessity.

"Sole and a green salad," she told the waiter, "and bring me coffee now."

She sat motionless in her chair, resting in her usual secret fashion by withdrawal into her own universe. Her private goddess there just now was Lise Meitner. She would have liked to call that stubborn goddess her friend, but upon the one occasion when they had met, the great scientist had looked at her with gaunt eyes and from a distance. They were suddenly only two women, one young and shy, the other worn and famous and as distant as the stars.

"You are too beautiful," the gaunt eyes said, and looked away.

And Marie Curie, had she known this sadness?

From her handbag Jane drew a book, *Madame Curie: A Biography*.

She began to read.

"Pierre was exhausted with the long struggle. For all their labor there were to be seen only a few grains of the precious material. But he did not know the stubborn persistence of the born scientist. Marie was determined to finish the work she had begun. Steadily she pursued her search and with infinite labor she continued. In the year 1902, nearly four years after the day on which the Curies suspected the existence of the new element, she prepared a decigram of the reality. The incredulous brotherhood of scientists was compelled to accept the fact. A woman, with superhuman effort and obstinacy, had brought into affirmed existence the element radium." *

"May I sit here?"

She looked up from the page she was about to turn. Stephen Coast stood looking across the table at her.

"Please do," she said.

She closed the book. "I usually read while I eat. I'm glad to have someone to talk with."

"Since it is obvious that we shall be working together," he said, "it's as well that we get acquainted. . . . Have you ordered?"

"Yes," she said.

* By Eve Curie. Copyright 1937 by Doubleday & Company, Inc. Reprinted by permission of the publisher.

"Steak," he told the waiter, "mashed potatoes, green beans. Coffee."

She was absurdly relieved. Now that he sat before her, now that she could look at him, she had no feeling for him. Good-looking, certainly very good-looking, and she liked dark eyes and dark hair and a smooth brown skin. She was conditioned, perhaps, by her own childhood in India, but the dangerous closeness she had felt for him in her thoughts was chilled. She was wary. He was a young scientist, very talented, she knew, they all told her that—oh, you must watch young Stephen Coast—and Burton Hall had insisted that he was to go with the project. But there was no longing in her to touch his hands clasped there on the table as he leaned toward her.

"I'm glad you're going with us, wherever it is we're going." He had a clean frank smile, white teeth, and the hint of a cleft in his chin. "I'd like you to know my wife Helen really well. I hope you'll be friends."

She drew a deep breath. No, she was quite safe. "I'd like to know her better," she said in good honesty. She moved the vase containing a red rose to the side of the table. "One of the disadvantages of being a scientist is that I have so few friends among women."

"Tell me—I'm frankly curious—how did you happen to be a scientist? Rather unusual, isn't it, for a woman—"

"It seems to be."

A petal fell from the rose and she crushed it in her fingers. No fragrance!

"I grew up in India," she said. "My father was an engineer there, working on hydroelectric power. I went to an English school but my favorite professor was a young Anglo-Indian—fresh from Oxford. He taught science. I suppose I had a crush on him—most of the girls did—but at least it made me work hard for him. Then suddenly I found I loved

49

science quite apart from him. That led me eventually into physics. I studied it at Radcliffe and then with Fermi at Columbia. He and Burton Hall are friends and Burton Hall borrowed me for the project here in Chicago. It's a simple story."

"I have an idea you're not simple," he said.

She smiled at him shyly. "None of us is, I suppose, if I may include myself in the noble brotherhood?"

"We're single-minded," he admitted. He blushed suddenly. "Do you know what I did this morning? I thought out an equation while I was dressing and entirely forgot where I was—went downstairs, ate my breakfast, thanked my wife for the good meal under the impression I was out to dinner somewhere. Lucky she understands!"

She laughed with him and felt a pang. The understanding wife!

"You're lucky," she said soberly. "Not all of them can. It's not easy, I suppose, unless one belongs to the brotherhood."

"Ah, but we don't seem to marry within the circle!"

"No," she agreed too quietly. "Not all women, either, are as lucky as Madame Curie. So we don't marry at all. I'm not sure whether we are the wiser or you, who marry anyway. Our standards are too high, doubtless. We insist upon companionship."

"Stop," he said. "You're going too fast for me. You're the first woman scientist I've ever met, remember. I'm not familiar with the breed. Are you different from the rest of us merely because you're a woman? Does sex matter that much even in science?"

"I'll leave you to find out," she said. She recognized a wary admiration in his eyes and smiled at him against her will.

The waiter appeared with his tray and they busied themselves for a moment. He looked up from his steak.

50

"One thing troubles me."

"Yes?"

"I've a conscience against allowing this—this atomic—"

"I know—you needn't mention the word—"

"To be used for war," he said.

"Are you a pacifist?" she asked.

"No, I'm not. That's the odd thing about it. I'm a realist, actually. I took boxing lessons once, secretly, when I was a kid, my father being a Quaker. I suffered a lot of ragging from the fellows and I had to knock them down, you know. So I did and never told him. No, it's not that. It's something different, a resistance. This new power—I don't want to see it used for beastly destruction. I want to devote my share in it to—to enlightenment, the good of mankind, and so on, if you'll forgive me for being corny."

"Why are you afraid to say you want to do good and not evil?"

"Sounds pompous," he murmured, attacking his steak again.

"Not pompous," she said. "Simply honest."

"I suppose you're right. But here in America we're ashamed of seeming to do good—too many pretenders, I daresay."

"You're no pretender, and you know it. So do I." The dangerous warmth was creeping about her heart again. He looked up and meeting his eyes suddenly she was reckless. "I can't tell you what it means to find someone like you. A scientist—and a good one—who dares to say what he feels as a human being."

She had gone too far. He was shy again, he withdrew. "Oh that," he said. "It's not as rare as you think."

She allowed proud silence to fall between them like a curtain. He must make the next advance. "Have you read that report by Macmillan and Abelson?" he asked after a moment.

"Yes," she said. "Element 93. But what's important is that it is only one in a series of discoveries. We'll develop one element after another in a swift process of creation in the next ten years. We've opened a box of secrets."

They were at ease again, upon safe and familiar ground. The warmth subsided. She was not going to fall in love. For this, thank God.

*　　　*　　　*

At home that night, Stephen had a vague guilt nevertheless. He examined his memory of the day and turned to his wife.

"By the way, I had lunch today with that new girl."

"What girl?" Helen asked.

She was tearing lettuce leaves for a salad, a small task she disliked.

"The female scientist," he said.

"Oh." She reflected. "And what did you have for luncheon?" she asked pleasantly, pretending no interest.

"Steak."

She whirled on him. "Stephen Coast, how dare you! You know I always have steak on a Wednesday night—to pep you up for the rest of the week."

He looked blank. "Is it Wednesday?"

She stamped her right foot. "Of course it is."

"My God," he said. "Twice in one day I've been an idiot."

She opened the door of the broiler and drew out a half-browned steak. "Didn't you smell it?" she demanded.

He shook his head.

"We won't have it," she said firmly. "Neither steak nor salad. It's omelet for you, my boy, just plain old omelet and some leftover fried potatoes. And I hope you'll get so fat and ugly that no girl will ever look at you. And I won't, either. So there!"

"Honey—" he began.

"And don't you honey me," she cried.

He watched her while she did exactly what she had said she would do. In humble silence he watched her break four eggs and beat them fiercely into froth and pour them into a hot buttered pan. And still in silence he saw her slice cold boiled potatoes into another pan. Guilty, that's what he was, a poor sort of man for her to marry, this brilliant restless talented girl, but he had fallen in love with a violence from which he had not yet recovered. And he had tried to be honest. "Honey," he had said on that glorious night when it had occurred to him to kiss her, and he had done so, and had found her only waiting to be kissed, an amazing state of affairs, since he was only one of many men who wanted to kiss her. "Honey," he had said. "You ought to know something—I'm an awful fool when I'm working in the lab."

"Who cares!" she had cried. "Oh Stephen, I thought you'd never ask me. Do you know I nearly gave you up?"

"Maybe we shouldn't have got married," he said now.

Her anger flared instantly. "And how dare you say such a blasphemous thing as that!"

She flew at him, deserting her pans, and collapsed on his breast in tears.

"How can you—" she sobbed. "How can you, Stephen— even think such words!"

Soothing her, his lips on the soft dark hair at the nape of her neck, it occurred to him that women should be kept as separate from men as the elements in his laboratory. Apart they were safe, non-critical mass and controllable, but, in conjunction, explosive. But was Jane Earl only a woman? Better, perhaps, to regard her as a known quantity, a scien-

53

tist, pure if not simple. He smelled the dangerous reek of burning eggs and heroically continued to soothe.

*   *   *

In the small office next to the laboratory, Burton Hall faced those intruders, the foreign scientists. They sat in a semicircle across the desk from him, cringing in the way he detested and although he understood why it had become a habit with them, he restrained himself from shouting at them: "Good Lord, don't you see I'm no dictator? I'm not even a government official, thank God! I'm a plain American, a scientist, who wants only to be let alone."

Instead he spoke in his suavest tones.

"What can I do for you, gentlemen?"

They looked at one another, each shrinking from the attack. It was Weiner who, at the end of the row, yielded with a sigh.

"Ach, we know how busy you are, Dr. Hall. It iss with greatest reluctance we come here today. But we know, also, your high influence in Washington. If you would please to approach the great President—"

He knew what they wanted. They were the most persistent, the most dogged, the most unbeatable—

"Gentlemen, I can't just walk into the President's office."

Szigny interrupted. "No, no, we don't ask it. First perhaps to go to the military?"

"As a scientist I have nothing to do with the military. It is a point of honor with us," Burton Hall said sharply.

Szigny broke in. "If you write a letter, I will ask Fermi to take it himself."

His eagerness was distasteful and the American withdrew from it. "Fermi doesn't need a letter from me. Everybody knows him."

"Nevertheless—" Szigny began.

"Oh very well," Burton Hall said wearily. "We've been through it all before. I'll write the letter. I only hope it won't sound ridiculous. The Navy has its own scientists, you know."

"They are very far from the main streams of what we scientists are doing," Weiner declared.

"They do not keep pace," Szigny added.

"I can scarcely tell them that," Burton Hall said dryly. He touched a button and a middle-aged secretary, grey-haired and with a pouting lower lip, came into the room, pencil and pad in hand. He dictated far too rapidly, while they listened with straining ears.

" 'The possibility of a chain reaction in nuclear energy is now sure. It remains only to experiment in the direction of control before an atomic bomb'—no, cross that out. Begin again after 'to introduce Enrico Fermi, famous' et cetera and so on. Pick up—'If uranium were used as an explosive it would liberate a million times as much energy per pound as any known explosive. My own feeling is that while the probabilities are against this—' "

"No!" Szigny was on his feet, waving his two arms. "The probabilities are not against this. We know these two months that Joliot-Curie in France, also German scientists are working already on fission."

"Joliot-Curie is Communist," Weiner began.

Burton Hall slapped his desk with his open palms. "Am I writing this letter?" he demanded.

The cringing again! What had men done to Weiner somewhere? This genius, clouded by fear!

He turned away.

"Pick up," he said to the secretary. "Where was I?" He continued in short bursts of words, whirling in his desk chair as he talked. Suddenly he stopped and stood up abruptly.

55

"That'll do. Type it off and bring it back at once—"

He stood, waiting until the woman had closed the door behind her, and then turned to his guests. "Have you read Meyer and Wang in the last *Physical Review?* Carnegie Institute—"

Their heads nodded. "Delayed neutrons," Szigny said.

Burton Hall broke in. "That means we have a margin for control before explosion."

Weiner clapped his hands softly. "Exactly. Let us only hope that Nazis have not also discovered it."

"Foolish such hope," Szigny groaned.

＊　　　＊　　　＊

Three weeks later Burton Hall agreed with them. The morning mail had brought from Washington a reply, perfectly typed upon handsome heavy paper.

"We appreciate your interest in the cause of atomic science but—"

In an excess of shock and rage Burton Hall leaped from his chair and strode down the hall, the open letter flying in his hand, to find Stephen Coast in the laboratory.

"Listen to this," he shouted. He roared out the letter, pausing to emphasize every syllable of courteous folly, and then tore the letter to shreds and dropped them. The wind caught them and scattered them over the floor and he flung himself upon a high three-legged stool.

"The damned foreign scientists are right," he groaned. "They are always right." He shot up the window shade behind his stool and let in a blinding beam of sunlight. "Know what that ignoramus of an admiral in Washington said?" he demanded.

"How can I know when you haven't told me?" Stephen inquired.

"He told Fermi—Enrico Fermi, mind you—the greatest— yes, I'd say greater than Einstein in some ways—practical ways, you know, applied science. Fermi is a first-rate mechanic as well as a genius scientist. He can make his own tools when he has to—knows what he wants down to the last millimeter. Fermi explained to those dunderheads that it's entirely possible to get atomic power from fission with slow neutrons, and we can make an atomic bomb by fast neutrons. Well, this damned uniform told Fermi that the war was going on all right as it is and anyway these new scientific weapons couldn't be got ready in time. We expected victory before long—all that rot, as though the Nazis weren't planning to blow us all up by tomorrow noon if possible!"

The telephone rang and Burton Hall snatched the receiver. Szigny's heavy voice crackled over the wires. He winced and held the receiver three inches from his ear.

"Yes, I know. . . . Well, what can I do? . . . get straight to the President somehow, but how? He's surrounded. All potentates are, in Washington or Timbuctoo. They only know what they're told. . . . Well, maybe Einstein—but tell him to drive it into the presidential brain that fission will not only power his precious ships, if that's what he wants most —he's mad about ships—but it will make bombs—powerful ones. One bomb could blow the port of New York off into space, tell him. And tell him the Nazis know it! Rub that into his handsome noggin. No, put it all in a letter, black and white, something the President can read. He doesn't listen to the human voice unless it's his own."

He dropped the receiver into place and groaned loudly.

"Szigny again! Wants Einstein to go straight to the White House. Einstein's too soft-spoken to appear in person. Besides, his English is curious. One gets to listening to his accent instead of what he's saying. Much better to write it all

57

down. That's concrete. God, the money it will take to get it all going!"

"Where's the money to come from?" Stephen asked soberly.

"Where else but government?" Burton Hall retorted. "Nobody else has it in the quantities we'll need. But the Washington bigwigs will have to be shown that it's necessary. We'll have to scare the liver and lights out of them first. I hope these European longhairs know what they're talking about. I guess they do. . . . They ought to, after all they've been through."

"How does it shape up to you now?" Stephen put the question with caution. He respected money and tried to ignore it. His own research had been done on pittances begged, borrowed, and scraped out of his own private till. Once under Helen's protest he had rebelled.

"A fellow can't steal his own money," he had grumbled.

"Don't forget that you endowed me with all your worldly goods," she had replied too smartly. . . .

"You mean millions," he said now.

"Billions," Burton Hall said grimly.

"I can't think of billions in dollars," Stephen said and added, "only billions in atoms."

"Same thing," Burton Hall retorted carelessly. He looked at his watch. "Time for lunch. Mollie's expecting me. By the way, I'm having her cleared. We'll all have to be cleared, we men, but I suppose it doesn't matter about the women. I want Mollie cleared because she worms things out of me. No, that's not fair. I talk too much. I have to talk everything over with her. Used to it— And she's a trusty soul when she knows she has to be. She will be now. When she knows what we're about she'll be too scared to whisper."

Burton Hall slid off the stool and strode out of the laboratory. Stephen sank into thought for a full fifteen minutes and then was startled by the opening of the door, into the next laboratory. He lifted his head. Jane Earl stood there in her white coat. She met his blank gaze, stepped back and closed the door softly. His thoughts were broken nevertheless and he rose and fumbled for his briefcase. He paused to examine a sudden wish he discovered in those regions within himself that he seldom explored, a sudden wish to open the door again. He shook his head doggedly. Better not, he told himself. Why was she here at work in the laboratory next his own? By whose command?

Behind the closed door Jane Earl quietly continued her new experiment. She worked steadily for two hours and then wrote a conclusion into her notebook in her small even handwriting.

"It seems evident that Seaborg, McMillan, Kennedy and Wahl are correct. The emission of an electron by neptunium converts it into element 94, plutonium. It is probable that plutonium will be the next material for experiment."

She closed the book, unbuttoned her long white cotton coat and brushed back her hair. Then she went out to lunch. Avoiding the restaurant where she had met Stephen, she entered a drugstore and sat down at the only empty seat at the counter.

"Ham sandwich," she told the clerk, "and a double malted milk."

Upon a dangerous impulse she had asked to be transferred to Laboratory B on the pretense—let her be honest with herself, at least—that the electrical outlets were of stronger voltage than those in the laboratory to which she had been first assigned. The real reason, uncontrollably transmuted with emotional impulse, was that Stephen Coast worked in Laboratory A. She was permitting herself a folly again, as if her lesson had not been bitterly learned in India. Dark eyes set in a sensitive masculine face, a male body, strong and graceful, a brilliant mind, speaking a language she understood, these she had sworn to resist, in India or anywhere in the world. And reminding herself in anger, she had opened the door and seen Stephen Coast and as quickly shut the door again.

"Fool that I am," she whispered between set teeth. Fool to open the door or fool to close it again? Never mind the question, she argued fiercely in her brain, and so never mind the answer. She subdued her wild thoughts and dispelled them as enemies, and returned to her usual companions, the atoms, those unseen and unseeable units of life, which in multitude and energy created the universe. Which or who? They had become living creatures in her imagination, each containing within itself its own universe complete. It was now apparent that if they moved in unison toward an explosive point of critical heat, a power never known before would be thrust into the hand of man. Chain reaction.

Across distances she heard a voice at her ear, a high fresh voice, the voice of a girl.

"I said to him, 'Well, if that's what you want, take it.'"

"Oh Marge, you didn't!"

A duet of laughter caused her to inquire. She turned her head to see two pretty girls, their slender figures encased in flowered summer frocks, thin arms bare and pony tails of blond hair flying against their childish necks. She looked at them with vague familiar envy. She knew them so well, not their names, but what they were, the gay little girls with whom she had tried to play games when she was herself a child, if she had ever been a child, their games never hers, their doll games, their games of playing house, mother and children, cooking and cleaning and visiting. Under an Indian sky the games were the same, and starved for companionship she had played until she acknowledged her loneliness was not healed. She was born under another star,

60

a different creature, but no less woman. That she was beginning now to discover. In the years after she had left India and come to her own country to study she had almost forgotten it again, in those years when she began to know what she was, her own talents, diagnosed by her physics professor at Radcliffe. In those years and in her excitement in the search she had not thought to ask whether she was woman, and indeed that she was a woman was a circumstance for impatience, an impediment, and still an impediment when she sat lonely among men.

The drugstore clerk slammed a plate before her with the ham sandwich and mixed the malted milk and set it down. The liquid slopped and wiping it away, he joined the conversation on her left.

"Hey, you kids, how's about a double date tonight? Me and Ernie."

"Ernie!" The name was a shriek. "I wouldn't go nowhere with Ernie!"

"Aw, come on, Ernie ain't so bad. A little too fat, maybe—but—"

"Fat! He oughtta be in a circus."

"Yeah, that's where Ernie belongs—"

"Ole sloppy lips—"

"Sa-ay, how do you know what kinda lips he has?"

She withdrew her mind and the habit of withdrawal enclosed her again in a curtain of unhearing silence. . . . Plenty of uranium 238, so the problem was not there. The resonance absorption of neutrons would lead, wouldn't it, to plutonium? Fast neutrons were easy enough but uncontrolled they might blow up the globe. There had to be control.

Control—control—control—that was the word. It rang through the recesses of her brain like a bell tolling.

On the way out of the store she bought a newspaper. The headlines caught her eye and she stood at the door reading.

61

Washington, April 24.—Scientists of the world are in an international race today for the solution of a riddle which would yield an explosive one hundred million times as powerful as TNT or any known explosive. A quick solution of the problem might lead to victory in the war. It is known that the physicists of Great Britain, France and Germany are all working upon the problem. But so are the physicists of America and fortunately from our point of view American physicists are in the lead. The new explosive which may also be the answer to the search for the release of atomic energy is one of the isotopes of uranium. Less than one per cent of a sample of ordinary uranium consists of this particular isotope. The only success reported so far has been at Columbia University where an amount so small as to be invisible to the unaided eye now reposes upon a glass slide.*

Over her left shoulder a voice spoke, a high fresh voice. "Say, what's iso—isotopes?"

She folded the paper. "Isotopes are elements that are identical chemically but have different atomic weights."

The duet of laughter rose again on the left. "Gee, whaddya know—"

They went down the street, hand in hand, and from the counter the clerk yearned after them while Jane Earl went her lonely way.

*   *   *

"What you have to remember, Stephen," Burton Hall said, "is the difference between the German concept of progress and our own."

* Reprinted by permission of Dodd, Mead & Company from *Atomic Science, Bombs and Power* by David Dietz. Copyright 1954 by David Dietz.

"Strange notion of progress," Stephen retorted. "Total destruction! And I can't say that we're much better, with all our plans and purposes shaping toward a weapon designed to end humanity."

It was the end of the day, early summer again in its soft warmth. They had met at the top of the marble steps of the university, where they had gone separately to hear Enrico Fermi lecture on cosmic rays. Burton Hall, meeting Stephen by accident, had said half ruefully, "The little man still knows more than any of us."

"I wonder if he knows how the atomic chain reaction can be made to work," Stephen had replied.

"Why don't you ask him?" Burton Hall suggested.

"If he were ready to tell, I suppose he would," Stephen said.

From such desultory talk, they had arrived at the weapon itself, Burton Hall pondering the possibility of the Nazi discovery of the secret. "If they have it they will use it in a matter of months, say four, in which case the rest of the world might as well give up hope," Stephen said.

"Not at all," Burton Hall retorted sharply. They stepped from the marble of the last tread to the soft green lawn and strode together into the brilliant sunshine between the shadowing trees. The noise of the city, usually so distant, broke into a sudden siren screech, and a fire engine roared down the street. Burton Hall continued. "The final aim is the same —peace and the products of peace. We all value peace, knowing that only in peace can we live comfortable and reasonably happy lives. Therefore the Germans destroy their enemies, or potential enemies, in order that they may progress in peace thereafter."

"And we?" Stephen inquired.

Two boys raced by pursuing a ball, and the men swerved to let them pass. Stephen recognized Jim Weiner, the son of

63

Ernst Weiner. But the son had eaten American eggs and meat and had drunk his fill of milk and he was inches taller already than his foreign-born father.

The ball was caught and Jim whirled back and Stephen stumbled over his flying foot.

"Careful, Jim," he cried. The black-eyed boy threw him a bold and careless look and ran on without apology. This was the look he had learned here, the American look, and how different it was from his father's cautious courtesy! Ernst Weiner had learned to cringe and to apologize, and the son had never known the need of either.

"We Americans," Burton Hall was saying, "build weapons for defense, not destruction. We want peace, too, peace in which to progress, but we don't create a desert around ourselves for safety. We simply hold our weapons—and let the rest of the world know we have them."

"You think we'll never use the bomb?" Stephen inquired.

"Whether we do or not," Burton Hall said firmly, "doesn't mean we can afford not to make it. We must make it, and as fast as we can."

They walked in silence for a moment until their ways parted and Stephen stopped.

"What do you want me to do?" he asked.

Burton Hall looked at him, unwavering. "I want you to make a study and write a report. I want you to tell me whether ordinary uranium can produce a chain reaction. Will you do that?"

Stephen did not reply. A grey squirrel ran to his side and he stood looking at the small expectant animal. The bright black eyes, the quivering brush of tail, the two pleading paws folded like miniature hands, moved some part of his unthinking mind and he felt in his coat pocket for the peanuts he usually carried. There were two left and he dropped one on the grass and watched the little animal peel the shell away and nibble the white meat.

"I wish you wouldn't ask me to work on it." He did not lift his troubled eyes.

"I need you," Burton Hall said firmly. "There's no one who combines your intuition and your precision. A fellow who can measure cosmic rays twenty-five hundred feet underground in a mine and have them within a decimal fraction of accuracy is the fellow I want to tell me what can be done with uranium. I count on you, Steve."

Stephen threw his last peanut to the squirrel.

"Very well," he said. "I'll go that far."

Burton Hall stooped, picked up a pebble and threw it at the squirrel. "Good. Then I shan't give you another thought. When you're ready you'll report."

Stephen nodded and walked away. It was evening and over the lake clouds were moving up from the horizon, black, heavy and fringed with silver. Out of them a fork of lightning sprang at him and he heard a growl of thunder.

*   *   *

The storm made Burton Hall restless. He faced the lake and as he entered his house the violence of the wind was already beating the water into white-crested waves. The rising rhythms of the elements roused in him a troubled excitement. He was always aware, subconsciously, of the infinite spaces beyond this globe where in black darkness the forces of explosive creation continued their ferocious play. Directed or undirected? Controlled or uncontrolled? This was the question of his eternal soul. Eternal? Who knew? He had traveled far from the safe highways of his father's theologies, and yet the farther he traveled the less convinced he became of purpose. Purpose! But what purpose, and whose,

65

and where was the powerhouse of control? Could it be in the infinitely small nucleus of the atom? Was what his father called The Divine Will concealed within that microcosm? Fragmented or whole? Or, as the Asians declared, pervading matter with spirit and energy? Was energy spirit and spirit energy, and this energy, as Einstein had shown, transmutable and even interchangeable with matter? . . .

He shook himself like a big dog. Let him remain a scientist. This was where he had split with his father. Oh, the long interminable and angry arguments he had fought through with that man of God! His father had never yielded. "No son of mine shall be an atheist," he had roared. The final argument had been on a Sunday afternoon Burton Hall remembered, when he was twenty. It was after a church service always too long, a sermon full of wrath and storm, and he and his father had argued for the last time.

"I'm agnostic, not atheist," he had shouted in reply. He stood as tall as his father, six foot two, and his shock of red hair made him taller. He remembered because their eyes met on a level, his father's brilliantly blue, and his tempered by his mother's brunette darkness into the sea green. She had died when he was fifteen, and his father had never married again.

They had stared into each other's eyes, father and son, and in momentary silence had discovered each the other's invincible will. Then his father lifted his arm to strike him and he stood ready to receive the blow. Instead his father's arm had dropped.

"God forgive me," he muttered. "But get out of my sight."

He had turned then and left the room—left the house, for that matter. He had packed his things into his suitcase and gone away. He had gone back to his old college, paying his own way by a night watchman's job in an apartment house where he could sleep in snatches. It was the last argument

66

he had ever had with his father. Two years later his father had died in triumphant faith, certain of himself and his God. . . . Where in this stormy universe could a man lay hold on faith? Perhaps God Himself was in creation, proceeding to unity through the infinity of nuclei in the infinity of matter. Perhaps God was everywhere, as his father had taught him, but only because God was Everything.

He turned away from the storm before his eyes and went into the living room. Mollie was sitting in the armchair, crocheting or knitting, he could never remember which it was. Two needles for knitting, a hook of some kind for crocheting—it was crocheting. Accustomed in her girlhood to the streets of a quiet suburb in Westchester, New York, she considered Chicago a center of the wild west, and she disliked the vastness of a lake which was as big as an ocean. She had drawn the shades against the storm, and had lit the lamps.

He sat down and in silence watched her smoothly moving fingers. She had plump capable hands. Long ago, when she had been a pretty girl, he had found the hands enchanting. Now they were only comforting. His mind slipped away into its own life. He began to talk, his eyes fixed upon the steady hands.

"Mollie, here's the problem. We've got to get enough of this uranium stuff to experiment with. Not just any uranium, but uranium 235. And you may ask me why uranium 235?"

Mollie did not look up. She never asked such questions. She let him ask them and answer them while she counted her stitches and kept her pattern. She was not interested in uranium whatever its numbers, but he needed somebody to talk to or he talked to himself and that made him look crazy. She counted silently, not moving her lips.

"Because, Mollie, the nucleus of uranium is not stable. It yields when a neutron attacks it, it divides into two the way a drop of water divides. Gamow says—"

She interrupted. "You told me that before, Burt. I remember now."

"About a thousand times," he agreed.

"What I don't see," she went on amiably, "is why you don't just let things alone. Call wood what it is. It's wood."

"Because it isn't what it is," he retorted. "It is changing—everything is always changing. Wood changes into fire and smoke and gas. When we had dinner with Niels Bohr in Copenhagen, don't you remember he explained that nothing is quiet or the same? Electrons are always whirling around the nuclei of atoms and atoms are vibrating inside the molecules and molecules are—"

She remembered very well that evening in Copenhagen. They ate from beautifully polished wooden plates and she had asked where she could buy them and the very next morning she had gone to a shop and bought twelve of them. She used them for service plates though she'd never liked eating off wooden plates. How could one be sure the wood was clean? It sounded silly to say that something inside the wooden plates was always whirling around—so unsettling! But even on her honeymoon she had made up her mind she would not let Burt and his strange scientist friends unsettle her. They were all a little crazy—Thompson, for instance, who walked down the street touching every telegraph pole with his forefinger, which he first licked with his tongue. Now what made him do such crazy things? She was ashamed to be seen with him. They were all touched; she pitied them, though, and found them lovable.

"Go on," she said absently. "I'm still listening." She finished an exquisite shell-like shape of pale pink wool. The woman next door was expecting a baby and wanted a girl.

"We run a terrible risk," Burt was saying. "We might blow ourselves up."

"Oh dear," Mollie murmured. She spread the tiny sweater

68

on her lap. It was almost finished. If Burt kept talking long enough, the way he did sometimes, talking for hours, and it would have made her nervous just to sit and listen, she could finish it.

Burt raised his voice. "Mollie, do you understand chain reaction?"

"What chain, Burt?"

"Oh God," he groaned, "chain of energy, of course! That damned pink knitting!"

"It's not knitting, it's—"

"I know—I know you're doing it with a hook so it's crocheting. I wish you knew as much about my work as I do about yours! Chain reaction, my child-wife, is when the fission of nucleus in an atom releases a neutron—or two or three—which in turn attacks other neutrons that attack other nuclei in a chain—"

"Sounds more like a fight to me," Mollie said.

Burt roared. "Exactly! Mollie, why do you ever act stupid? The fight is the explosion—see? Bang—bang—bang! The only trouble is we haven't much uranium 235, only enough to show us that it can be done. We haven't as much yet as the size of a pea."

"Gracious," Mollie said. "I hope they won't lose it somewhere—down a drain, or something."

"They're working on uranium in General Electric," Burt said, not listening. "When big industry goes after something they get it. They have the money."

"Speaking of General Electric," she said. "I wish you'd look at the refrigerator. It's freezing everything solid. I had to throw out a quart of milk this morning."

"Sure."

They got up and walked toward the kitchen. He put his arm about her plump shoulders. "It's a comfort to talk to you," he said. "It clarifies my mind. Let's have dinner early tonight, old girl. I've got some thinking to do after all this talk."

"I do hope the dessert isn't frozen," Mollie said. "It's your favorite custard."

"If it's frozen it'll be ice cream," he said amiably. He was not deceived by his Mollie. She did not understand one word of what he had said. But then she did not try to deceive him. She made no pretense of understanding. And his mind was clarified, nevertheless.

He opened the refrigerator door. The storm was over. A ray of evening sunlight fell across the room to illuminate his household task.

*   *   *

At four o'clock in the morning of the same night the telephone beside Jane Earl's bed rang three times. She woke instantly, alert and aware. That was Burt's call. Three times and he'd put down the receiver if she did not answer and then take it up and call again, waiting to hear three rings. It was the signal between them.

"Yes, Burt," she said quietly.

His voice was harsh and abrupt at her ear. "I'm worried."

"What's happened?"

"That's what worries me. Nothing's happening. We'll have to get the go-ahead sign from the very top. We've got to scare the Big Boss himself, no less. These old birds from Europe—they're right, tall girl."

"You're right," she said. "You're always right. So who can get to the top? I can think of only one man."

"Old longhair himself?"

"Right. . . . And you're the one to make him do it."

"He won't listen to an ordinary American."

70

"Waiting for me to say you aren't ordinary? Well, I won't say it. You're already as vain as a rooster."

"Who do you suggest to talk to the long-haired buzzard?"

"Italy and Hungary."

"Okay—you sleeping alone?"

"I always sleep alone."

"Say the word, tall girl—"

She laughed. "Good night." Then she hung up the receiver and lay awake until dawn, thinking of no man in the whole world. Instead equations crawled through her brain in endless succession, leading inevitably to the conclusion that she had discussed with Fermi only that day. Chain reaction was possible, explosion inevitable. And control? she had inquired. Graphite, he had said, blocks of graphite interlarding the sticks of uranium that didn't yet exist. Much better than the heavy water the Germans were using.

"You don't mind getting your hands dirty, do you?" he had asked. "Graphite's black as soft coal."

"How often have you seen my hands dirty?" she had retorted.

He had laughed without answer. Plenty of times, he might have said. She had sacrificed her slim and pretty hands as she had sacrificed herself. And to what? To the eternal curiosity that made her a scientist, in spite of being a woman, and she would never know if science was worth it.

*   *   *

On a September day in the White House the Big Boss looked across his desk at the small crumpled figure opposite. He lit a fresh cigarette, thrust it into his cigarette holder and held it in the corner of his mouth and jutting it at the same angle as his own formidable jaw, he listened to the mild voice, speaking of vast annihilation and immeasurable

71

catastrophes, a voice as mild as a child's. The day was hot, September in Washington could be damnably hot, and he sat in his shirt sleeves.

He broke in affably. "Take off your coat, won't you?"

The small figure shook a shaggy head. The gentle voice trailed off into apologies. He had taken too much time, he was sorry, but these were important facts and it was to be hoped that something would be done, and in time—

The man behind the desk, tall, heavy, handsome, stared at the small grey scientist. "So all matter is composed of atoms, eh?"

The small man nodded.

"And what are atoms composed of?"

"Electrical particles, sir."

"What's the difference between electricity and magnetism? You see, I've been boning up on you!"

"They are aspects of the same force."

"The Chinese had the same notion—did you know?"

The shaggy head declared a negative. No, he did not know.

"They called it yang and yin. Yang is the male principle, which surely is electric, and yin is the female, which is magnetic, just as surely."

The cigarette tilted extravagantly and the big man laughed. "Rather clever? My grandfather—maternal—made his fortune in China—Hongkong and Canton. Opium, I'm sorry to say, but in the fastest clippers that sailed the high seas. Ships are in my blood."

He threw a sidewise look at the little man. A patent clerk, eh? With not enough to do, probably, for how many patents were issued in a patent office in Switzerland half a century ago? So in boredom that brilliant mind, so utterly concealed in an undistinguished skull under a lot of uncut hair, had begun idly, or fervently, to consider the universe.

And here he sat, the only living man among the great dead scientists of the past, the only one who could be sure of his place among the imperishable saviors of mankind, Hippocrates, Archimedes, Euclid, Copernicus, Galileo, Newton— and Einstein.

"I wish I could stand up in honor of you," the big man said abruptly. "But at least your mission is fulfilled, I will move to act."

The small man rose and bowed in his deep European fashion.

"Thank you, sir," he said in his soft voice. "Thank you very much."

He bowed again, he turned and opened the door and closed it behind him so quietly that it was hard to believe he had been here at all. The big man slumped a little in his chair and a grey pallor crept over his face. He took up a paper from his desk and read it, chewing at his cigarette holder. Two years ago the Germans had invaded Poland and for sixty days the bitter battle had been waged in the streets of Warsaw. The Russians? Idle, playing cards, eating and drinking and lighting fires at night, their army had watched from the banks of the Vistula, opposite the beautiful, dying city. Russia and Germany! The little man was right. There was no time to waste and a long way to go. To find the men was the problem. Always the problem of the right men for a job! The little scientist, sitting there across the desk, prophesying—yes, a prophet. He dared not disobey the prophetic warning. Whatever these scientists were doing, he was compelled to heed.

The big man sighed. Then he pressed a buzzer firmly and spoke.

"Tell Harry to come here. . . . I want to talk to him—or hear him talk. And send word to my missis that I won't be home for dinner."

His cigarette was ash and he fitted another into the holder and tilting it toward his left eyebrow he blew out clouds of furious smoke.

*   *   *

In his small study off the living room Stephen Coast was finishing his report for Burton Hall. He had checked and re-checked his calculations, and as far as they went he was prepared to stand by them when those bulletlike questions, to which he was by now well accustomed, were flung at him by his superior. Yet his conclusions were far from re-liable. The mind could imagine and abstract, but the flashes of insight, expressed in the figures of equations, had yet to be affirmed by physical measurements of atomic nuclei, thus far never measured. He had no wish and indeed no courage to measure them. The power that was still locked inside the invisible nucleus of an atom was something he preferred not to think about, much less to be responsible for releasing into the world of man. He sat, frowning and troubled, before the sheets of paper where his close reasoning lay revealed in equation upon equation in his small fine handwriting. If he could go back again to his youth in a quiet Pennsylvania street he would have chosen any calling but this in which he found himself, a scientist. But his father, that silent man of business, had given him no warning and his mother had only been proud of him for winning a scholarship to Harvard that he did not need. Who was there to warn him of future destruction? A child? A child playing with matches—

Across his questioning thoughts the light laughter of women fell with disturbing music. What had possessed Helen to give a party only for women, today of all days, was be-yond his understanding, and the more because she had not only avoided asking his permission, but she had not so much

74

as told him. Suddenly at three o'clock in the afternoon women had filled the house. This, in view of the procedure accepted between Helen and himself that when he was working at top speed upon a difficult assignment, and now on the most difficult and dangerous of all, the house should be kept quiet. Instead of the quiet so necessary to him, when he was wresting from the recesses of his brain abstruse and remote concepts, to be expressed only in the precise terms of relativity, he had to contend with this chitchat of women's voices in the next room.

He put down his pencil impatiently. At the sight of the red soft lead pencils with which he worked, he remembered that for at least a week Helen had not kept those pencils sharpened, a task of love which she had begun in their honeymoon, a sign of repentance for a fit of anger because the honeymoon had been interrupted by Burton Hall, demanding that the bridegroom submit a plan for a machine or tool or instrument or perhaps only a method for extracting radium easily and quickly from pitchblende, on the basis that there was only one Madame Curie, a woman who had had the patience to do it ounce by ounce, and by hand. Only a woman—

His scattered and irritable thoughts were suddenly focused by Helen's laughing voice, clear and cutting.

"Now, Jane—I may call you Jane?"

"Everyone calls me Jane." He recognized that calm voice!

"Well, then, Jane, do you really, really and truly, understand Einstein's theory of relativity? You needn't lie, we're only women, and we'll never tell."

Now this was outrageous of Helen! It proved what he had begun to suspect, that however passionate and singlehearted she might be in love, she was also capable of extreme malice and torture, of herself, he admitted grudgingly, as well as of others, and whom she was now torturing he did not know,

75

Jane or herself. He repressed an impulse to leap from his chair and face her in the presence of all her female friends —how female a woman could be! Instead he turned his head to hear Jane's reply. He was amazed to hear her laugh, and hearing that soft and pleasant sound, he realized that he had never heard her laugh before.

"How can I answer such a question?" Jane said. "If I say I do understand, you will hate me. And, please, I want you to like me. So I'll say that Einstein has just led us further into our own universe and perhaps he has thrown a guiding light on a universe beyond ours—in terms of mechanics, I mean. I suppose I could say, too, that Einstein is always trying to simplify the complex ties of everything that exists, and bring them into a relationship, a unified field, he calls it. Time, distance, and mass—these are the materials he uses —I suppose they add up to everything—everything that's physical, I mean—and mass means weight or, rather, resistance to motion. Einstein understood somehow, with his purely conceptual mind, that relativity between these three proves that this mass or resistance is not unchanging, as we thought it was, but that its weight increases with velocity, relative to the one who observes it."

The lovely voice flowed on and on in total listening silence. Across it Helen's lively tones cut like a sword across silk.

"I can almost understand what you are saying—but only almost. It's like creeping up on a bird ready to fly, with a handful of salt for its tail. Tell me—do you understand what my husband is doing?"

Now why, he asked, did she use the two words, "my husband." He was always and only Steve. "My Steve," she might have said.

Jane hesitated. "I am not sure I know exactly what he is doing, at this moment. We haven't talked—"

Ah, she was telling Helen delicately that she had not met

this husband recently. So that was Helen's question. It was true that he had not met Jane for two months, nor thought of her, his mind pre-empted and preoccupied.

"Haven't you? Really?"

"Not lately, Mrs. Coast."

"Will you call me Helen?"

"If you wish—"

"Well, but tell us about this uranium. Oh, I'm stupid—"

"I'm sure you're not. . . . What shall I tell you?"

"Anything you think I could understand."

So once more the lovely voice began. "There is so much to tell, and yet so little we know. I suppose that is what Dr. Coast is working on."

"Don't you call him Steve?"

"No. . . . You see, the natural uranium ore as it comes from the mines can't be exploded atomically. Only one of the isotopes of uranium can be exploded—uranium 235. It's a magic sort of thing, so rare that of the isotopes of the 92 elements existing in nature, only this one fissions when it is struck by slow neutrons—so far as we know now, of course. Unless we can separate 235 in pure form we can't get the energy we need—for whatever we need it for."

"Weapons?"

Ah, Helen was being shrewd! He rose to rescue Jane. No one was sure yet that weapons could be made, or should be made. To explode by fission a fairish-size piece of uranium, enough atoms had to be split at the same time. Neutrons were the solution, of course, as Fermi had already discovered. If fission itself released neutrons, they could create fission again and there would be a chain, linking one fission to another. . . . That was not woman's talk.

He went into the living room and stood looking about him. Six women, among them Mollie Hall, knitting at something pink. Would she report to Burton Hall what Jane had said, or was she too stupid to know what Jane had said? One never knew whether Mollie Hall was stupid.

"May I have a cup of tea?" he asked.

He met Helen's defiant eyes and hardened himself. There must be no shenanigans in times like these. With elaborate and unusual courtesy he went the round of the guests, shaking hands with each, and then seated himself beside Jane.

"I have finished my report," he said, "and if you can spare me an hour or so, I'd like to discuss a few points with you before I turn it in."

"Of course," she said.

He met Helen's eyes fixed upon them and gave back her look. She turned away.

*   ❖   *

At midnight he was still talking with Jane. Two hours ago Helen, restless and moving about the house out of earshot of their voices, knocked at the half-open door of his study.

"I'm going to bed, Steve."

"I'll be up soon."

She came in then and unexpectedly kissed Jane's cheek. "Good night, Jane."

"Thank you, Helen—"

"For what?"

"The kiss—"

"Oh that—well, I don't often kiss people."

She went away, enigmatic, and they fell to talk again as though she had not been between them.

"You have no doubt now," Jane said, "that a bomb can be made."

"None."

She bit her lip. "That means any nation can destroy any nation, and cheaply, as warfare goes."

"I'm afraid so."

"Have we control of the raw materials—possibly?"

"There's uranium everywhere, probably—and probably thorium—so that's beyond our control."

"And there's no controlling science. We may keep a secret for a few months, or years—not more."

"There's no stopping the minds of men," he agreed.

She gave a deep sigh. "Is this the end of mankind?"

"I refuse to believe it so."

"But you are profoundly troubled."

"Every sensible person must be."

"Yes—"

Silence fell. She broke it at last. "I feel terribly responsible —as a woman. I wish I weren't so alone."

"At this moment you are only a scientist, no more woman than I am man."

"Except that you belong to one half of the human race and I to the other. And your half is awake and in action. And mine—sleeps. Bearing children, keeping house, all asleep, the children to be thrown to the fires of atomic explosion and the houses to be ashes! How shall I wake them?"

Tears welled to her eyes and slowly rolled down her cheeks. He could not bear to see her weep in this concentrated agony, and did not dare to put out his hand to comfort her. Instead he tried to speak lightly.

"Aren't these tears premature? What we are talking about may never come to pass."

"We mustn't let it come to pass."

She rose and put out her hand. He took it, and felt it warm and quivering in his own. Yet only for an instant for, mutually aware, they parted, and he saw her into her small car outside.

When he went upstairs Helen was asleep, or so he supposed. She was on her right side, face turned from the door, and she did not move. He did not wake her, and then lay sleepless in his bed. Jane was right. They must not let it happen.

*   *   *

"Here's my report," he told Burton Hall next day. "I finished it last night and checked it with Jane Earl. We agree that chain reaction is entirely possible. The explosion it creates may be beyond control, but only a test will tell."

"What'll we use for moderators?" Burton Hall inquired. He ran his pencil through his bush of red hair and stood it on end. The morning sunlight, blinding bright through shadeless windows, caught his head in a blaze.

"I've made suggestions in the report," Stephen said. "I think Fermi's graphite is the best, probably. Simpler than heavy water or any of the others—"

"Hm—" Burton Hall was riffling the papers of the report. "A very thorough job. . . . Your next assignment."

Stephen broke in. "I want to be taken off the job, Burt."

Burton Hall stared at him with eyes as green as glass. "What do you mean?"

"I want no part of the making of this weapon."

"Who does? It's devil's work. But suppose other devils make it first? I'll bet the Nazis have seized Norway just because of the heavy water supplies there. I can't sit around and see my country blown up."

"Every man has to decide for himself," Stephen said doggedly.

"Not today," Burton Hall declared. He pushed the report aside. "We live or die together."

Stephen Coast did not reply. He sat, his lean length relaxed and, facing the window, he watched the students

80

sauntering across the campus. They were lively with the bright day, the cold wind whipping their cheeks, the girls' hair flying. Unreality! But which was the less real, these creatures of flesh and blood, so fragile and quick to die, or the unleashed force in a particle so small that only its shadow could be seen upon a photographic screen?

"As of today," he said, "I will have nothing to do with it."

Burton Hall's ready temper burst into a roar. "You call yourself a scientist! Will the fact that you decide against the weapon prevent its being made—and used?"

"At least I shall not be responsible," Stephen said.

Burton Hall's strong white teeth snapped like a dog's.

"You are already responsible," he snarled. "You are so damned responsible that if the bomb is dropped on us first before we can drop it on the enemy, you are to blame—you and your damned breed! You are the real warmongers! You pacifists—warmongers and defeatists. I don't forget your father was a Quaker. Milk in your veins!"

Stephen Coast did not reply. He rose to his feet, reached for his hat under the chair and left the room.

That night when he went home he kissed Helen briefly in the kitchen. She was making dinner, her cheeks were hot and red, and her mood, he surmised, was not entirely calm.

"When I think of my lovely big kitchen in the house I'll never have," she complained. "I wonder why I ever married a scientist."

"I wonder, too," Stephen said. "In fact, I wonder why I am a scientist."

He waited for her to inquire what was the matter with him, but she was engrossed in the handling of a nicely browned cake which she was drawing from the oven, in the course of which she burned her fingers. He searched for baking soda and applied it damp and decided that it was no time to speak of atomic explosion.

81

"How long before dinner?" he asked instead.

"Half an hour," she said, "and don't speak to me again. I have hollandaise on my mind."

"I'll be in the study."

In that safe retreat he sat with his head in his hands and tore apart his inner soul. Soul? He remembered a favorite saying of his father's. "The Chinese," the stubborn Quaker had declared, "know man better than we do. They declare that each of us has three souls and seven earthly spirits, in continual war."

"Three against seven?" he had inquired. "Isn't the conclusion inevitable?"

"Ah," his father had replied. "Who knows the strength of a soul? The proportion may be right."

Upon an impulse he reached for the telephone and called Jane Earl, aghast somewhat that he remembered her telephone number without having written it down. He could not remember where he had heard it but here it was, carved in his memory.

"Jane?"

"Yes, Stephen."

"I'm glad you call me that—I've been wanting to ask you to."

"It seems natural," she said calmly.

"I gave my report to Burton Hall today—and told him I wanted to go no further with the weapon. I'll do anything else in the way of research but I'll not work on that particular job."

"I'm glad," she said. "That means there are two of us."

He heard the soft click of her receiver and then silence.

*　　　*　　　*

It was long past midnight. Burton Hall rose from his desk and gathered the sheets of paper upon which he had been making notes and equations. He had completed the first step to any project he undertook. He had sat alone in the untidy room he called his library and here, surrounded by open books and scrambled paper and laboratory apparatus, he had created a plan for his own brain. The next step was to find Mollie wherever she was, wake her up if she was asleep and talk aloud to her. At this hour—he glanced at the clock on the dusty chimney piece above a fire long ago ashes —she would be asleep in the huge old-fashioned double bed which he had shared with her since their wedding night twenty-three years ago. However far they traveled together, she faithfully his helper wherever he went, the thought of that bed was to him the thought of home. In its depths, Mollie's sturdy body warming him, he could sleep as he slept nowhere else on earth. Climbing the stairs, he sighed. Sleep! When would he be able to sleep again without nightmare dreams? He stood upon the threshold of fearful knowledge, from which there was no retreat.

He put out the light in the upper hall and opened the door of the bedroom. The bedside lamp was lit, but Mollie was asleep, her even breathing stopping just short of a snore. He put his papers on the table beside the lamp and undressed in silence. A hot shower to relax him, five minutes of exercises—he mustn't take any chances with his health now—and he crept into the big bed beside her.

"Mollie!"

Accustomed to the summons, she struggled up from the depths of slumber.

He waited for her. "Mollie, I want to talk to you."

"Yes, Burt," she mumbled.

She was awake, he decided, bleary-eyed but awake. He

83

leaned over and kissed her forehead. "Poor woman—married to me," he said with rough tenderness.

"I'm all right," she mumbled. "Go on and start. I'm listening."

She forced her eyes open, gave him a wavering grin, and bolstered herself on her pillow.

"Mollie," he said. "I've bit off more than I can chew this time."

"Have you, Burt?"

He had taught her long ago never to waste time by contradicting him. She must not annoy him either by praise or by unwise faith. "I know my own weaknesses," he had snarled at her. "Your praise doesn't do a thing for me—it only makes me mad because you don't know what you are talking about, and I know you don't know. So when I say something—anything—about myself just agree, for heaven's sake, so that I can work myself out of it."

He proceeded now to self-destruction.

"I know my cosmic rays and all that stuff. I'll even go so far as to say I know a good deal about the possibilities of atom-splitting—not as much as that little giant, Fermi, but enough to talk with him and to understand what he's talking about, anyway. Not that we talk in this damned secret world we live in now—I don't even know what he's doing about trying to make this chain reaction business work. But here I'm asked to—no, I have to—do a job which has to use top scientists, a job of top secrecy, which will probably result in my having to make, or help make, a weapon which may blow up the world, you and me included—"

Mollie yawned loudly. "What do you do it for, Burt?"

"Don't ask silly questions," he retorted. "Do you think I'd do it if I didn't have to? The Nazis will blow us up—that's why! And the boys getting to military age!"

Mollie woke up at the mention of their two sons. "Don't

84

you get them mixed up in this! I don't want them to have
anything to do with your old science."

"Is Tim still set on being an actor?"

"Yes, he is, and Peter wants to be a doctor."

"Good. Now, Mollie, don't talk about the boys or anything.
Just listen, will you? Or we won't get any sleep. Here's the
situation as I see it at this hour of the night. We've got a
hell of a lot of work to do and no time to do it in. What we
could have taken our time about in the next century has to
be done inside of five years at the most. Let's aim for four
years. So where do we stand? We have a dim idea where the
greatest energy in the world is hidden. We're scared to let
it out because we don't know how to control it. So that's
the first problem, see? Control!"

"Control," Mollie murmured and fought off sleep.

"So how can we get control? Well, we have to have a
nuclear reactor first. A nuclear reactor, Mollie, is nothing
more nor less than a great big oven."

She opened an eye at him. "Oven? Like a kitchen oven?"

"Exactly the same but millions of times hotter, and so hot
that if the heat got out of control everything would burn up
and keep on burning because the heat is the same heat that
keeps blazing away in the sun and the stars—eternal flames
of burning helium gas."

"Oh mercy me," Mollie exclaimed and opened both eyes.
"Why do you have anything to do with it?"

"Will you keep quiet?" he snapped. "So I have to get
someone to build a reactor. I have to get a lot of men to do
a lot of things all at the same time. Now who'll I get for
that reactor? What do you think of Ted Parkes? He's stuck
in Washington with the Navy but I could pull him out. This
is bigger than any Navy project. He knows his nuclear
physics. We've worked together on X-rays. And I like him.
He listens to me, but he thinks . . ."

"He writes poetry," Mollie said irrelevantly. "I saw some poetry of his in a magazine. It was nice but I couldn't understand it."

"Then what's the use of its being nice?" he asked impatiently.

"It sounded nice when I read it out loud to see if I could understand it," Mollie said. "I couldn't, but still it sounded nice."

He stared at her. Was or was she not as stupid as she seemed to be? Married to her for nearly a quarter of a century he still did not know.

"Shall I go on or do you want to talk about poetry you can't understand?" he inquired with sarcasm.

"I haven't anything more to say, Burt," she replied.

He proceeded. "Whether Ted writes poetry is none of my business and not to the point. Now where was I?" He studied his notes. "Oh yes—here—control of atomic power. Now then, Mollie, there are several ways in which we can control this deadly power, but we don't know just how or which is the best medium of control. For example, there's beryllium or carbon. Both of them slow down atomic explosion. But beryllium is so damned scarce—I don't know where we'd ever get enough. Still, if it's the best moderator, we'd have to get enough—yeah, I guess that's what I'll ask Ted to look into. But carbon is dangerous—too close to the limits of what's needed as a moderator, if we get a chain reaction really going. Now, Mollie, I'm sticking my neck out. The Committee in Washington has been working a year and a half on uranium fission, trying to find a way of getting a controlled nuclear reaction and they don't think of getting anything ready in time for use in this war. But, honey, we're going to have to get it ready for this war, because from everything these European longhairs tell us, the Nazis are making big plans. So the Committee is still thinking only about peacetime use of this hot oven power if they are thinking at all! It's so damned secret that nobody knows about it and maybe they don't know themselves. There's such a thing as keeping a thing so secret that you stop thinking. But—are you listening, Mollie?"

"I'm listening," she said and swallowed another yawn.

"Mollie, I have a hunch!"

She looked at him hopefully. When he had one of his hunches it meant he was nearly through talking.

"I have a hunch," he repeated. "If we can once make a controlled nuclear reaction we can get any amount of radioactive material and we can make such a bomb that it will end a war at any minute we choose to drop it. . . . Maybe we won't have to drop it. Maybe we can just tell people we have it and scare the liver and lights out of 'em so they'll lay down their guns and get to work on peace. And Lord, won't that be worth doing!"

He leaned back and clasped his hands behind his head. His notes went fluttering to the floor.

"Know what that simpleton of a Stephen Coast said today? He said he didn't want to work on it any more. Handed in a report saying he was sure it could be done but he didn't want to be the one to do it. So with his damned foolish notions of not fighting he left me. Wants to work on things that won't kill people. . . . Let him go. . . . No, I can't let him go. I need all the top brains I can clutch. I'll keep arguing with him. Meanwhile I'll work on Ted. . . . We'll have to get pounds of U-235, pounds and pounds. But we'll do it. Yeah, and Thompson has a hunch of his own, too—you still listening, Mollie?"

"Yes, Burt, but I'm awful sleepy."

"Listen one more minute. . . . Thompson says that his experiments show that we can maybe make plutonium out of uranium 238. That means we can make chain reaction units out of a hundred pounds of the stuff instead of a hundred tons of the natural uranium. And if we get enough of the plutonium we can expect a chain reaction with fast neutrons instead of slow ones, which means such an explosion, Mollie, that we'd not just have a bomb—we'd have a super-bomb. . . . Yeah, that's what we've got to work on, honey. It's clear to me and now you can go to sleep."

He leaned over, smacked his wife's cheek with a loud kiss, and turned off the light.

＊   ＊   ＊

"Gentlemen!"

The clear English voice, the clipped English accent, reached every corner in the conference room.

Burton Hall was in California again. "I'm a sort of human spider," he had told the English scientist. "I weave a web across the country—New York last week, Chicago, Washington, and now here to meet you. The fellows in Washington don't want me to fly any more. They have some notion that I'm valuable. They're threatening to make me go by train, with a bodyguard!"

"They are right," the Englishman had replied.

Burton Hall settled himself now in the uncomfortable wooden chair to listen to the famous scientist and continued instead to think out his secret plans. The web must be woven far beyond the limits of one country. Science must narrow itself—no, call it focus—science must now be focused upon one single military project. A plutonium bomb must be made. . . . Strange how dreams became reality, given time and necessity! Alchemists in ages gone had wasted their lives in trying to make gold from baser metals. Now the transubstantiation was possible, but not for gold. The necessity was life itself. The urgency was war—possible war.

He corralled his thoughts and fought off sleep. The air in the conference room was warm and still. He had not slept well since the last night in the big old bed with Mollie. Coffee had lost its effect and he did not dare to try any of these "pep" pills that college kids used. He could not risk euphoria. Reality was too grim. And he had to know what this English fellow was saying. He'd had too important a hand in developing radar in England, and radar was the most valuable of all the scientific developments so far for the war. How many British lives it had saved nobody knew, the Nazi raids announced in time for fighter planes to soar into the darkness of English skies to meet the enemy attack. And what would they have done without that proximity fuse of radar to give them the warning?

"We have measured the scattering and capture of fast neutrons as they pass through uranium 235," the cultivated English voice was saying, "and we find that the amount needed for chain reaction is many times smaller than we first thought. We now believe that a bomb can be made with the resulting plutonium."

Americans had flash and flair, a daring genius, a brilliant improvisation, but these English fellows were substantial and sound. Burton Hall leaned to mutter this under his breath to Ted Parkes, sitting next to him.

"This makes it unanimous, doesn't it?"

Ted nodded. "England, Italy and U.S.A.—"

"Italy?"

"Fermi—remember? Everything he said confirms what we've just heard—less than a hundred pounds of plutonium."

Burton Hall nodded. His web had included Fermi in the last fortnight, and Weiner. Sitting alone with Weiner in his barren cement-floored office in an eastern university, he had gazed at the great Hungarian scientist. A timid man, he had thought at first, a man too ready to apologize and bow and excuse. . . . And about that he had been entirely wrong. The brain was brilliant, the thinking as lucid and swift as light.

"In a controlled reaction, where a moderator is used, it is the slow neutrons that are most important. We are making tests—"

He had listened that day while a grey autumnal rain pounded against the windowpanes of the high shadeless windows. Outside on the campus the leaves were falling from the maple trees. Students in raincoats hurried past, their heads lowered against the driving wind.

He had been startled by the sound of a cough—or perhaps a sob? He looked at Weiner, and saw tears on his pallid cheeks.

"We have no time," Weiner was saying. His voice sank to a whisper. "Believe me, I know what these Nazis will do. They give us no time. I know them so well how they are. There is no mercy in them—no humanity. . . . I have seen them—they killed my old parents—my old father, tortured by—no, I cannot tell it to you—" He had turned away, mopping his wet face with his handkerchief, his hands trembling —extraordinary hands, sensitive, delicate, the hands of an artist. There was an artist in every true scientist, and Burton Hall knew it because he had none of it in himself. He was a scientist by the chance of a too facile brain which could have made him a success at any one of several professions. A scientist pure and dedicated was a theoretician, a dreamer dreaming out of the universe great abstract possibilities.

"Maybe you'd better tell me," he had said that day. "Maybe I need to know. It's hard for us to believe what we read in the newspapers."

And so he had sat through the somber autumnal hours, listening to Weiner, seeing a man dissolve into crumbling terror as he remembered that from which he had barely es-

90

caped, leaving behind him every human being whom he had loved.

"'Go,' my father told me when I did not want to go. 'You must go,' he said, 'because you have in your brains something which can help to save the rest of the world. Go to America—tell them—'

"So he made me leave him, and leave everything—except what I carry here—"

He had tapped his forehead. He tried to smile.

"Excuse me. I have not allowed myself to remember and yet I cannot forget. . . . So you see why I say we must proceed quickly to make this bomb, to be ready for war."

"Maybe we won't have to use it, if we have it," Burton Hall had said.

"We don't decide that now," Weiner had replied. "But if we must we shall do it."

Into the pale grey eyes, still wet with weeping, there had come a look as grim as steel.

And from there, still within the web, he had flown back to Chicago and called in his men and through three days of racking thought and planning they had sat, quarrelsome with sleeplessness, to agree at last that plutonium could be made but only with much money and a huge plant, but it could be made, reduced to the pure metal needed for the bomb. A Polish scientist exile, expert on explosives, had stood up again and again.

"We can deliver a small atomic bomb in one plane, sparing the four hundred planes or seven hundred and fifty, maybe even one thousand planes usually carrying incendiary bombs to do such damage, or maybe even with the one bomb we can do fifteen times as much damage as all these. We cannot know until we try."

Silence had fallen upon them.

"It may be we shall never have to try," Ted Parkes had said.

"We shall have to try," the Pole had replied. "I have seen too much in my own country."

The meeting was breaking up, the Englishman had finished what he had to say. Scientists moved toward him, not in applause or disapproval but in grave concern. Burton Hall did not rise from his seat. A problem had surged up out of the depths of his restless mind. The fission energy of one pound of plutonium was equal, say, to about ten thousand pounds of TNT. Suppose the bomb blew itself apart before it could be used? What about the gas pressure, the specific heats at what temperatures—who knew the forces of inertia, the transmission of radiations and particles through the metal itself—how could such questions be answered or even calculated? Who knew anything?

He rose silently and tiptoed away. He had to be alone somewhere, for hours, out of sound of human voice, somewhere beyond this small world and near to the stars again.

*   *   *

On the flying platform in the chamber of the great telescope Burton Hall stared at shadows upon the vast and silvery background of the mirror.

"So that's the expanding universe," he said.

"That's it," the young astrophysicist agreed. He was new. Reuben Patterson had been found dead one morning at the foot of the circular stair. Some time in the night, or at dawn, dazed with what he had seen in the sky, or exhausted, his foot had slipped and he had been hurled through space to death.

Another scientist, without delay, had taken his place. He was a careless-looking youth, his rough tawny hair in need

92

of cutting, his round boyish face grey with fatigue. "The nebulae are all moving away from Earth," he now explained. "The more distant they are, the faster they're going. But they're all evenly spaced from each other. We don't know why."

"Billions of them," Burton Hall said, absorbed in the night.

"Billions of them," the young scientist agreed.

Burt's sea-green eyes narrowed into infinite distance. "Where did they start and where are they going?"

"If we knew that," the young man retorted, "we'd know where we began and where we're going. Which we don't! They repel each other, and that, if we're to believe Eddington, is why the universe is expanding."

"I don't believe repulsion is the whole secret of the expanding universe," Burton Hall said. "There's a stronger force than that—an attraction somewhere beyond, which even this telescope can't reach."

"It may be," the young man said. "We haven't got that far yet."

They went back to the rotunda as they talked, and the young man led the way to his private office, a room comfortably furnished with a cot and a desk and a blue and white lounging chair.

"Quite a boudoir you have here," Burt said.

"A lonely one, you bet," the young man replied.

He threw himself into the blue and white chair and motioned to the cot for Burt. "I worked here all night and hadn't time to clean up. I'm my own housekeeper."

Burt stretched himself on the cot. "Not married?"

"No time," the young astronomer replied. "Besides—where would I put a woman? Work all night and do mathematics all day. That's my life."

"No sleep?"

"Cat naps, between stars. . . . I saw a new nebula last

night. Golly—she was a beauty. . . . Blue-green, jeweled with tiny lights. I'd been looking for her."

"How did you know she was the one you wanted?"

"I'd set the telescope for her. There she was. I felt good about that."

Burt fell silent, contemplating this life for a young man not yet twenty-five. How explain to anyone such satisfaction as finding a blue-green nebula you've been looking for? But he understood it perfectly. The young man slept one of his cat naps and woke suddenly and sat up. "I've got to get back to the top."

"Before you go," Burt said, "tell me where the loneliest place in the world is, barring the top of your telescope where you swing among the stars. You know your western deserts."

The young scientist scratched his head and yawned cavernously and reflected for a moment. "There's a place in New Mexico," he said. "I used to go there to camp—golly, I was lonely among all those kids! Miles from nowhere it was—"

*   *   *

Burton Hall let the reins drop from his hands. He turned in the high western saddle and surveyed the scene behind him. Ahead were the mountains and the high mesa for which he was headed, but below was the magnificent desert spread of the Pajarito Plateau. In the distance the bare and rocky mountains of the Jemez range, that southernmost span of the Rocky Mountains, were iridescent in the afterglow of sunset. He must make the top of the mesa before nightfall. He faced the road again and took the reins. The horse pricked up its ears and broke into a mild trot. On either side of the narrow trail the walls of volcanic tuff rose shoulder high as he rode. Ahead of him, beyond the mesa top, a rim of mountains, pale gold in the last light of day, marked the crater of the largest volcano in the world, now extinct. What explosion, that, millions of years ago, when the boiling center of the earth upon which he rode so firmly today brimmed over into what was then probably an inland sea! Clouds of steam must have poured into the heavens and enveloped half a continent. Not more of a spectacle, though, than this dry valley, encrusted now in many feet of tuff! He'd see if there on top of the mesa was the spot for the great experiment. Uranium alone—ah, there was enough. He had come here by way of Colorado, where he had stopped to explore. If this mesa was to be the place, then within distance as easy as possible the old uranium mines, all but abandoned, must be opened anew.

For there in Colorado, a hundred and fifty million years ago, giant reptiles had stalked through the waters and their bones became fossils in the twisted and corniced rocks. The seas dried and the sands were petrified. Yet from the deep inner springs of the now-dry sea he had seen the mineral waters still bubbling to the surface, bearing the precious ore of carnotite to lie in pockets of powder in the solid sand. Yellow, green, grey, uranium was there, waiting to be mined. Ancient Navajos and Utes had smeared their bodies with the colored dust and in the First World War the two Curies had sent for small shipments of the mineral. Then with their death, prospectors searched for gold instead of uranium, and the work died. Now it must begin again in bitter vigor, mining and milling and shipping.

He climbed to the top of the mesa and here he paused and turned once more. To the east he saw the valley of the Rio Grande, the waters pale in the gathering dusk. Ahead the trail led through a forest of pine and when he had followed it to its end, the shadows darkening across his path, he saw a wooden building of logs. From the chimney a faint blue mist of smoke curled into the evening air. He had found the place he sought, far from roads and highways, distant from cities and remote from men. Here, in safety and secrecy, the great experiment could be made.

The door to the lodge opened as he reached it. An old man stood there in a torn grey sweater and dirty blue jeans, a stubby pipe clutched between his broken teeth.

"Can you shelter me for a night?" Burt asked.

The old man took the pipe from his mouth. "I reckon I can," he said.

✱   ✱   ✱

"It's the end of another day, Jane," Stephen Coast said. "And time to stop. We have our data down on paper, at least. There are four ways in which the stuff can be made, or so I figure. We'll need some hundreds of pounds of it. We have to remember that. The Germans are using the thermal diffusion method—terribly expensive, if I'm to trust the reports from the Naval Research people in Washington. They're working on that, too. England's using gas diffusion, so's Canada. But the problem there is the porous barrier. It's got to be perfect for the uranium in gas form—a material absolutely and uniformly permeated by holes less than one ten-millionth of an inch in diameter."

"Not to mention that the gas is frightfully dangerous and corrodes everything," Jane said and sighed. She sat down on a high three-legged laboratory stool and pushed back her hair with both hands. "I hate the very color of it," she went on, vehement with weariness.

"Sickly," Stephen agreed, "and it'll be all but impossible to make the pipes leakproof and corrosion-proof. But I have some ideas on that. . . . Then there's centrifugal separation and electromagnetic separation. And Burt has everything in mind now, in orderly form. I spent Sunday evening with him. Just to make sure, I outlined the four methods for him and where the laboratories are which work on each one of them. Amazing how much is being done in a scattered haphazard fashion all over the country! Co-ordination is the next thing. That's Burt's job, but he can't move until the government knows it. . . ."

"I went to a Beethoven concert on Sunday evening," Jane said. "I couldn't stay alone in my apartment, for some reason."

"Am I ever to see that apartment?" Stephen asked. He was washing his hands at the sink, his back to her, and he did not look around.

She considered this question and decided to accept the advance. She who had long ago acknowledged loneliness was finding it unbearable at last.

"When would you like to come?"

He retreated again. "Some time . . . when I have nothing on my mind. Maybe Helen will come with me. . . . Well, Jane, we know a lot about the stuff, I should say."

"We know a lot," she amended, "but maybe not enough. Shall you work on it, Stephen?"

"No," he said. "I'm still not working on it. I've done all I'm going to do. Oh, I'll work on a project of my own, of course. I've notions about the medical use of isotopes, for example."

She made no reply.

Stephen turned to face her and staring at her suddenly saw her. "Your nose shines," he said.

"Is that relevant?" She wiped the nose with her sleeve.

"Don't," he said. "I like it shining. It's a pretty nose. And your hair is in little wet curls."

She turned away and gathered pencils and sheets of paper scrawled over with figures and put them into the drawers of the table.

"It's time to go home," she said.

"I suppose so."

He idled for a few minutes about the laboratory, whistled under his breath, sharpened a pencil, cleaned the pencil sharpener for tomorrow.

"I had a letter from Burt today," she said.

Stephen did not turn his head. "Where is he?"

"In New Mexico. He's found the place if the project goes on."

"I suppose he wants you to go with him."

"He'll give me the choice."

"Are you going?"

"I don't know."

"You'll be working directly on the weapon if you go there."

She did not reply. He put down the pencil sharpener and taking off his work jacket, he reached for his coat.

"Well," he said. "I'm off."

Then he paused at the door. "I thought there were two of us. You said so once. . . . Two against all the rest of them. . . . It seems there's only one. I stand alone . . . don't I?"

She was studying a final sheet of paper, her straight brows drawn into a faint frown. Suddenly she exclaimed. "Stephen, I see where your mistake is!"

In three strides he was at her side. He snatched the paper from her stained hands. Over his arm she pointed her pencil at an equation.

"You've taken it for granted that the strength of the shock is determined only by the amount of energy that develops. But, it's not mass that matters. It's the energy, straight thermodynamics—"

He slapped his forehead and groaned. "God, how stupid can I be—of course! It's the same principle that Burt used,

98

years ago with General Electric. The force that bursts a photoflash bulb!"

"Right," she said. "The same formula for a tiny bulb and an atomic bomb."

He left her, clutching the sheet of paper in his right hand. She waited and when at the door he did not look back, she smiled. Left alone, she opened a drawer, took out a dusting cloth and proceeded meticulously to wipe the table as clean as though it were a kitchen sink.

*   *   *

"Do we have to live in that desert, Burt?"

Burton Hall put down his knife and fork and looked with exasperation at his wife.

"Will you please not talk about such things at the table, Mollie? The maid has ears as big as scoops."

"It's her day off and there's nobody in the house but us, Burt," she argued.

"Get into practice then," he retorted. "The boys will be home for Christmas next month."

She opened her china blue eyes roundly. "But will I have to live in the—"

"No!" he roared. "Nobody's going to live in the desert for a long time—maybe never, if I never hear from Washington, D.C.! Damn them, you'd think they'd all gone to sleep down there. All these months—"

"You don't have to swear, Burt, not at your own government," she protested, "especially since I only asked if I had to live in the—"

He broke in sharply. "And I said no. There's a lot of work to be done first. Besides, I'll put somebody else in charge there—probably."

She looked at him with wifely reflection. "You're so bad-tempered today I guess things aren't going well, are they, Burt?"

He wiped the egg from his mouth. "Too slowly, that's all. I've been waiting weeks for that call from the White House. The English keep prodding me. They came in a year after us and now they're ahead of us. It'll take something big to wake us up to this war, Mollie."

She pressed her hands to her carefully waved hair. "Oh, I hope we'll never wake up, Burt! Think of the boys. Tim would have to go right away. I couldn't bear it. I do hope you won't let those English drag us in, Burt. It's not *our* war!"

"Shut up, Mollie. You don't know what you're talking about."

"But I mean it, Burt. How come they're ahead of us?"

"They're smart, that's why. They concentrated from the very first on a weapon while we're still interested only in simple atomic energy—dreaming up a lot of things to do with it, all wonderful, but not useful except in the long run. And God knows how long any of us has to run, if I'm to believe these foreign fellows."

"Oh dear—I wish you would all stop!"

He looked up from his ham and eggs to see tears in her eyes, and throwing down his napkin he went to embrace her. She sobbed into his bosom.

"I'm so scared, Burt."

"Honey, honey," he muttered. "Don't—please don't. What I'm doing is only to keep you from being scared—you and everybody else. If we can get ahead of these goddam Nazis—"

She drew back suddenly. "Don't muss my hair. I've just had a new permanent. Do you like it, Burt?"

He looked at her with quizzical tenderness. "It's beautiful, honey—just beautiful."

100

An hour later, alone in his study, he got the telephone call for which he had been waiting all through the dragging months of an autumn heartbreaking in its late beauty. He snatched the receiver from its hook and heard the harsh dry voice crackling at his ear.

"That you, Burt?"

"It's me, Van—"

"The answer is, yes."

He sighed in a gust of relief. "Thank God—and you!"

"Don't thank me," the voice barked. "Not yet, anyway. We've got to sell the whole idea to the la-de-das, up yonder. How soon can you get here?"

Burt pulled the desk calendar toward him.

"Let's see—this is the fourth. I'll be there day after tomorrow. Oh God, that's a weekend."

"A weekend is nothing in my life."

"Nor mine—now. I'll bring the committee report with me."

"Fine. I'll be waiting."

"All right—but—"

"But what?"

"You know all this is going to cost hundreds of millions of dollars, don't you?"

He heard a snort of rueful laughter from Washington. "Don't mention that now."

The conversation was ended. He heard the distant click of a receiver replaced and he hung up his own.

"Mollie," he bawled. "Oh Mollie!"

Her voice came shrilly from upstairs. "I'm up here, Burt—"

"Well, get up then, girl. I'm on my way to Washington, at last—at last!"

* * *

Twenty-four hours later he knocked at an office door in a great marble building in the capital. It was Saturday afternoon but a pretty young secretary was behind the desk. She looked up and smiled.

"I'm waiting for you, Dr. Hall."

Burton Hall's green eyes comprehended the slim figure, the neat bright hair, the ready mouth. Very nice!

"I'm sorry you've been kept here on a Saturday afternoon," he said.

Their eyes met, communicated, measured, and he rejected the possibilities. No time, alas!

"You run along now," he said. "I'll let myself out."

She reached for her small blue hat and he went into the inner office. There behind a large governmental desk sat the tall spare figure he knew very well, the straight mouth, the shrewd stone grey eyes, the big hands of an old engineer. They exchanged a handshake and Burton Hall took a thick envelope from his briefcase and sat down.

"Here it is, Van. . . . Want to talk or shall we wait until you've read it?"

The engineer looked at his watch. "It's my wife's birthday. I promised I'd be back early. But if it's serious, I'll read it tomorrow and telephone you in the evening."

The two men looked at each other.

"It's serious," Burton Hall said. "You know us scientists. We're cautious. We hedge every statement with a barricade of ifs and buts and it's possibles. That's self-defense. We work in the realm of the unknowns and perhaps the unknowables. We don't know and we don't know when we do know. A new fact can destroy all we thought we were sure of yesterday. But why am I telling you?"

"Because you're as sure as you can ever be sure that things are blacker than you hope they are."

"Yes. Exactly."

Silence fell. The engineer reached for a pack of cigarettes on a bronze tray on his desk and lifted his fine eyebrows.

"No, thanks—" Burt said.

A flicker of flame, a puff of curling rings of smoke and the engineer spoke. "I take it you're staying over."

"I certainly can't leave until you finish the report and get some sort of comment from the higher-up."

"Good. Where are you staying?"

"The Wardman Park."

"Well, I'll be in touch with you. Let's go."

They rose and walked away together, their footsteps echoing down the empty marble corridors. At the street they parted and Burton Hall took a taxi to his hotel. There in his room he was restless. The air was dry and too hot with superfluous furnace heat. He threw open the window and leaning out he drew in great gulps of the mild November air. A heavenly day, still early, and what he needed was a hard game of tennis. Why not? And if he could get old Hank who lived here—but small chance at that. The Vice-President would scarcely be free, even on a Saturday afternoon. They were friends, at least more than acquaintances. He had defended the man through years of crackpot ideas that seemed to turn out all right, somehow. No harm trying, and lifting the receiver he dialed briskly and by a miracle heard the familiar nasal drawl. "Yes?"

"Hank?"

"Speaking."

"Burton Hall speaking. Want a game of tennis?"

"What are you doing here?"

"Official business."

"Sure I'll play tennis. I'll meet you downstairs in fifteen minutes."

"Fine. You ready to be walloped?"

"I might do the walloping."

"Not a chance."

They made mutual grunts of male laughter and he hung up.

Two hours later, when the sun was fire in the western sky and he was cleansed by sweat and fatigue, he said what he had to say.

"Hank, I've handed in the report from my committee. You'll see it. I've signed my name to it. When it comes under your eyes, give it your full attention, will you? It's possible—I'm the cautious scientist again—no, it's probable, that the way we act on this report will decide whether the war is to be won or lost by us."

"Sure," his victor replied. "I'll do that."

He put out his hand and Burt took it with the usual mild but inevitable disappointment. The hand was cool and limp, the hand of a dreamer who could not make his dreams come true.

*　　　*　　　*

The next morning, a mild grey Sunday morning, he woke to the sound of church bells ringing mellifluously through the sleeping city. He lay, pleasantly relaxed between the sheets, and meditated upon the endless number of friends whom he might inform of his presence. If he called one, a host would assemble and the day be frittered into broken conversations, hilarity, joking, useless talk and camouflaged questions as to why he was here. And he needed solitude. Ahead of him lay the greatest and most grave task that the mind of man could conceive, the making of a weapon capable, unless calculations were wrong even to the thousandths of a point, of destroying the planet. Fire from the gods, no less! And if the men at the top refused their approval, then he had the task, greater maybe, of convincing them of their complacent folly, when across the ever-narrowing Atlantic a madman was rousing the latent madness in every human being within sound of his raucous voice and sight of his bestial face. That lock of greasy black hair hanging over his crazed eyes! God, how could anybody not see what the mountebank was? And why the hell did he have to think of Hitler this Sunday morning in the still-peaceful capital of his own country!

He flung back the covers, impatient with himself and everything else, and padded barefoot to the bathroom. . . . No, he wouldn't talk to anybody today. He'd wander about the city alone, maybe go and look at Lincoln's marble face in that marble memorial hall. Better still, he'd visit Mount Vernon and walk the paths the founding father had walked and gaze out over river and hills and renew his soul. Gird up my loins and pray, he thought. Shades of my own dead father and how he would laugh in his grave, the old cuss, or wherever he is at this moment, if he is, to see me reduced to prayer! But I am reduced, O Lord!

The vague nostalgia of his religious childhood crept out of its hiding place in his soul and he dropped to his knees as he had not done since he was a child, and there beside the hotel bed he gripped his head in his elbows.

"Oh God—if there is a God—"

Then as always when he got that far he was silenced. What was the sense of mankind if there was no God? He knelt, tense and still, his whole being straining toward that great Unknown, and he heard no voice. Then after minutes he felt his muscles relax here, there, throughout his body, and slowly he was relieved, refreshed, almost renewed. What was this? Nothing, perhaps, except the refusal of physical particles to continue in the grip of the sustained energy of his will. Matter and anti-matter, whatever it was, he was ready to begin his day.

*   *   *

When he returned at nightfall, he was resolute again, clear in mind and purpose. All day he had moved among crowds, solitary and silent, observing and taking no part. He had eaten a sandwich at noon, sitting on the stone bench in front of the modest mansion and, facing the Potomac River as he munched bread and cheese and an apple, he had let thought and feeling subside in him. He had existed in and absorbed one of the rare days of his life and from its calm he perceived that George Washington, the owner and creator, had been willing to leave its rest and its beauty or, unwilling, had left it and had fought for his people because they were worth fighting for. He saw them today, men and women, trailing their children after them, not clouds of glory by any means, but dirty-faced, crying, laughing, quarreling minuscules of vitality, and yet as they wandered through the beautiful old rooms, their repulsiveness subsided. He observed their eyes of wonder and reverence, their wistful efforts to learn their own beginnings in a strange land, pausing to consider and to comprehend, to explain to each other in hushed voices, "Look—there's where he slept—" "That's his desk—his chair."

They, too, were here to be renewed, they longed for greatness, to be near it if they could not achieve it, and they were still worth saving, these people of his and George Washington's. They were not to be sacrificed to ignorance and complacence and delays or to the small prudence of saving dollars and balancing budgets.

106

Upon an impulse he ended the day at the feet of Lincoln and gazing up into that craggy face, those huge hands outspread, he heard a small voice murmuring somewhere at the level of his own knees.

"Mighty big, that Mr. Linkum—kinda scary."

He looked down to see a dark and scrawny child, a boy of six or seven, maybe four or five, who had wandered away from his parents, he supposed.

"If you got closer," he said to this child, "you wouldn't be scared. Shall I lift you up?"

The child nodded and he stooped and lifted him up in his arms.

"I touch he foot," the child whispered.

"All right, go ahead—" Burton Hall said.

The child put out a filthy left hand and touched the huge stone foot of the statue.

"Mr. Linkum don't mind," he observed.

"Not a bit," Burton Hall agreed.

The child slid out of his arms and ran to his mother, now approaching, a thin black woman in a cheap black dress, and not wanting to hear another voice, Burton Hall turned abruptly and walked away.

That night the telephone rang beside his bed. He waked instantly and glanced at his watch on the bedside table—half past two. Then he lifted the receiver and the dry harsh voice scraped at his ear.

"Burt? Van. I spent the day with the Boss. I've just left the big house. He says if the—gadget—can be made then we must make it first. . . . Meet me tomorrow at nine in my office. I've asked three other fellows to be there. You're to be a new committee. Fission research. Report back to me not later than a month from now. Maybe the world will look different to us then—better or worse. If your report is favorable—and the world looks worse—the nation is behind you—unlimited."

"I'll be there," he said.

"Good." The distant receiver clicked at his ear. He hung up and sank back on his pillow. Mission fulfilled.

*   *   *

On the sixth day of December, he signed his name to the final report and was proud of the speed with which they had worked. Days, not weeks, and the seven men had met here in his office or in Washington, sandwiching their conferences between inescapable tasks and journeys, two of them scientists who scuttled between the office and laboratories in England, checking and rechecking the testings, findings, recommendations.

Burton Hall wiped his pen on his handkerchief.

"Wonder your wife stands for that," a man observed. "Mine wouldn't."

"Nor mine—"

"Nor mine—"

"Mine's given me up," Burton Hall said briskly. "Besides, I've improved. I used to wipe my pen on my pants. . . . Well, gentlemen, we've finished the first part of the job. I don't know if this is an historic document or a waste of time. But I think Mr. Big will approve."

He heard a murmur of agreement, a scuffle of chairs shoved back, feet moving. He continued.

"I never voted for that fellow in the White House, never met him, never even saw him. But I say we're lucky at this moment of our history. He's brave and he's intelligent and he likes people. That's rare for a president."

The murmurs again, handshakes, men departing and eager to be gone. A good committee, he thought, watching their crowding backs, a college president, a politician of the better sort, the research director of a great industry, the rest of them scientists like himself, only better. It was clever of the President to dilute science with some everyday human material. He couldn't deny that scientists were queer ducks, he among them, though they insisted that they were not. We're like everybody else, they always began, and then proceeded to prove by word and act that they were different, a clan, a brotherhood, never in true communication except with one another. They could get off the beam quicker than any other members of the human race and yet they were the only ones eternally right in the end. A paradox of mutation!

He pressed the buzzer on his desk and the door opened on his plain-faced, middle-aged secretary.

"Get this report off tonight, Rosie," he said.

"Yes, Dr. Hall," she said docilely. Her mouth pouted as she took the papers from his hand. "I was going to the fight tonight. I have the tickets—my sister and me."

"Well, go on," he retorted. "I'm not stopping you. But get the report off."

She left with an air of profound injury and he observing it asked himself irritably why when the city was stuffed with pretty girl secretaries he kept Rosie Molloy in his office year after year. She was a good secretary in her stubborn complaining fashion but he'd had her so long that he knew her entire meager history and she continued to tell him every detail of her spinster's life. He was sorry for her, he supposed. Then he grinned suddenly. He knew himself thoroughly. He couldn't allow a damned pretty woman within his daily reach. He knew his weakness and he must not mess up his life now. Maybe later, when he retired and had time, if there ever was to be any time in his life, or anybody's, for that matter.

*   *   *

The next afternoon at four o'clock while he was dozing on the living-room couch, half buried in Sunday papers and his shoes off, the telephone rang. It was Rosie again.

"Dr. Hall, I don't like to bother you on Sunday—"

"So you're doing it," he growled.

"Yes, and only because the fight was so marvelous. Snaggy Bartlett won—did you know? I had a bet on him—twelve dollars. I'm going to buy—"

"Did you get that report off?"

"Yes, I did, Dr. Hall. Before I went to the fight. You know I wouldn't—"

"I don't know—"

"What I called you up for now is, they have the fight on radio right this minute—It's being broadcast again by the best sports commentator in—"

"Thanks," he snorted and hung up. Idiotic woman! Rosie and Clara! Why did silly women look at men's fights? His own sensible Mollie was upstairs in bed, deep in her Sunday nap, her hair in curlers and her face smeared with cold cream, as he very well knew, because they were going out to a buffet supper tonight somewhere or other. He yawned and turned on the radio to a football game, not to the fight. He wouldn't give Rosie that satisfaction tomorrow morning when she'd ask him.

Of course I didn't hear it. Think I have nothing better to do?

Football? No, there was some interruption. He heard the voice of a news commentator, excited, high—

"We stop this program to announce that Pearl Harbor has just been bombed by Japanese planes—"

110

The words, stark with horror, fell upon his heart like blows of iron upon bare flesh. He rose to his feet and stood immobile, the tears streaming down his face. All questions were answered at last. The nation was at war.

II

He woke on the morning of the next day, the eighth day of December, 1941, and was conscious of a clear mind, a calm heart. The great decision had been made and not by him. All over the country men and women were waking in this mood of certainty. Argument was dead. The enemy had declared himself and they saw him plain. That he had appeared in Asia was meaningless. The enemy was still the man with the ragged forelock, the spoiled and discontented child, carrying his discontents into the idle and unsuccessful youth, clinging to his discontents in a man who was still the spoiled child, refusing the disciplines of life. Now, in his revenge, he was drawing others like him everywhere in the world into rebellion against mankind. The weak had chosen the weak man whom they understood, and he used them. Had there been no Hitler there would have been no Pearl Harbor. Long ago the enemy was defined. He sighed, stretched and relaxed in the big bed beside his sleeping Mollie. Five more minutes and he must get up. Let her sleep! Last night she had astonished him by a fit of tears,

115

begun in subdued sobbing after he himself had fallen into a preliminary doze. He had turned over with a great heave.

"What's the matter with you?" he demanded.

She refused to answer, maintaining a silence broken by strangled sobs until, propelled by indignation, he had bounded out of bed.

"Let's have this out," he ordered.

She had refused to get out of bed, however, and propped on pillows had at last made unwilling revelation of why she had wept.

"I don't want to bother you, Burt, but it's Tim."

"What about Tim?"

"He'll have to go to war."

"Of course!"

"Burt, don't you *care?*"

"Mollie, it doesn't matter whether I care or not now. Every mother's son will have to go—why not yours?"

She wept afresh. "I wish I had no sons. I wish Tim and Peter had been girls!"

This from his Mollie! His mind leaped back to the days of birth. She had wanted boys, only boys, as proud to be the mother of sons as any Asian woman was. He tied the string of his pajamas tightly about his waist and paced the floor.

"Mollie, stop crying. And stop saying you wish you had no sons. Besides, the girls are going to have to get into this war. Not even sex will save them."

"You mean—"

"Yes! Bombs fall upon male and female alike."

Terror had dried her tears. She said no more, and watching him pace the floor with the loping stride of a hound-dog, she said at last in a small sighing voice, "Come back to bed, Burt. You'll catch your death of cold."

It had been three o'clock before he slept and now the day had come, a day like none other to which he had ever

116

awakened before. Still reluctant to begin it, he heard the doorbell ring. He glanced at his watch on the bedside table. Barely seven o'clock! A telegram perhaps—no, that would have been telephoned. He got out of bed, his dressing gown about him, found his slippers and went downstairs. The day was still dim, a grey and foggy morning, and he snapped on the hall light as he opened the front door. There in the chilly mist he saw a small thin figure, hatless, and enveloped into an overcoat too large. He recognized him. On any other day he would have shouted his welcome.

"Yasuo, old boy—come in—come in! Man, you'll freeze standing there."

This morning he was silent, shocked and immobile. Yasuo Matsugi was an artist, a great artist, whom he had known for years, ever since he began to be interested in Japanese art in college. All but penniless, in his senior year he had bought a small painting by Yasuo, reeds black and white against an off-white background, and on a reed an emerald-green cicada. He still had the picture in his study. He would have said twenty-four hours ago that Yasuo was his friend, and he certainly a friend to Yasuo. It would not have occurred to him to connect the artist with a potential enemy or any enemy. Now he could not speak. Nor could Yasuo speak. They stood staring into each other's eyes. In this deadly silence tears began to roll down Yasuo's face. He put up his hand and wiped them off. Then he turned to go away, his head lowered against the cold wind from the lake.

Upon that bent and solitary figure Burton Hall could not close the door. "Yasuo! Come back!"

He was horrified to recognize that even as he spoke he was stabbed by sudden inner alarm. What if someone passing by heard him summon a Japanese? What if a neighbor looked out of a window? He recognized the horror of fear, a small and ghostly fear compared to the certain danger in

117

Germany, say, if Yasuo were a Jew instead of a Japanese and he himself a German instead of an American. But this was how it began! He would not yield to it. He was an American and not a German.

"Come back," he repeated.

Yasuo returned, doubtfully. He stood inside the door and waited.

"Come into my study," Burton Hall said.

He closed the door and led the way. "Sit down," he said.

Yasuo sat down, huddled in his overcoat. Burton Hall did not look at him. He busied himself with building a fire, laying kindling across the dead ashes of last night. When the flames caught from one stick to another he sat down in the worn red chair whose springs were shaped to his body. He looked at Yasuo and saw him waiting and speechless.

"I don't know what to say, Yasuo. Nothing is changed between us, basically. Except that—"

Yasuo nodded vehemently. "Everything is changed. In you—not in me. I feel so. I am here to say I understand so. Please. I know how. I don't say forgive me, my country. It is not possible. I cannot myself forgive my country. They attack me also when they do such attack on America. . . . I only say—please, I love America like Japan. I am not changing. I am artist. I am thinking only eternal art, the same, everywhere, always. I am not enemy. Never. You are not enemy to me in my heart. Never."

The stone-still figure was suddenly urgent and alive, the words pouring forth, declaring, pleading, promising. Burton Hall tried to smile and failed.

"Thank you, Yasuo. . . . I suppose people like us are trying to say the same things in your country and mine. You can go on being an artist. . . . But I—"

He broke off and rubbed his hands over his unwashed face, his red hair on end.

118

"Yasuo, I have to be somebody else now. Not just a scientist. I beg you to understand, when you hear of my doing something you wouldn't have believed possible for me. And I suppose we mustn't see each other any more until this dreadful business is over—and your country or mine is the victor. It has to be mine, Yasuo—at all costs. Because your country chose to side with the mortal enemy—not only my enemy but yours, too."

The Japanese listened, his eyes black with tragedy, his pale face drawn. He wanted to talk, to communicate, to reveal himself somehow, now while he could.

"Something will happen soon," he said. "I don't know, but something. Maybe they send us back to Japan. Then I have no opportunity for friendship with America. . . . I want now to speak all my friendship for Americans."

He folded his arms and closed his eyes.

"So—I begin. . . . I come here. I am seven years old, when my mother in Japan is dead. My father is butler in Mr. George Kincaid's house, San Francisco. Mrs. Kincaid having no children, she was like my mother. So, thanking her, I make pictures for her, small pictures of her little dog, her Persia cat, and so forth. She tells me I must be an artist. So, I take lessons, and I am an artist. That is how. When I was seventeen, Mrs. Kincaid dying, Mr. Kincaid sent me to Paris for three years. When I came back, I felt America my home. My father was very old and I told him he must not work. I am a good artist, I sell many pictures, so we have a home together. All my life is here. America has been good to me, buying my pictures, giving me such friends as you. Sometimes at night in a bad dream I thought Japan perhaps may fight the war with America. Now it has come. But I have no war. I love this America. She is my country, my mother. . . ."

Burton Hall felt his heart wrenched in his bosom. "I don't know how we got into this," he muttered. "God knows I

119

don't hate anybody, and I can never hate you, Yasuo. . . . Let's go in the kitchen and have a cup of coffee."

They rose and walked down the hall together, Burt's arm across Yasuo's shoulder.

"Let's not talk about war," Burt said. "It will all end some day, and we'll still be friends."

He made coffee and toast and scrambled eggs and in the middle of it Mollie came down in her quilted pink bathrobe, her hair in setting combs and a net, and for her there was no war.

"Hello, Yasuo," she said. "Burt, you sit down there at the breakfast table. My goodness, why didn't you call me?"

An hour later Yasuo left them, comforted and tearfully grateful and Burton Hall went to the window and stood watching that desolate figure, bent against the bitter wind blowing in from the lake. Thousands of them, it occurred to him suddenly—thousands of Japanese, who had become Americans, farmers, students, teachers, cooks and restaurant keepers, servants to the rich, and, like Yasuo, artists—he had forgotten about them in the singleness of his mind. Then he put them away from him. They were not his responsibility. He had but one task—to build the bomb as fast as it could be built. . . . And the next time he saw Yasuo, it was behind the barbed-wire barriers of a concentration camp in the deserts of Arizona.

*   *   *

To find the men he needed was now his task. He must search for young scientists, the younger the better, under twenty-five if possible, minds daring and unwearied, imaginations free and bold enough to explore the illimitable. And how could he persuade Stephen Coast, how cope with the too tender conscience? He needed that young intuitive spirit. More than anyone he knew, unless he excepted Fermi, Steve had the authentic genius. Was this to be lost because a Quaker had fathered him? How little it meant to be a father! His own two sons, both solid, hard-working, reliable, were Mollie's children, not his. And Stephen's father —he had met the man at Stephen's wedding, a cautious child of God, living meagerly in spite of a big bank account. He smiled a crooked smile. That wedding—expensive simplicity! The ancient meetinghouse, primitive in its plainness, was a comic contrast to the sumptuous wedding party, Stephen in morning coat, ascot tie, and striped pants and Helen in a gown from Paris. And afterwards he had gone to the reception at Stephen's parents' home because Helen's parents were dead. That house on the Main Line in Philadelphia— plain? It was furnished in a fortune of antiques, all inherited, the old man said, but he had clung to them. He knew the worth of every piece. And though there had been no music in the church, there was a superb band at the house, and only to play a few melodies—no dancing, of course.

Suddenly he thought of Jane. She could help him. There was something between Stephen and Jane, or had he imagined it? He divined a comprehension when they were together, even upon that day when they had first met, and since then in an interchange of looks, an atmosphere of understanding flowing between them, surrounding them like a magnetic field. He took up the receiver and dialed the laboratory—a little late, he thought, glancing at the desk clock, but she worked late. . . . Ah, she was there and recognized his ring.

"Yes, Burt?"

"Jane, I want you to come right over. . . . Is Stephen there? No? Good. I want to see you alone. Business, of course. There's nothing but business from now on to eternity, for all we know. All right. . . . I'm alone, too. Mollie's gone to some women's hubbub. . . . That needn't scare you, tall girl."

He laughed raucously and hung up. Some day he'd have to wake Jane up to the fact that she was a beautiful woman but he had no time for it now. Nor had she. He was struck by an idea, loaded and brilliant. Why shouldn't she be his assistant? Brains—that's what he had to have near him now, someone who could argue with him. He liked the idea of that person being a woman, anyway Jane, but that was all. She wouldn't be jealous of him, as these young fellows could be. In spite of their preoccupation with the hugeness of science, his fellow scientists could be beastly small, envious, competitive, as petty a lot as could be imagined, he sometimes thought in gloom after a conference somewhere, and this pettiness included the habit of being argumentative with the boss. And if the military had to be in on the deal, as they would have to be, for the government would insist on that, and then big business, he had to have someone to whom to explode. Mollie wouldn't be enough. . . . Ah, Jane was a fine idea.

He lit the fire and paced up and down, waiting for her. He had not left the room all day. Mollie had brought his meals in on a tray and had gone away again. He had frowned furiously and on purpose and she knew better than to stay. Now what Jane must do, as her first job, was to persuade Stephen to take over the creation of plutonium.

He heard the doorbell ring and he threw another log on the fire before answering it. When he opened the door, Jane was standing there in her fur coat, her dark hair flying in the wind.

"Come in," he said brusquely. "You've taken a damned long time to get here."

She slipped off her coat. "The traffic was heavy—Christmas shopping."

122

He snorted. "Christmas! Don't tell me we have to have Christmas this year."

"We can't escape it." She warmed her hands before the fire, delicate strong hands, stained to the bone with laboratory acids.

"Want something to drink?" he asked.

"No, thanks, Burt."

"I suppose that goes for me, too," he growled.

"Yes, please, Burt—so you won't grow mellow."

"All right. . . . Then I'll get down to business. Sit down, will you? You look about seventeen standing there warming your little paws. Your cheeks are apple red."

She sat down and looked at him calmly. "What is it, Burt?"

"I want two things of you," he said. "First, you have a new position. You're my assistant from this minute on. That includes everything. You'll be in my confidence. I'll have no secrets from you. Your powers are unlimited so far as I am concerned. You can argue with me if you think I'm wrong. Don't pay attention to my tempers. If I make a fool of myself, anywhere, any time, stop me. You'll pinch-hit for me whenever I need you. You'll read all my letters. You'll be—everything."

She looked at him with a gaze cool and reserved. "For how long?"

"For the duration. After that, we'll see."

"Is this necessary, Burt?"

"Absolutely."

She turned her gaze to the fire and was thoughtful for so long that he lost patience.

"Well? Well?"

"All right, Burt," she said. "I'll do my best. We all have to do our best now."

"Right." He looked at her with a stir of curiosity. What

123

was she? A scientist, of course, and if she had been a man she'd rank with the top. A physicist first, but a fair biochemist, too. Look at those hands! A synthesizer, that's what she was. Pity she wasn't a man, and yet—

"What's the second thing?" she asked.

"You're close to Stephen Coast, aren't you?" It was a sharp thrust and he meant it to be.

She lifted frank dark eyes. "I don't know what you mean by close. If you mean personally, then no."

"Are you close to anybody personally?"

"Perhaps not. There doesn't seem to be time."

"Ever think what it may be like when you get old, Jane? A spinster, living alone, missing life!"

"What was it you wanted, Burt?" she asked.

He sighed. "You won't let me divert you. Well, what I want is to get Stephen Coast to head up the—plutonium job. He's respected, in spite of his queer religious views. Maybe he'll get over them when he sees what we're up against."

"You've decided on plutonium?"

"Everything points to it, Jane. Of course we'll try everything else, too. We've wasted a lot of time in committee rooms. We should have stuck to our labs. We'd be further along. Szigny called me up last year—last year, mind you—and said he was fed up. No new work on chain reaction between July 1, 1939, and March, 1940! He keeps prodding me, thank God. Fermi has taken the lead, bless him—that pile of his at Columbia—and Parkes of course, on uranium cleavage. That business in the Berkeley laboratory seems to have given us the final proof—uranium into neptunium into plutonium. We have it. A new element—God, how the old alchemists must want to rise out of their graves! Transmutation of elements, no less! Well, I mustn't get off on that. . . . You see what I'm after."

"Uranium 238 into plutonium, depending upon the number of neutrons that evaporate from the splitting of one uranium atom," Jane said.

He flashed her a glance of admiration. "What am I explaining anything to you for?"

"I'm in touch with Fermi," she said quietly. "Don't forget he was my professor at Columbia. If as many as three neutrons are given off, it will allow for chance. He says we can count on 3.5."

"Yes, but if no more than one, then we're sunk. We can't count on one neutron hitting a target. . . . Jane, day before yesterday, the last day possible, the Committee decided to go all out. Two of our men just came back from England—you know whom I mean. They say the British are making terrific progress without us. And they were told that the Nazis have ordered immense quantities of heavy water from Norway. If the whole thing at Pearl Harbor weren't so horrible, I'd call it luck. . . . I wonder if Stephen would say God had a hand in it!"

"I haven't seen Stephen," she said. "Where will the product be made?"

"Good girl. So we don't use the name of the stuff any more? Yes, it's 'the product.' It'll be made right here in Chicago, at first anyway. Headquarters in Eckhart Hall. Symbolic, eh? Where we first discovered uranium 235—without which we cannot stay alive today, my beauty! So will you persuade Stephen Coast to head it up?"

"I will try," she said.

He waited but she said no more. He sat watching her, a lovely woman, delicate, graceful, with hidden fires, he was sure. With a brain like that, and a body, too—

She looked up involuntarily and met his concentrated smiling gaze.

"I'm trying to explain you," he said. "I'm trying to imagine the genes which went into your being, those recessive genes from somewhere, generations ago, meeting by chance in you. There's a lot about chance that we don't know yet. Did you ever ponder that, tall girl? You're the chance of a lifetime for some man. Maybe me, some day, who knows?"

He felt the familiar urge, the impetuous response of body to brain, passion of the body after passion of the mind. His body caught fire from his brain, his blood swelled into veins and arteries, draining the centers of thought and control. He leaped to his feet and, ignoring her startled eyes, he lifted her into his arms.

"Jane," he muttered thickly.

He felt her hands against his face, pushing him away with a terrible strength.

"Let me go, Burt."

"But Jane—"

"Let me go!"

He let his arms fall and instantly was ashamed of himself. He turned his back to her, fumbled for his handkerchief and wiped his face.

"You're damned cold—"

"Whether I'm cold is not the question, Burt."

He could not look at her. "It seems very much the question at the moment."

She spoke steadily. "There's only one question, so far as I am concerned. If I am to work with you, I can't fight off this sort of thing, too. You'll have to take your choice. Control is essential."

He tried to laugh. "Where have I heard that word before? Control! It's what they're talking about in the lab, isn't it? Very well. I'll control. I can't do without you—on this job."

"Thank you. . . . When do I report?"

"Tomorrow morning, at nine."

"I'll be there."

She put out a cool slim hand and he did not take it. He saw the glimpse of a half-wistful smile and then she was gone. No, the door opened to admit her again.

"I understand you better than you know," she said, and closed the door finally.

And he stood looking at that closed door and cursed himself. Damned ass—letting my glands take over at a moment like this!

*　　*　　*

"Where shall I meet you?" Stephen asked.

He is still angry with me, Jane thought. That is good. It means he will do nothing for my sake. He will decide against me, if possible. Then I shall not be responsible.

"I don't want to take you away from home in the evening," she said. Her voice was cool, literal, matter-of-fact. "Shall we make it luncheon? Though why we should always eat, I don't know, except that one relaxes a little, perhaps. Whatever you say—"

"Helen has an alumnae meeting tomorrow night. I was going to work."

"Tomorrow night, then. We might go to a small Indian restaurant where I sometimes go alone. Do you like Indian food?"

"I've never eaten it."

"It may amuse you. I'll order ahead and tell them not to use too many peppers and chilis."

"I'd rather eat it the way you like it."

"All right."

This conversation was unreal and caught between the pressure of new demands the next day. The laboratory was tense after the somber weekend, the world changed, people facing the known future, and how much worse the known than unknown.

127

Nevertheless she prepared for dinner at the Rajah restaurant, a narrow building confined between two tall skyscrapers where sometimes she went to spend an evening of nostalgia. Here she could speak in Hindi, the language of her childhood in India, and here she ate the hot spiced foods that she had learned so early to love. It was a family restaurant, the proprietor an elderly and dignified gentleman from Bombay who had never revealed even to her how it was that he had sunk to the level of restaurant keeper. He himself did no more than watch the cashbox and keep a critical eye upon the waiters. Nor did he demean himself to speak to his guests, except and only to Jane.

Now when she came in, a little early, so that she could choose her table before Stephen arrived, he ambled across the room to her, spotless in his knee-length black coat and white trousers, upon his head a turban of silver tissue. He held his hands palm to palm in greeting and she replied with the same gesture.

"Good evening, Ramkrishnan," she said. "I hope you and your family are well."

"All well, thank you and thank the gods. Where will you sit?"

"A quiet table, please—I have an important guest."

"Behind the curtain, please. I have a table there reserved but you shall have it."

"Thank you."

She followed him behind a heavy curtain of gold tapestry and he beckoned for a waiter.

"Take away all places except two," he commanded. "Do not allow another to sit here. Remember also that this lady is like ourselves. Do not serve her the food that common guests eat."

The waiter murmured and obeyed, sweeping knives and forks and spoons from the table.

"You will eat as we do?" Ramkrishnan continued.

"Yes," she said.

She seated herself and he leaned toward her. "When will the war begin?"

"It has begun," she said simply.

His large eyes, black and heavy-lidded, lightened from within. "In this war we will take our independence from the British," he said.

She looked up, startled, into the darkly bearded face. "I suppose so," she agreed. Who could blame them? It was only one of many wars within this war, old quarrels simmering to the surface, deep angers finding vent. All through her childhood she had been conscious of revolt everywhere about her, breathing through men, women and children in a fiery determination for independence. Gandhi was not yet dead.

"You wish it?" Ramkrishnan asked.

"It is inevitable," she said. "It is karma."

He put his hands together again, palm to palm, and she smiled and replied with the same gesture, its meaning instinctive from her childhood. I worship the divine in you—

At this instant Stephen put aside the curtain. Ramkrishnan inclined his head as she introduced him and disappeared. Stephen sat down opposite her, somewhat ill at ease, as she could see.

"Helen sent her greetings," he began. "She said to tell you she envies me. She's never eaten Indian food."

This, as she very well knew, was his defense. He was a good man, purehearted, wary of disloyalty in slightest degree to his wife, guarding himself not only against her, but against his possible feelings toward her. Had she been only a woman she might have been amused and even tempted to try her powers of attraction. For that he was vulnerable she divined, and vulnerable not as Burt was, through the blood and the flesh, but through the intricacies of thought and mind. She had an instant's idle wonder whether, or how, Helen's mind and his could meet—not a stupid woman, Helen, oh not in the least, but not a scientist. It was as scientist that she, Jane Earl, had the advantage. The woman for Burt, the scientist for Stephen! She had very much the advantage.

"Helen must come here with us next time," she said.

He relaxed. "I'll tell her so. She'll be pleased."

"I don't know what we're eating," she went on, "Ramkrishnan will order for us. Oh, and we must eat with our fingers. He's had the silver taken away."

"Eat with our fingers?"

"I'll give you the argument. There is nothing cleaner than your own right hand, especially if you're an Indian and keep your right hand separate from your left. The right hand is for clean tasks, the left for the lowly ones."

Stephen stared at his right hand. "Do I have to eat with that?"

She laughed. "The Indians think it filthy to use knives and forks and spoons that other people have used."

He was awed. "God, the differences in people! How can we ever get along together in the world?"

"There's a lot to do before we can."

"How'd you happen to grow up in India?"

"My father was employed by one of the Rajas to build a dam in the upper Ganges, and we stayed on."

The waiter came in with three silver dishes, steaming hot. Over two of them was a film of liquid silver, over the third a film of gold.

"What's this?" Stephen demanded.

"Silver and gold," she said.

"Real?"

"Real."

130

"We can't eat it, surely."

"We can. It's quite healthy."

"Popadom," the waiter said. He put down on the table a tray of paper-thin cakes and went away.

"Now," Jane said, "like this—"

She showed him how to roll rice in a silvery ball and dip it into the curries. "Two fingers and your thumb," she said.

He tried, clumsily at first, and then with increasing relish. The meal became gay. He liked the food, skillfully modulated with spices, and he ate with appetite. When they had finished, the waiter brought in a silver bowl of scented water and two hand towels.

"Now you may wash your hand," Jane said.

He was impressed with the elegancies. "Do they eat such food as this every day?"

"No. It is in your honor and mine. Ramkrishnan and his family are old friends of mine—a nice simple wife, two sons, their wives and children."

The waiter came in now with the sweet, a custard that he dipped into bowls and placed before them.

"We may drink it," Jane said.

"What is it?"

"Almonds ground up with cream and a little powdered sugar."

The meal ended, the moment drew near and she faced it with resolution.

"Stephen, Burton Hall wants me to be his assistant. I have accepted."

He straightened the shade on a candle. "You'll do what you wish, I suppose."

"He is planning to ask you to be responsible for the production of—the product."

"I can't do that."

"It will be produced without you."

131

"Of course. But I shan't be responsible in that case."

"You might have a responsibility for the way it is used."

He sat back in his chair. "Jane, must we argue? I'm responsible for only one person and that is myself. I will not create a weapon with which other people can be killed. If another man is willing to do it, let him. But not I."

"What will you do then?"

"I'll go back to my own laboratory. I'll work on something that doesn't damage anybody."

"We must argue, Stephen. Indeed we must. Because radioactive material can cure as well as kill. Even in a bomb it might save rather than destroy. Nobody has said that we'll use the bomb. If we make it, if we show that we have it, perhaps it will end the war without being used."

He stared at her, unbelieving. "The arguments of Alfred Nobel when he made dynamite!"

"Dynamite was the worst explosive he could make in those days. The bomb will be so much worse that no one will use it."

"You believe that?"

"I believe that. . . . It is the only reason I can go on. I feel as you do. But being a woman, I'm more practical. I do believe if we make war as horrible as it really is, as horrible as it can be, men will stop fighting."

"I wish I could believe it, Jane."

"Oh Stephen, if men like you don't work with—these others, what hope has any of us? It will be made, there's no doubt of it. We're in a fearful race. The Nazis will make it if we don't—before we can, maybe. And they'll use it—no doubt of that. That's the problem. And where is there a man like you among them? Not one—not one. We've got to make it, Stephen, but we don't have to use it. Demonstrate it, maybe, so that the enemy can see what we have—that's all."

He listened, his eyes on her pleading face. "How can I

say you are wrong?" he said, slowly. "How do I know if I am right? Give me time, Jane. I have to re-think my way."

"There is no time, Stephen."

"Until tomorrow."

"Very well," she said. "Until tomorrow. Will you tell Burton Hall yourself?"

"Yes."

They rose. There was nothing more to be said. He left money on the table and they walked away in silence to part at the door. He did not take her home, and she understood. He could not because he would not allow the slightest possibility that there was anything between them as man and woman. Better so, she thought, and then was startled that something in her heart, a vague stir, a sudden pang, caused her unexpected pain. It was not important, scarcely more than a moment's loneliness, and to loneliness she was accustomed.

❈   ❈   ❈

Stephen Coast opened the door. He listened and heard no sound. Helen had not come home yet. He was vaguely relieved without knowing why, and infused with something like a mild remorse, for what he did not know, he hung up his top coat in the closet instead of dropping it as usual on a chair. Echoes from his childhood sounded through his memory, his mother's voice calling Stephen, hang up your coat—though Helen, to do her justice, had never scolded him for small failings. He strolled into the living room, lit all the lamps and sat down.

With plenty of work, he was restless and could do nothing. Until this evening he had been sure of his own moral rightness in refusing to have anything to do with making an atomic bomb. He had been reinforced by Jane's agreement. Now, unaccountably, she had deserted him—not him,

133

but his moral stand. Had she simply and clearly gone over to the other side, capitulated to Burton Hall, he could have accepted the desertion. But in an unreasonable womanish fashion she had not capitulated. Instead she had thought up an entirely new moral stand, her own and yet involving himself so cleverly that he could not deny there was something in what she had said. She had thrust upon him another burden. The bomb would be made. So far she was right. Nothing he could do would prevent it now. Nevertheless, if it were made by men who had no compunction about using it, would he not therefore share in their moral guilt? If, as she reasoned, he stayed with them, influenced them while he worked with them, might he not indeed present to them the alternative of announcing its accomplishment without using it in a sneak attack which would surpass the attack upon Pearl Harbor in its devastation and destruction of human life?

He leaned his head against the cushions of his chair, he groaned and closed his eyes. He could not deny that logic was on her side, a practical logic in contrast to his lofty and selfish idealism. Yes, selfish was the word. He had sought an escape in idealism and she had discovered it and presented it to him. He could have hated her except that he was too honest not to admire her for the piercing quality of her mind, never paraded in exhibition but used with the swift and silent skill of a rapier in the hand of a master swordsman. She was right, of course. He had now only to decide how his services were to be used for the making of the bomb.

The door opened at this moment and Helen's gay voice called through the house.

"Stephen, are you home?"

"Here." He hoisted himself from his chair and went to meet her and overcome by the vague remorse he put his arms about her and kissed her with such vehemence that she stepped back.

"What's this?" she demanded. "You haven't kissed me like that since you proposed to me."

"The house seemed horribly empty when I came in," he said. "Suddenly I missed you."

"Suddenly," she repeated, and then, shrewdly, "What have you done, Stephen?"

"Nothing," he said, and then because she still gazed at him mystified, if not actually alarmed, he said too hastily, "Let's go to bed, darling."

She flung off her fur jacket and sank down on the bottom stair and looked up at him.

"Now I know there's something wrong. You'd better tell me."

He tried to laugh. "Idiot—just because I want to make love to you—"

"It's not like you," she insisted.

"It is like me," he retorted. "Do I have to be always the same?"

She wrapped her arms about her knees and reflected, her eyes very clear, very blue, upon his face. "You're hiding something."

"I'm not," he protested. "I was going to tell you. I have to work on the bomb. I'm convinced."

He sat down on the step beside her. "Everything is changed now, Helen. Pearl Harbor changed it. What was possibility only day before yesterday has become certainty. There is no longer hope of escape. The only hope left is that if we make the bomb we can tell people we have it and what it will do and it may be enough as a threat and not as a weapon. I have not lost my concern, as my father would say. I've only changed its focus. Since the bomb must be

135

made and that I cannot prevent, my duty is to do all I can to keep it from being used."

He reached for her hand. It lay passive in his palm, a competent, pretty hand, and he smoothed it.

"I can see what you mean," she said after a thoughtful moment.

"I'm grateful for that," he said, and was indeed very grateful. He put his arm about her and tilted her face toward his. "Now shall we go upstairs?"

He was amazed to see no sign of the joyful yielding he expected. Instead she shrugged herself out of his grasp. "You still haven't told me everything."

"What else?" he demanded.

"You haven't," she insisted. "You haven't told me why you want to make love to me all of a sudden."

"It isn't all of a sudden," he muttered.

"It is, for you," she said. "Remember? Only day before yesterday—in the afternoon?"

He had forgotten. It had indeed been only Sunday afternoon when, in a mood of unusual relaxation, they had gone upstairs. After the hour of love she had turned on the radio to listen to the Sunday concert, and while they lay quiescent and dreaming in each other's arms the music had been cut off sharply and a commentator's frightened voice had announced the bombing of Pearl Harbor, and she had burst into tears.

"I had forgotten," he confessed.

"Well, I haven't," she said. "I've been thinking ever since. . . . Stephen, I don't want a baby now."

*   *   *

"Skip Christmas," Burton Hall said. "It's the only sensible thing to do on a year like this."

"We will not skip Christmas this year of all years," Mollie retorted. "It may be the last time we can celebrate it together."

He persisted in the argument until his sons came home, Timothy from Yale and Peter from Andover, and subsided only with their presence in the house. He did not write to his sons. He left such correspondence to their mother and it was his guess now that she had said nothing whatever about the possible future of the family. She did not believe in crossing bridges, as she put it, and justified this by adding, somewhat fretfully when pressed, that there was always a bridge ahead of her, so far as she could see.

Burton Hall was compelled therefore by the ignorance of his sons to put on a show of casual good cheer. They arrived three days before Christmas, Tim announcing as usual that he must leave the day after Christmas to make the round of houseparties in and around New York, with which he filled his holidays.

"I don't know why you come home at all," his mother said, after she had presented her cheek which he kissed as distantly as possible.

She maintained the ritual of family kisses against Burton Hall's intolerance of such a show. "I don't want to kiss anybody but you," he had once told her.

She had given him one of her rare looks, a compound of shrewd surmise and patience which made him laugh and redden at the same time. "Why do you look at me like that?" he had demanded.

"Like what?" she had asked too innocently.

"Oh, you know!"

"I don't know what you're talking about," she had replied. "Anyway, you need a haircut."

"Hello, Tim," he now said to his first-born son. "You've

grown some more, haven't you? I thought you'd call it quits when you got to be a senior."

"It's time for me to leave such goings-on to Peter, I'll agree," Tim said.

He was a tall young man, sand-colored and pleasantly good-looking like his mother.

"Where's Peter?" Burton Hall asked.

"Out in the kitchen. He was yelling all the way home about being hungry."

Peter came in, a wedge of pie in his hand.

"Hi, Dad."

"Hi, yourself," Burton Hall said. He repressed a desire to rumple his son's hair. The boy was still enough shorter than himself, but remembering his own father's caress, he restrained his impulse.

"Are you leaving us immediately after Christmas, too?"

"I haven't anywhere to go," Peter said, stuffing his mouth too full.

"It's only a question of time, Mollie," Burton Hall said, "when you and I will be as deserted as though these two had never been born."

Mollie bloomed into a smile. "They'll marry and then it'll all begin over again."

He was struck into silence and crushed into reflection. This woman, a creature of instinct and not impulse, took for granted a future as invincible as though Pearl Harbor had never been, as unchanging as though he were not contemplating at this very moment the creation of a weapon, by means of a force so immense, so cosmic, that there was no way of knowing for a certainty whether it might not explode of its own power and create of Earth a planet as bare as the moon, all life gone. And this had made no impression on Mollie, who had nevertheless lived here with him night and day as a witness, if not a partaker, of his continuing agony. He had a strange creeping relief, a minute faith, that nothing man could do would, after all, destroy life. Instinct, female instinct, might prevail. Unpredictable chance!

He turned abruptly to his elder son. "There's to be a conference in New York three days after Christmas. If you can be persuaded to abandon your pleasures, however briefly, I should like you to accompany me. It may be well for you to know what is going on."

Tim looked up politely surprised from a magazine he was reading. "I'd like to, Dad," he said.

*   *   *

Somehow he got through Christmas, but only somehow, Burton Hall thought with inner grimness. He had been shaken to discover that he had to cope with forgotten scenes and emotions he had thought worn away by the years, but which were only sleeping and were awakened by the immanence of the unknown future now so near. The bells of Christmas morning, for example, ringing out the carols of peace and good will, those ancient and meaningless words, should have aroused in him only a humorous irony. Instead he found himself thinking of his mother of whom he had not thought for half a lifetime. One morning, in particular, a memory which he had considered nothing but a childhood dream, appeared to him again as reality. He was seven or eight that Christmas and he had waked to find her hovering over him in her white nightgown, her long fair hair, a reddish gold, about her shoulders. Confused by sleep, he had some notion that she was an angel, a Christmas angel, and he had been half afraid, so that he burst into tears and when she asked him why, he said distractedly that he thought she had come to sing to him.

139

"But where is all the heavenly host?" he had sobbed.

She had gathered him up out of bed and into her arms and she had sung to him, "What child is this—" He could still hear the words in her soft soprano. He had hidden his face in her fragrant bosom. . . . The worst of Christmas was this stir of memory, this recall of what was no more.

In such mood he had endured the family day, manufacturing a false good cheer which he suspected his family understood well enough but to which they responded decently until night, when Tim went to a dance, too early, on the pretext that a girl wanted to do something else first, and Peter demanded a movie, and Mollie went to bed. He sat through a Christmas show at Peter's side and wondered how long this sort of thing could go on in a world where romance had ceased to exist. And that night he had been sleepless with nostalgia, after all, for who knew where they would all be next Christmas at this time, or if they would be anywhere except in floating cosmic dust.

The next morning arrived again as usual and as though the world were safe from friend and foe alike. He packed his bag briskly with garments fitting for a conference and a possible theater in New York and at noon set off in a train with Tim, who sat in another seat under the pretense of having to study for a term paper. Glancing at his son now and then while he busied himself with his own figures and equations, Burton Hall pondered the immeasurable distance between the generations, and especially between himself and this son, once only a minute particle in his own body, now grown to an independent being and demanding separateness by instinct if not by conscious choice. In terms of matter and energy, what did it mean? What equation could express the principle of growth, or for that matter, the pain of separation to the parent, which Tim could not understand until he himself was the father?

140

It was not until two days later that he was savagely compelled by this son to face a desperation of hatred against pure instinct, and all the more frightful for being that. In his longing to share his life with his son, he said the first morning in New York when they breakfasted at the Harvard Club—and that was another battle that his son had won, for he had supposed that of course Tim would go to Harvard, but no, he had chosen Yale—he said:

"Tim, how would you like to go to the conference with me this morning?"

Tim cracked the top from his egg with precision, an affectation, Burton Hall thought, but this was an affected generation, whether the beats or the casuals.

"Am I allowed at such summit?" he asked as, pepper and salt carefully applied, he tasted his three-minute egg.

"It's not summit exactly," Burton Hall replied. "It's reconnoitering. We have to get four operations all going at the same time, with the hope that one will be successful. I've asked Stephen Coast to take charge of the one I consider most probable. There'll be some Washington fellows there this morning and I'll introduce you as my son, though it's not necessary."

"Thanks," Tim said and proceeded in silence to absorb methodically a large breakfast, each item critically appraised before he consumed it. When for the third time he called the head waiter to inform him that something was not perfectly prepared, this time wheat cakes with a maple syrup less pure than it was announced on the menu, a father's patience broke.

"You can't expect a university club to offer you a gourmet's heaven, for God's sake, Tim!"

"I expect to get what I pay for," his son replied.

"Well, I'm paying for it," Burton Hall blurted.

Tim scorned to reply to such gaucherie. He finished the

wheat cakes drenched in the despicable syrup and sat back replete and in condescending good humor.

Hours later, when the morning conference was over and they sat at the bar in preparation for yet another meal before the afternoon session, Burton Hall turned to his son.

"Well, what did you think of us this morning?"

Again and again during the morning he had glanced at Tim, sitting silent and watchful while his elders argued and planned. It was impossible to tell from that expressionless young face what was going on in the brain under the sandy blond crew cut. For further shield Tim had put on a pair of large dark glasses which gave him the look of a Hollywood director, a theatrical impression Burton Hall felt sure was purposeful.

"You are all a bunch of stinkers," Tim said now.

"What—"

"I said stinkers," Tim repeated. "A bunch of old men plotting to kill off my generation!"

Burton Hall put down his glass of Scotch.

"See here—"

"There's no other way to look at it from where I am," Tim said.

"Are you a pacifist?" Burton Hall demanded.

"No."

A blow of memory from the past now fell upon Burton Hall. He had argued this out years ago with his father when the country entered the First World War. To his astonishment, his father had taken a militaristic attitude.

"Those Germans started the war for their own benefit. They don't give a hoot for anybody. The only thing that they recognize is force and it's got to be a bigger force than they have. We'll have to lick them."

"You're a nice kind of Christian," Burt had snarled.

With all his heart he had resented the possibility that he

142

might have to get into a war that as yet meant nothing to him, at the very moment when he was beginning to realize what a marvel, what a wonder, life could be if one were a young male.

"There are people in the world who don't understand anything but a licking," his father said.

They had argued until Woodrow Wilson brought the United States into the war at last not by force but by guile, by the winsomeness of the notion that it was a war to end all wars, and then Burt, the young scientist, had yielded to the magic of idealism and had worked night and day on designing better airplanes. And when the war was over the idealism had scattered like dust to the winds. He acknowledged his father had been right and wished that he could tell him so. But his father was dead by that time and perhaps if he had been alive the primeval antagonism between males, old and young, would have kept him from acknowledgment.

"I'm not a pacifist," Tim was saying, "but I don't want to die."

"There are things more important than life," Burton Hall said.

"I don't know what they are," Tim retorted, "and if they're so damned precious, why don't you old fellows do the fighting? You've had your lives and we haven't." He twisted the glass around and around slowly between his hands, watching the flow of golden liquid between the cubes of ice.

"Your ancestors, and mine, came here to escape military duty in Europe," Burton Hall said. "It wasn't necessary then to bear arms for freedom's sake. One could escape and the sea lay between us and the enemies. But we are now where Europe was then. The Nazis are as close to us as the nations in Europe were to one another two centuries ago. We must keep this country free, a place where men and women can still come for freedom."

143

"Why should I die to save them?"

These words were muttered so low that Burton Hall demanded to have them repeated, whereupon Tim lifted his head and all but shouted them out.

His father stared at him. "Who's asking you to die to save anybody? Today we must hang together or we'll hang separately. Trite but never before so true! We can't live separately any more. The two halves of the world are pressed together. We mingle, the interstices are filled with one another, like particles in compressed matter."

"Oh, science," Tim said under his breath. "I've had enough of that!" Suddenly he lifted his head and looking straight at his father he spoke with fierce clarity. "Your science ought to tell you why you want war—old males in the herd always want to kill off the young ones, don't they? So they can have everything for themselves, that's why! Including the young females!"

Burton Hall banged his glass on the counter. "You're impossible. . . . I shall have to wait for you to grow up."

He turned abruptly and went away to lunch alone.

*   *   *

Two days later he found himself recounting the whole incident to Jane Earl in his office in the university.

"And I don't know why I take up our incalculably valuable time in telling you," he growled. "I ought to know from my own experience that a son can't agree with his father or even approve him until he, the son, is old enough to have some sense. I know now that my father was much more right than I was."

"You expect Tim to have reached the same point when he is half your age. Is that reasonable?"

He yielded suddenly. "No. And I'm not dead. I didn't

144

begin to agree with my father until I saw him in his coffin.
. . . Well, let's forget it and get to work."

He paused and forcibly detached his mind from his son,
closing one compartment and opening another.

"Here's the picture, Jane, as we left it at the end of the
conference. The Committee met with a representative from
the President and another from the Pentagon. They listened
while we talked, but we parted in agreement. My job is two-
fold. I'm responsible for designing the bomb itself and then
for getting it made. I'll need some hundreds of pounds of
plutonium. And how do I get it? Three problems—how can
we induce a nuclear chain reaction with the normal uranium
we can get, how can the plutonium produced by this reaction be extracted from the uranium it's embedded in, and
how the devil can we do it on the scale we have to do it if
we're to build the bomb?"

"You'll use Fermi's graphite as moderator, of course," she
said.

He lifted his heavy red eyebrows at her. "Argument?"

She replied in the prompt and concise fashion to which
he listened with mixed amazement and amusement, incredulous of such words in a woman's voice.

"Heavy water takes too much time to make, as the Germans are finding out, I am sure, and beryllium, satisfactory
enough, is too hard to get."

"Good chemist—but dare I trust Fermi's Columbia tests?
Pretty small, aren't they?"

She would not grant it. "His graphite and uranium piles
are below the critical size for chain reaction, yes—but they've
shown us how much the neutrons multiply and how the
multiplication is affected by impurities in the material or by
different ways of constructing the pile."

Burton Hall gave a hollow laugh designed to tease. "Why
is it that Italian fellow can do no wrong in your eyes? I ask

you, how in heck can we get enough of the pure graphite and uranium? Impurities are poison. They'll stop the whole works."

He broke off and sighed.

"Fermi will do it," Jane said.

He pretended pettishness.

"Change the subject, for God's sake. . . . Fermi, Fermi—"

He tossed a sheet of paper toward her. "Read that aloud, will you?"

Obediently she read. "Sources of pure uranium at present are as follows: Lamp Division of Westinghouse; evaporation of uranium solution."

"Damned expensive," he put in.

"Canada; purification of uranium by crystallization."

"Damned slow!"

"Deuterium—"

"Damned slow again—heavy water problem. But we'll let the Canadians try it, just in case Fermi's magic doesn't work. They'll call me back to Washington on this, though, Jane. Deuterium will sound good to them. Then I'll have to fight them."

"Tell them there is plenty of graphite. Tell them we'll have to delay again if we wait until we make enough heavy water to get the deuterium."

"R-right," Burt said. "The argument in a peanut shell. But still we'll keep it as an alternative. And now, my chemist, recite the results of what you've done in your lab, with all your collaborators."

"You know the series, Burt—why should I repeat it?"

His eyes caressed her. "It sounds so wonderful coming from a woman's lovely lips."

"Don't—"

"Don't what?"

"Keep making me remember I'm a woman."

146

"Why should you want to forget it?"

Her lips trembled. Then she lifted her head and looked at him steadily and recited tonelessly as a child recites: "We had enough plutonium salt last spring so that we could see it under a microscope, so we knew it could be made. We knew what it was because the rays are different from those of uranium. The first element in the series was neptunium. That was 93. Plutonium was 94. But we had so little that we were afraid we would lose it. So we used bismuth in the solution. It precipitated and separated from the uranium and carried the plutonium with it."

"R-right, and very clearly and simply put, so that even Washington will be able to understand it and the multiplication constant I've worked out—if it checks with yours—is even better than Fermi or any other fellow has predicted. But . . ." He paused to point an impressive forefinger at her. "We can't take the risk of depending on any one method of making the product. We must do everything at once. So we'll proceed by four parallel methods, call it four horses in a race, and let the winner win. That's why I want Stephen Coast to take the one I am betting on."

"He will win," she said.

"You'll see to that, I daresay!"

To this feeler she made no reply and after a sharp sidewise glance at her he proceeded.

"Magnetic separation at one university, gaseous diffusion at another, centrifuge at the Standard Oil laboratory—but in co-operation with a third university and Stephen here in Chicago under your eye and mine. No, the race horse metaphor doesn't hold. These four aren't in competition. They're co-operating, matching results, eager to congratulate the winner. There's nothing personal now, in the whole world."

"Nothing," she agreed.

"The Committee will meet every two weeks in Washing-

147

ton. Top level, of course, terribly secret, but we'll have the best men with us from Europe and England. We are ready to go. And we've been in the war for six months! Japan has the Philippines and Singapore and Indonesia is next. The Nazis have Europe and Rommel the Fox is trying to take North Africa. I haven't slept for weeks. . . . And what would I do without you!"

He yawned a whale's yawn, leaned back in his chair and was instantly asleep. He was wakened by the telephone and he snatched the receiver from the desk, his eyes still shut. Mollie's voice was at his ear.

"Burt, aren't you coming home tonight?"

"Yes, of course. Good God—"

He forced his eyes open and looked at his watch. Nine o'clock! Jane had left a note on the desk pad. "I am going home. Call me if you want me to come back."

"I fell asleep, Mollie," he mumbled.

"Well, it don't matter, but Washington is trying to get you. . . . Didn't you hear them ringing you?"

"I've been asleep, I told you!"

"Are you alone?"

"Mollie!"

"Don't get mad, Burt, but I wonder sometimes."

He snapped at her. "Ever since I had the cot put in the filing room—I know! You don't believe I work all day and night and drop asleep for an hour and get up and work again. Oh goddam, I haven't time or strength for this sort of nonsense. I'll call Washington now and get home when I can. You go on to bed and expect me when you see me."

He slammed the receiver down, waited a moment and then called the number in Washington. He was put through at once.

"Sorry you've had trouble finding me, Van. I went to sleep here at my desk. Been sleeping like the dead."

"Never mind. . . . You need it, I guess. Who doesn't? Can you catch the ten o'clock train?"

"Emergency?"

The voice hesitated. "Yes, I suppose you'd call it that. Everything is, nowadays. Maybe several emergencies."

"I'll see you tomorrow, sure."

"Good."

He hung up again and rubbed his face with his fists like a sleepy lion with its paws, and went into the men's room and doused his head with cold water. Then he went back to his office and called Jane.

"You not in bed yet?"

"No, I've been expecting you to call me."

"Yeah, well, I've to take the next train to Washington. Damned nuisance their not letting me fly any more! You take a plane in the morning and meet me at the hotel. By that time I'll know what's eating them down there—I hope."

"Yes, Burt."

"Good night, tall girl."

"Good night."

An hour later he swung himself on his train and dropped into a berth. No use worrying about Washington—no use worrying—no use worrying—the words echoed in his brain, went into a tailspin of dying sound and he fell into the blackness of sleep again.

The consequence of such sleep was that the next morning he entered the inner office of the government building with his usual bounce and his verve restored. The same pretty secretary looked up from her typewriter and smiled. He gratified her expectation immediately.

"Say, don't you and I have a date tonight?"

"Not that I know of, Dr. Hall."

"No? I've been remiss. Some other night? How's your boss this morning?"

149

"Overworked, not too cheerful."

"Thanks for the warning."

He strode into the inner office. Behind the huge desk the chief engineer of the government was waiting for him.

"Hello, Van."

"Glad to see you, Burt—sit down."

He chose the most comfortable chair and took his pipe from his pocket and lit it.

"We've run into a snag. That's why I sent for you."

"Snag about what?" Burt asked.

"About you. Just glance at this." He handed Burt a typed sheet. "The Dies Committee includes your name in a report to Congress on subversive persons. So Military Intelligence won't clear you."

"What!"

"Read it."

Burt read and began to bellow. "Of all the damned silly —why, I've never so much as heard of these organizations! Me? I never joined anything—not even the Methodist church! American-Soviet—who the hell are they? Never heard of 'em. They stole my name. But I'll be glad to quit. Get somebody else for this thankless job you've unloaded on me."

The grey-faced engineer gave his meager New England smile.

"Take it easy, Burt. I know you're no communist. Of course you can't quit. We can't spare you. I just wanted you to know, that's all. I'll return the report with my comments."

He scrawled a few lines on the bottom of the sheet and handed it to Burt again. "Read that and calm down."

Burt read. *This report is of no value. Further investigations must be made by the proper military authorities. Attention Attorney General.*

"Thanks," Burt said. He put the report on the desk. Then

suddenly he laughed loudly. "What do you know! Mollie's cleared and I'm not! Wait till I tell her."

Across the narrow bleak face of his friend the thin smile broke again. "I kind of like to hear you laugh, Burt. It clears the murky air of this town. I have only one more thing to say about this commie business and then we'll never mention it again. Are you sure of all your foreign scientists? What about Fermi, for example?"

Burt cried out, instantly impetuous. "I just swear they're all right, that's all. Fermi—why, that fellow left his country after he got the Nobel Prize in Sweden. What does he put first? What does any real scientist put first? Science! And that means he has to live in a free country. He belongs here."

"And the others? You've got a lot of them."

Burton Hall flung out his big work-stained hands. "Don't imagine I haven't thought about this myself. God knows, I'll be grateful for any information you get or the intelligence services can provide. But I have to take them one by one. I weigh each man against his value to us. If he's indispensable, I take a risk. If he's only valuable, I don't take the risk. There's a fellow from Canada—he's a good fellow, but I suspect him. He wants to know too much. I'm letting him go. Yes, I'll let you know his name—on paper. On the other hand, there's Vogel—a German Jew, his work on electrical gases helped us all to understand basic atomic structure much better than we could have. He fought as a German officer in the First World War, then went back to his university as a professor of physics. He got the top award of the year in physics and trained a lot of good men and was headed for the Nobel Prize when Hitler came in. He tried to keep out of politics and stay in science. But he's a Jew. I trust him as I trust myself, or you." He got up and paced the floor, gesturing with pointed forefinger. "Take Max Planck! The whole world knows him. When the Nazis began to say

151

that scientists must only work on what would help Germany instead of what would help mankind and Hitler screeched that serving mankind by scientific truth was a dirty Jewish notion, Planck resisted, old as he was. It was only when Heisenberg, the most brilliant young physicist among his students, began to put Einstein's theory of relativity into universal proportions and was attacked by his Nazi students who told him, 'Even if you aren't a Jew, you think like a Jew,' that Planck knew he must leave. But before he left, that brave old man published warnings to his fellow scientists."

"Stop—you've convinced me." Van's bleak eyes twinkled. "Your father couldn't have preached better. Now let's get down to business. The Boss has made a summit decision, all by his lone. . . . Brace yourself."

Burt took a deep breath and sat down. "You are putting me on the rack this morning."

"No time for anything else. All right, here it is. He has decided that the Project must be put under military control and administration. Now."

"No!"

The engineer nodded his grey head. "It has to be. There's no argument. It's been discussed at top levels after it was decided."

Burt stammered in dismay. "B-but I can't hold my scientists. It's against our whole tradition. They'll never work under military command. They'll snarl at me—I can hear them—'Say, what's this? Are we in Nazi Germany?' You don't know them like I do. Dammit, I'm one of them. We're the worst s.o.b.s in the human race when it comes to freedom and independence. Why, we question God himself. It's our job to rebel against dogma and red tape and—"

"That's your problem, Burt—not mine. And I want you to

152

meet the General in charge. We'll begin by going to his office."

He touched a buzzer, murmured into it and rose. Without a word but with a heart blazing in his bosom, Burt followed him into another building and into yet another inner office. There behind the square block of a desk sat a huge man in uniform.

"General," Van said, "meet our top scientist, Dr. Burton Hall."

The officer put forth a large plump hand. He spoke and his voice was deep and velvet soft with a Mississippi accent.

"I'm pleased to meet you, Dr. Hall—I'm mighty pleased."

"Now," Van said. "I'll leave you two together. You don't need me any more, Burt. But if you think you do, let me know. I'm here—for all eternity, as far as I can see."

And casting a wintry glimmer in Burt's direction he walked softly away.

*   *   *

"And left me there with that behemoth, Jane," Burton Hall said that night over a small dinner table set up in his sitting room at the hotel. "I was flabbergasted, flattened out, I hadn't anything to say. He was my boss—me, a scientist, free and independent, and I have to take orders from a General. And I'm only a halfway sort of scientist compared to some of these pure ones, these theoreticians, Thompson and Parkes and Eaves and all the rest of them, not to mention Szigny and Weiner and even Fermi—"

"They'll be difficult," Jane agreed. He had dismissed the waiter and she was serving him quietly, pouring coffee, mixing the salad which she had ordered because left to himself he would eat nothing green, declaring that such stuff was only rabbit food.

153

"You're the only person in the world who knows what I'm up against," he groaned. "Those longhairs are the worst about yelling for freedom. One minute they're dissecting the universe, all brains and scintillation, but cross them somehow, press them a little, let them get the notion they have to listen to you, and they're naughty boys, capable of the smallest kind of mischief. You wouldn't believe—"

"I do believe," Jane said. "I know them."

* * *

"But what do you know about this fellow Eaves that you want to put in charge of making the weapon?"

The General pursed his lower lip and stared.

. . . Patience, O God, Burton Hall muttered inside himself. Aloud he said pleasantly, "He's a man I've known for years—a student in my classes here in the university, and a person of such human understanding that he can keep a bunch of high-strung scientists working smoothly and happily together on top of a mess in the desert where they'll have no contacts with the convivial world."

"You're an undisciplined lot, all of you," the General grumbled. He was in fine fettle this morning, his full face rosy and his small blue eyes bright as the buttons on his uniform. He had lost ten pounds in the last month and his belt felt comfortably loose for the first time in years.

Burton Hall swallowed hard. He would be grateful, he was grateful. The General was not stupid. He even had a rudimentary sense of humor. He had been to college, and he had been successful in military administration. But he did not know scientists. And there was always the dangerous chance that he might have heard the irreverent names that the sulky scientists were already calling him behind his back, old Saggy-pants, old Bubble-guts.

154

"General," he said, "I can see my chief role in the Project. I'm to be the buffer between you and the scientists."

"They're a damned cocky bunch," the General growled. "They think they're God's little wise men. Nobody else knows anything. Well, I'm a Harvard man. I don't mind telling you that I graduated *cum laude*. I wasn't a bookworm in college, either. I was also on the varsity football team. Even in prep school I took a math prize and I've done some reading on this science stuff. And I'm going into training for my new job—diet and exercise and so on. I'm a soldier by choice and profession. I practice my own discipline. And I don't intend to take back talk from a lot of eggheads who think the Project can't get on without them."

"It can't, can it?"

"Sure it can! After the initial idea, I don't need 'em. Now it's a matter of production and for that I'll go to big industry."

"General, no!" Burton Hall moaned.

"Of course I shall. Who else can do it? I've already approached three companies."

"General, I don't know how I'll break this to the men."

"They're under discipline like everybody else," the General snapped.

Burton Hall stared. "What do you mean by that?"

"They'll have to learn how to take orders as well as to give orders," the General said flatly. "If they don't, I'll put them into uniform—commissioned officers under my command."

Burton Hall considered. Then his gorge suddenly rose. He was a scientist, born and trained, and for his brothers he would speak.

"You are right, General. We don't know how to take orders or give orders. But we are disciplined. We have the hardest discipline in life—self-discipline. Nobody can tell a

155

scientist what to do because what he has to do depends on facts discovered and proved. His discipline is to make himself do what he sees must be done, without anybody telling him to do it."

"Sounds nice," the General retorted, "but I'll have to tell you, Dr. Hall, that from now on the full responsibility for the Project rests on me and only on me. You scientists needn't worry any more. You're not responsible for anything that develops from this atomic stuff."

Burton's red eyebrows bristled. Outrage swelled into his veins and he felt his eyeballs hot. He thrust his clenched fists into his pockets, but his voice, when he could speak, was as smooth as molten metal.

"We accept your responsibility for the Project, General. But we can't escape the responsibility, now or ever, for the release of atomic energy upon the world. We have a lot to think about in the development and use of what we have discovered, and no one can relieve us of that."

"I don't get you," the General said.

Burton Hall choked slightly. "You will, in time," he said.

      *   *   *

He was dashed some weeks later, nevertheless, to observe that his Mollie took to the General and the General to her, and with a mutual warmth that both shocked and amused him. For the General, earnestly pursuing his duty, asked to meet the officials of the university, the scientists and their families.

"I want to know the men I have to handle and I want to know their wives especially," the General said. "You can learn a lot about a man if you know his wife."

"And I like the General, Burt," Mollie said. "He's a kind of man I can understand. And he's polite—not absent-minded and thinking about stars and atoms and things, like a lot of you."

Burton Hall, driving her home from a cocktail party at the General's headquarters, laughed loudly. "Bless you, Mollie. Have a good time with the General."

"Now what do you mean by that?" she demanded.

"Anything you like," he said and was suddenly cheerful. "If the General likes you, he likes me."

And seizing the moment he sped past the car ahead and missed it by the fraction of an inch.

"There, there," he said when Mollie screamed.

. . . He reported this conversation later to Jane in the office, and she laughed mildly and then took a letter from her briefcase.

"You'll be interested," she said, "to know that I happened to get a letter today from India, from a man that I know there, a biochemist. We went to school together when we were children. I haven't seen him in years, but he writes that he has had a report from Germany, by way of Japan, that German scientists are saying American scientists are not planning to develop the bomb. They believe this, they say, because at the last international conference American scientists were giving no thought to military aspects of nuclear fission. I thought it might cheer you."

"It does," he said. "We'd already stopped talking about fission or writing about it, as you very well know. I was careful myself even at the symposium on cosmic rays. We talked about everything else with German scientists except defense."

"Very different from our American scientists coming home from Berlin that year—remember?"

"Do I remember?" Burt sighed. "Isotope separation—direct road to atomic bombs! How can Fermi say he doubts

157

the Germans are making the ferocious weapon? Think he's all right, Jane? One hundred per cent?"

"Absolutely all right," she said. "If I must doubt him, I doubt myself—or you."

"Okay—okay—" He frowned at her hideously and pretended furious jealousy and she laughed again. A mist of tenderness came into her eyes. There was something adorable about this big man, something touching. She could love such a man, perhaps, providing love were necessary.

*   *   *

He was never again to be free of the General, and to this he must resign himself. Daily, or almost daily, Burton Hall was confronted at nine o'clock in the morning as he entered the elevator by a neatly uniformed lieutenant colonel. So it was on this Monday after the cocktail party.

"The General would like to speak with you, sir."

Burton Hall nodded, diverted his direction and found himself in the General's presence. In that presence also was a slender man of about thirty-five, who had a handsome profile and whose dark hair was prematurely silvered at the temples. The General announced him.

"Meet Christopher Starleigh, executive vice-president of the Canaday-Farrell Company. . . . Dr. Hall, our top scientist in charge."

Burton Hall recognized the name of the firm as one of the three greatest industries in the country. He shook hands in unsmiling silence and sat down. The General proceeded to announce his decrees.

"I've decided on Canaday-Farrell to put us into production on a big scale. We need their facilities and their engineering skills to build and operate our plants. I've been studying the whole situation. This radioactive element—

158

we've got to protect the communities as well as our own people. A big chemical concern like this is used to working on different kinds of big jobs, and I'm convinced—"

Starleigh broke in. He had a pleasant voice, a good baritone singer, Burton Hall imagined.

"I've made it clear to the General, Dr. Hall—or I hope I have—that we're ready to go ahead but under certain conditions. He must realize and you, too, sir—the enormous size of the project. The engineering alone is formidable, even for us. Plants must be designed and built and entirely new processes developed about which as yet we know nothing. Even the equipment has to be designed and installed and operators trained. There'll be incalculable delays in getting materials. In fact, I very much fear the war will be over before we can get under way."

Burton Hall was cold. "I am surprised. The scientists have estimated that without your help we ourselves could have the atomic bomb ready before the end of the war. We're used to making our own tools and equipment. We improvise new ones for new needs."

Starleigh spoke with tolerant kindness. "Is that practical? You don't even have a laboratory demonstration yet of your product, do you? You think the experiment will succeed, but you've only proved it on paper. Very well, suppose it succeeds. Then a pilot plant must be built and tested. Can you do that? It will take months to accumulate enough plutonium. The product has to be separated from intensely radioactive material by a chemical process that you scientists haven't worked out yet. Then we have to take the stuff, learn how to reduce it to a metal and find out how to make the metal into a bomb that will explode. It will take ten years. The war will certainly be over."

Burton Hall lit his pipe, his hands trembling with anger.

159

"It will not take ten years. I promise you that. Of course if you—if you make it take ten years—"

Starleigh's handsome profile turned haughtily to the General. "We will begin our work the moment your scientists present us with the product."

"Within six months you'll have it," Burt declared. He drew hard on his pipe for a moment. "And I'm not going to lose my temper at anybody," he added and grinned at them both.

The next day, a grey November day, Stephen Coast heard the tale of this encounter retold. He listened carefully until Burt repeated his final declaration. Then he spoke, his eyes fixed on the bare college landscape outside the window. "I believe we can make the chain reaction right here in Chicago."

"Let's hear your analysis," Burt said.

"Well, it's brief. Control is the important factor, as you know, Burt. And the possibility of control is in those few delayed neutrons in fission, the ones that aren't emitted at once but come off a few seconds later. You know what that means when conditions are right for a stable chain reaction. There's a time lag and that gives us opportunity for adjustment. I've checked Fermi's calculations a hundred times. We'd be working under conditions so close to constant that we'd have several minutes before the reaction doubled its power. That would give us time to get control."

Burton Hall gasped. "But Steve, Chicago, in the middle of a big city—we'd be relying on only a marginal fraction of all the possible neutrons!"

"I can't see what could go wrong," Steve said. "We'd allow the reaction to grow only very slowly, so there'd be no chance of its getting out of control."

Burton Hall's rugged face fell into haggard lines. "I ought to go to the mayor, or anyway to the president of the university, or somebody. But I can't. They'd have to say no.

160

Anybody in his right mind would say no, because he couldn't take the chance."

Stephen did not reply. He continued to sit motionless, his hands in his pocket, and gazed out of the window at the grey and windy sky. He was conscious of a vague headache, a deep malaise, a depression of mind or body, he could not be sure which, and perhaps it was both.

Burton Hall sighed in a sudden gust of desperation. "All right, I take the responsibility. There's nobody else. Go ahead, Steve."

The door opened at this moment and Jane Earl stood there. She looked from one to the other, but neither of them looked at her. She stepped back and closed the door again.

✻   ✻   ✻

Stephen Coast pulled the thermometer from his mouth and looked at it with disgust.

"A hundred and three!" he muttered.

"That settles it," Helen said. "You don't get up."

"I must get up!"

"Well, you can't. And if I hear another word out of you I'll send for Burton Hall."

"He's in New Mexico."

"Does that matter?"

She disappeared briskly, and he lay fulminating. Who could have thought that as soon as Burton Hall had flown off three days ago to some unknown place in the desert, four of his own colleagues, men who he could have sworn would uphold him, now rebelled against Chicago as the place to make the great experiment?

"It's all in your hands, Steve," Burton Hall had said gaily as he departed.

All in his hands, and here he lay in his bed, felled by some

161

minute virus of influenza, germinating in that vague malaise, that wandering headache, three days ago in Burt's office. The meeting which was to decide everything was to have been in his office an hour from now. He dared not defy himself and get out of bed. It was too important for him to be well.

Helen came back with a bowl of soup which he had no desire to eat.

"It's all psychosomatic," she said ruthlessly. "You don't really want to make the damned thing, whatever it is that you have to make, and your conscience is taking revenge. So you get the flu."

He waved the soup away. "Nice and cruel of you to make such a diagnosis."

"You will too drink it." She set the bowl on the table beside him. "I'm going away for five minutes. If it isn't gone when I come back—"

"What'll you do?"

"I'm not telling."

"Helen!"

"Yes?" She paused at the door.

"I propose a compromise."

"Oh?"

"You telephone the fellows to come here. While you do that, I'll drink the slop."

She shook her fist at him in mock fury. "Slop! But I'll do it."

She went away and he drank the broth distastefully. Why did women insist upon stuffing men and children with food? It satisfied the possessive instinct in them, he supposed. She came back as he swallowed the last drop.

"They'll be here. . . . Shall I telephone Jane Earl, too?"

"No, she's with Burt."

"Oh—"

162

A very pregnant cunning *oh*, he thought. But he would not inquire into its meaning. He could not get involved now. He must save himself for the clash with the men. He tried to doze and seeing his closed eyelids she took the empty bowl and tiptoed away. But behind those eyelids he was far from asleep. His febrile mind, already at work, paused for one satisfaction. Helen was right about not wanting a child. He could not do with any creation now save the one conceived and nourished in his own solitary brain.

Half an hour later he was in the thick of it. Four men sat around his bed, all scientists whom he must respect and whom he needed. Their arguments beat against him, and with his invincible logic he knew they were all arguments which also he must respect.

"The main focus of this work is already in Columbia—"

"Or Princeton—"

"So what is the sense of moving it here?"

"The tempo here is too slow, Steve. You'll never get the chain reaction going in Chicago!"

"I'll have it going by the end of the year," Stephen said grimly.

"I'll bet you won't—I'll bet you a thousand dollars."

"All right, I'll take it—in the presence of these witnesses."

"Cut the stakes to a five-cent cigar."

"Agreed."

He sat up, his eyes burning holes in his head. "You fellows think I'm not serious. Well, I am. And I've listened to all your arguments, like Job in the Bible, and mine are better. The laboratory and the offices here are as good as any of yours. And this is where I am. You may remember that I am responsible for the product and the Project. It's got to be where I can be in charge and in control. And I can get scientists here in the Midwest. On the east coast the Pentagon has gobbled up all the good ones. I wouldn't know where to find my men there. And don't forget that where there are men, there are families. We can still find housing here. And most important of all, we're not as liable to be bombed as the coastal cities."

The blood was pounding in his skull. He felt his fever rising, his flesh grow hot. He lay back on his pillows. "I make the decision. It's final. We stay in Chicago. Here's where we'll see it through."

There was silence. A voice spoke.

"You forget one very important fact."

"What's that?"

"Fermi is in New York. We can't do without Fermi."

"Fermi will come here," Stephen said. He opened his hot dark eyes and stared at them, daring them to reply. No one answered. One by one they got up and said good-bye and went away.

When they were gone he took the receiver from the telephone by his bed. "Person to person," he told the operator.

He gave a private number and waited. Far away he heard the pleasant Italian voice.

"That you, Dr. Fermi?"

"It is I."

"Stephen Coast, Chicago."

Fifteen minutes later he had the promise he wanted. He hung up and turned to Helen, standing beside his bed, biting her lip and tapping her foot on the floor, and in her hand a bowl of broth on a tray.

"Another!" He groaned.

"Three hours since the last," she retorted.

He suddenly felt better, his head cooler, the pounding less violent inside his skull. "All right," he said. "Give me the slop. I'll drink it down. I've won my private war."

*   *   *

Burton Hall let the reins fall slack. The desert air was clear and autumn-cool, the distant mountains violet-dark against a sapphire sky.

"I keep coming back here, Jane," he said. "I keep coming back because I have a hunch that we're going to use this place—not this spot, but the top of that mesa yonder. I'm not taking you there because I don't want to rouse ideas in the people around here, but it's a place as good as a fortress if—when—we need such a place for the final putting together. Parkes has the design about ready and Steve has the pile about ready. When those two jobs are done, and the big test made under Fermi's eyes, and you and I will be there for the finals, then we're ready to go ahead and make the thing. And that's where we'll concentrate, right up there on the flat top. We'll get the cream of the crop of scientists up there, and the young ones, the pure experimentalists, and we'll put them together and let them burn each other's brains up."

"And then?" Jane inquired. She rode her horse well, but in the English fashion she had been taught by her English riding master in the mountains of Kashmir where she and her parents had spent their summers when she was a child. She had been a grave little girl, rather small then for her age, pale as white children in India always are, and she had taken her lessons seriously.

"Think of yourself and your horse as one," the Englishman had told her. "Learn the rhythm of his pace and make it yours. Then you know you are in control."

"Then," Burton Hall said joyously, "then, my girl, I shall go far away. When the bomb is made, I'll retire from everything I hate and fear and detest. I shall do only that which I love and enjoy and relish. And that may include anything —and more than you realize, tall girl."

She smiled at him. These months of working under his

165

willful brilliant direction had brought her perilously near to being in love with him and she knew it. There had not been a spoken word, but much was shared. Looking at him now, in the blaze of the noonday sun, his thatch of hair sunburned and tawny, his strange powerful eyes greener than ever in the hard sunlight, she knew that some day it might be impossible to resist him. She must prepare for the day, the hour, when the gathering tensions of their shared work were released. She must be very sure of herself, sure that she knew what she wanted. Mollie was to be considered. She was fond of that plump mother of men, a mother to Burt as well as to his sons, and there was a man in Burt who needed a mother, among the many men that he was. And she, Jane Earl, was not a mother woman. If Burt ever turned to her for mothering, she would leave him, repelled. A mate, yes, but not a son. She would create her own sons.

He broke across her thoughts. "Do you ever dream?"

"Dream?"

"Yes, dream!"

"I never dream."

"Your eyes are a dreamer's eyes."

"Probably dreaming of neutrons—"

"You can't escape me that way! Neutrons are the secret, my girl! Without them we couldn't transmute the elements and make the dreams of the alchemists come true at last. No explosion without neutrons—"

She laughed. "I admit the choice was bad. Neutrinos then, little ashen wisps, little ghosts of what has been and is no more."

He laughed with her. "Oh, I could love you, woman! I mean really love you. What enchantment can match what you and I have? I speak and you understand. You speak and I understand. It's enough, isn't it? And women waste time on rouge and permanents and—and—all that nonsense. . . .

When your brain answers mine on the instant, you incomparable female, I could—I could—"

"Wait," she said, "wait—wait!"

They interchanged a long look. He cantered his horse so close to hers that their knees touched.

"No, Burt," she said unsteadily. "I dare not."

"Why not?"

"I don't trust myself."

"Sure it's not me you don't trust?"

She threw him an uncertain smile and spurred her horse into a gallop ahead of him. Between them rose the cloudy dust of ancient volcanic ash, stirred into life again by her horse's flying feet.

❋   ❋   ❋

Stephen Coast shivered in the cold December wind as he waited for the streetcar. The second day of the month and already it was as cold as midwinter! This morning when he fed Spot, ice crackled under his feet. The dog's dish, he saw with satisfaction, was not frozen, a small satisfaction in comparison to much that was far from satisfactory. The thermometer was down to ten degrees and the bitter wind blew across the tossing whitecapped waves of the lake. It was the second day of gasoline rationing, too, and he had left the car for Helen. She had visits to make to the families under her care, since the scientists had come with their families to Chicago. There were sick children to be taken to the hospital and marketing to be done for mothers of small infants. The streetcars were crowded and the elevated trains were no better. Even the news from abroad was bad. An air battle was being fought fiercely at this very moment over Tunisia. The Dieppe operation was recently over, with what consequences no one yet knew, but an American soldier had

167

received the Distinguished Flying Cross from King George. In the midst of the bad news, the scanty good news was that an American destroyer had sunk a Japanese destroyer and four other ships and the Italians were losing morale under Mussolini. But throughout the world the Jews were in mourning. The State Department had announced that two million Jews had been murdered so far, and five million more might yet perish. . . . A terrifying world, and it might be yet more terrifying before night fell.

The streetcar screeched to a stop. Stephen Coast swung himself into it and propelled himself by force through the crowds. He was exhausted with sleeplessness. He had left the pile at West Stands only two hours ago to rush home and wash himself, eat and sleep for three quarters of an hour while Helen stood guard by the telephone. It would take a day of washing to get the grime of the soft graphite out of his skin. His nails were as black as a coal miner's.

"What on earth are you doing to get so filthy?" Helen had demanded.

"I wish I could tell you everything," he said, and so gravely that she asked no more.

He drowsed lightly now as he stood, his body upheld by the bodies of strangers pressed against him, and almost missed his stopping point. But not quite, for some hidden sense within him was awake and roused him. He swung himself down again and pulling up his coat collar he hurried across Stagg Field to the concrete grandstand under which for many weeks he and Fermi and all the others had been working. Fermi was the freely acknowledged leader. Under those dark and confident eyes the pile had been built in an abandoned squash court, the graphite blocks stacked layer by layer in alternate layers, the uranium imbedded, and through the center of the pile ran the control rods of cadmium.

The hour now was half past eight. The air in the court was damp and cold as he entered. The furnace had not been turned on, he had not found a way to keep it on, for no one could be told of the secret work going on under the grandstand. A few scientists were already there, up in the balcony above the pile, from where they could look down upon the pile itself. Upon a desk a meter was attached to a long electric cord. Others were coming in. Across the space he saw Burton Hall and then Jane Earl. He had not seen her for months. He caught her eyes now and nodded. She had been with Burton Hall every day. How could a man, emotional and susceptible in spite of his brilliance, be with her every day and fail to fall in love with her? And since she was still with Burt, what could it mean except that she responded?

He turned his back on them both and then found Burton Hall beside him, and was compelled to shake his ready hand.

"I wouldn't miss this for anything, Steve. It's the greatest day in human history."

Stephen defended himself with pessimism. "Something will probably go wrong."

"I'm betting on Fermi—and you."

"Thanks—it works on paper, but who knows?"

Stephen walked away, unable to endure talk, and examined the last neutron counter. Its ticking had accelerated last night and the critical size had almost been reached, a coffeepot ready to boil over, he had thought, and Fermi, wakened in the night to be told the news, had set the trial run for this morning.

Fermi stood before them now, a short but commanding figure. "Good morning, gentlemen. We have now reached the goal toward which we have so long been working. Chain reaction has been started."

He sat down at the desk before the meter, and motioned

169

to Jane to take the chair next him. The men gathered around.

Fermi lifted his head and began to speak. "We now make the supreme trial. Let us remember that the chain reaction has not only to be started, but most important it has to be stopped. It is necessary first for each man to take his post and to remember what he must do if the reaction gets too much. Otherwise—"

He shrugged his shoulders and smiled with a charming gesture of apology that they might all be burnt up in an instant. In silence the men took their places behind the controls that were already in the pile, one automatic that would shut down when the defined neutron count had been reached, another an emergency safety rod, with a rope to be cut if the reaction grew violently high, and a hundred feet away, behind a concrete wall, three men stood ready to thrust in the safety rods by remote control if the reaction overwhelmed the men nearby.

They began the rehearsal. Fermi stood by the table, watch in hand, straight as Napoleon before his armies, as critical and as careful, the calm smile fixed upon his pale face.

"Good. It is now a quarter to ten o'clock. We will begin the last tests."

In silence men stepped forward and pulled out the electrically operated rods to the point already set. Minutes passed. Fermi spoke under his breath to Stephen Coast.

"Be ready, emergency squad!" Stephen ordered.

A man stepped forward, ax in hand, ready to cut the rope.

"Liquid control squad!" Stephen called.

Three men stood ready to flood the pile with cadmium salt solution if the reaction went out of control. Fermi now read the meters and checked the reaction against his prediction.

"The data correspond to my calculations," he announced. "We have nothing to fear."

Stephen spoke. "Unless the final step is unpredictable, and the safety rods don't work."

"That is the chance we take," Fermi said. His beautiful childlike smile shone upon them all. "Meanwhile, we take the noon hour for a good lunch."

The men crowded toward the door, pressing after Fermi and Burton Hall, but Stephen did not go with them. Jane, passing by, touched his sleeve.

"No luncheon?"

"I can't eat."

She nodded and went, and he stayed on with two assistants. They did not talk beyond a word now and then.

"Ever see anybody like Fermi?"

"Never."

"Wonder what he was as a kid?"

"A terror."

"I'll bet."

At two o'clock the balcony was filled again. Stephen saw Burton Hall come in with Fermi and Jane Earl. She walked beside Fermi, her head bent, her lips faintly smiling as she listened. Fermi took his place and every man followed to his appointed position. The watchers grouped themselves against a wall, Szigny and Weiner and two others in front, nearest the pile.

"We will begin," Fermi announced. "Remove now the rods six inches."

The men behind the control rods pulled them out six inches farther. Fermi watched the indicators. The counters clicked as they registered the rays from the pile. A light from the galvanometer began to mount the scale of a recording meter.

"Another foot," Fermi commanded.

Stephen saw the recording stylus move upwards. Minutes passed. The big room was silent except for the ticking of the

171

instruments, the hum of the motor. The air was all but unbearable with the intensity of human minds, concentrated upon one momentous purpose. He glanced at Jane. She stood against the brick wall, her hands braced on a ledge behind her. Her face was white, her eyes black. She did not look at him and he looked away again.

"Again four inches," Fermi called. He beckoned to Jane and she came instantly to his side. He pointed to the sheet of his calculations and smiled. "Exactly—not?" She nodded.

"Another inch," he called. He turned to her again. "This will do it."

The meters showed the radiation approaching the danger point. Suddenly the level was reached.

Fermi shouted. "Throw in the safety rods!"

The cadmium strips went in with a roar. The meter readings dropped. The reaction had taken place—and it had been stopped. They had achieved control.

"What time is it?"

Stephen started. Jane's voice, at his side—

He looked at his wrist watch. "It is exactly twenty-five minutes past three o'clock."

"We will call it a day," Fermi was saying. "Lock the control rods in safety position. Then let us drink a bottle of Italian wine together. Jane, paper cups, please."

She fetched paper cups from the water cooler and into each Fermi, with ceremony, poured the red wine. He lifted his cup high and drank and stood waiting while the others drank. They drank, Jane noticed, with strange and different expressions, Thompson and Parkes as if they were taking communion in a cathedral before the Host, the General with relish, smacking his lips, Burton Hall casually, tossing it off. Stephen, holding the cup, did not put it to his lips and Jane, unnoticed, spilled her wine upon the dusty floor.

Fermi was speaking again in his usual mild and matter-of-fact voice.

"Come back tomorrow morning, please. We will start at once a new series of experiments."

What had happened was over. Fermi was already thinking of what must next be done. Burton Hall went to the telephone. Stephen heard his voice, pitched low but excited and full of confidence, speaking to someone afar off.

"The Italian navigator has landed in the New World. . . . Yes, yes, the natives are friendly."

He set down his paper cup, its wine untouched. He was shaken and doubtful, he wanted to weep. The exhaustion, the discouragement, the anxiety of the past weeks, welled up in him mingled with relief, reluctant pride, and the excitement of success. He was profoundly sad. In the center of his being he felt the conviction of tragedy. He wished that he had failed. What would men do with his success? How far was he responsible for what they might do? The General was talking with Fermi now at the door. Nothing but triumph on that florid countenance! Someone touched his shoulder with a light hand. It was Starleigh, the young industrialist whom he had just met today, his handsome face glowing as he spoke.

"Endless power! Enough power to heat and light the homes of the world for all eternity and run all the industries everywhere. Talk about a new ice age to come! We needn't be afraid now. We have the secret of the light of the sun and the stars combined. I congratulate you, Coast."

"Thanks," Stephen said. He was assuaged for a moment. "I'm glad you said that. I was thinking of something very different."

The quick brilliant smile came and went on Christopher Starleigh's face. "I can imagine. But don't let yourself think of a particular weapon, or a possible moment. Your interest

173

is in the ultimate values. So is mine. Did you know I was trained as a scientist? At Carnegie Tech. I've invented a thing or two myself."

"How could you give it up?" Involuntarily Stephen asked the question.

"I had to go to work—had a job in Canaday-Farrell—my first. Mr. Farrell was my boss, and I was his fair-haired boy, the successful young research scientist, you know, who came up with a money-making idea. He invited me to a weekend and I met his lovely daughter. Six months later we were married and I was an executive from then on—see?"

"Do you—"

"Regret it? No. I wouldn't want to be responsible for that monster yonder."

He nodded toward the pile, smiled again and walked gracefully away. And Stephen, left to ponder these weighted words, felt himself relapse again into his dark mood. He stood, forgetful, staring at the pile, and heard Jane's voice at his side.

"You've done it, Stephen."

He did not turn his head. "Please don't congratulate me. I couldn't bear it at this moment."

She did not reply. But he felt his hand taken into her warm strong clasp. He looked down, surprised, and saw her face tender and soft with understanding. For a moment they stood hand in hand. Then quietly she withdrew her hand and left him to follow Burton Hall.

All of them left him, and he stayed on with the pretense of a few last things to do, until he was alone, except for that dark pile, wherein burned now a fire, powerful beyond human knowledge. It was as ancient as eternity itself and as indestructible. But man, in happy ignorance, had not known it until today, and now knowing it, he could never be ignorant again. Nor happy, perhaps!

174

And suddenly, unable to bear his utter solitude, Stephen fled from the presence in the dark pile and hastened to his home.

"You're sick, Stephen!" Helen, meeting him at the door, cried at the sight of his white face.

"I'm going to sleep," he muttered. He dashed past her and up the stairs. "I've got to sleep. Don't wake me—not for anything."

Bronze Plaque at West Stands, Stagg Field
Chicago, Illinois, U.S.A.

———————

ON DECEMBER 2, 1942

MAN ACHIEVED HERE

THE FIRST SELF-SUSTAINING CHAIN REACTION

AND THEREBY INITIATED THE

CONTROLLED RELEASE OF NUCLEAR ENERGY.

———————

III

In the low mountains of Tennessee spring was in the air again. The crimson buds of Judas trees mingled with the white blossoms of the dogwood against the dark green pines. The mild air was windless. Across the pale April sky white clouds floated huge and slow, threatening showers into the sunshine. In the valley, through which a small river flowed riotously over its shallow bed, Stephen Coast stood listening to a burly contractor, who spread blueprint plans upon a rough plank table set up under a crooked buttonwood tree.

"This here," the contractor was saying, "is where the houses will go up, and there'll be a shopping center handy over here, and to the right and left a schoolhouse and a church. We'll cut the roads through the scrub oaks yonder on that ridge."

The roads were streaks of red mud through which great machines lumbered with groans that could be heard even here.

"What's that big hole over to the right?" Stephen asked. He was dressed for the woods, and his high boots were caked with mud.

179

"Big as a race track, ain't it," the contractor said. "That there is for some sort of a magnet they aim to put in, though what magnet can be as big as that is beyond me. What you reckon they're goin' to do with it?"

Stephen smiled. "It would take too long to tell you," he said.

"You don't want to tell, I reckon," the contractor retorted in good humor. "Well, we each has our part in this here, and mine is to build and ask no questions."

Stephen smiled again and was silent while the man's rough voice burbled on. He gazed into the oval hollow where the great instrument was to be set to do its work, the magnetic separation of uranium isotopes. Last week he had conceived an idea about that magnet. It had come to him one day while he ate a sandwich for his hasty luncheon in the laboratory. He missed Jane Earl more than he would allow himself to know, and he had taken to those sandwiches Helen made for him instead of going to a restaurant. Copper was the problem. He had sat thinking about copper while he munched his ham and bread. The war was consuming the national resources of copper and he needed copper for the magnet, quantities of it, for the windings. It was not to be had. He considered the metals that might be substituted. Silver, of course, but where could enough silver be found? And then he remembered the vast reserves of silver hidden away in the United States Treasury. There it was, and why could it not be used, borrowed and returned again without loss, or with very little loss? He had taken his idea within the hour to the General's office, and there, because the General was in conference, the perennial, inexhaustible, eternal conference, he had blurted it out to the General's assistant.

"How much will you need?" the dapper uniform inquired.

180

Stephen had considered. "I should think about fifteen thousand tons."

The uniform had stared at him sternly. "Young fellow, when you talk about silver you say ounces and not tons."

Another twenty minutes, nevertheless, and Stephen's earnest and careful persuasion prevailed. The request was sent to someone in Washington at the Treasury building and the silver was granted, on condition of the metal's return, the same metal, Stephen promised, and his guess was that not more than one tenth of one per cent would be lost. . . . These were the details of his job. And at this moment Helen came sauntering down the hill from the woods, her hands full of violets and windflowers, and her dark hair blowing in curls about her sun-browned face.

"I shall like it here, Steve," she said. "I shall like it much better than Chicago. I've always wanted to live on a hill beside a river."

"Here's going to be your house, ma'am," the contractor said and planted a thick grimed thumb upon a spot on the blueprint. Helen pored over it, and measured its lines against the hills and the river and sauntered away again.

All the way back to Chicago she talked about the house. "It's not our real house, Steve," she said, "not the one you're going to buy for me some day, but it could be a sort of practice house, and I intend to make it a home."

He could not talk to her about his job or any of the vast secrets over which he now had control and for which he was responsible. Yet he longed to share with her something of his life. Jane had taught him what it meant to have someone, a woman, who could share his innermost scientist's life. But Helen was not cleared. It had not seemed worth while, since he would have had to explain so much to her and for that he had no time. He hoped in the sober self-examination, which was the habit of his conscience, that

181

he was not making an excuse of her ignorance. At any rate, he had not asked to have her cleared. They had somehow not achieved the closeness in their marriage which made her indispensable to him. It was his fault, and perhaps his fate as a scientist.

The way revealed itself to him now. "I need help," he said abruptly, "and I've thought of a way you can help. . . . While you're making the house into a home, you could be persuading other women to do the same thing. Men are never happier than their wives are—d'you know that, Helen? A discontented wife can ruin a man's work. I've seen it happen in the lab again and again. And we can't afford to have any man hampered now by trouble at home. Can't you just hear women complaining about the mud and the cramped houses and being so far away from home and all they've been used to? It would be a big job for you and very important."

"Do you call me discontented?"

She flung the question at him over her shoulder, and the wind blew the words into his face. She had insisted that he put down the top of the car, the day being fine, and he had yielded, because it was impossible to talk in the wind, and he had to think, to plan, to solve a thousand problems.

"I shall have to be so busy that you may very well be discontented," he replied. "I should not blame you at all if you were. But if you are busy helping me, you will be happier."

"Yes," she said, "it is possible that I may be happier."

Her voice, carried direct to his ear, was cool and touched with irony. But he had no time to analyze its quality. There was too much to do.

*   *   *

182

In December he had acknowledged that Helen was invaluable to him. They moved into the small wooden house, one among three thousand others. In the months between spring and winter the plant was finished and the great magnet was already at work. The new reactor was built, too, and housed in corrugated metal under tall brick stacks. It was a small plant, its place upon the blueprint marked X-10, but in it was the pile, with its thousand kilowatts of atomic power. Not beautiful to look at, Stephen thought, but how beautiful in its smoothly functioning power, and holding what promise for future benefit for man, when this wretched war was over! This was his elixir, his tonic, his anodyne, when he contemplated what he was doing—the bomb, yes, but beyond it, another better world. And he would even consent to the bomb's being used.

He called. "I'll have to go down to the plant now, Helen. Can you manage the furniture?"

"Go on," she called back. She came out of the house to see him off, the car sliding in the mud, and when he was gone she stood for a moment looking at the hills and the floating clouds. The houses about her were filling with families of scientists and technical workers and laborers. Dazed wives and bewildered children clung together, and truckloads of furniture stood before scores of newly painted front doors.

Suddenly she heard sobbing. She turned and on the flattened half-frozen mud in front of the next house she saw a young woman weeping, her handkerchief to her lips. The house was still empty. A lieutenant colonel was to live there, an assistant to the General, but he and his family were not yet come. The woman was poor, her navy blue suit thin and sleazy and her straight hair blowing in faded blond wisps in the wintry wind.

Helen walked toward her. "May I help you?"

183

The woman turned her head, and tears hung on her scant white eyelashes. "My home was here," she sobbed. "I heard about it. I work in Knoxville in a factory and I heard about it and I come to see what was goin' on, anyways. The house used to be somewheres here, but it's gone. The bulldozers have scraped it clear away. It set on a little hill, now even the hill is gone. I can't find a trace. What are they doin' here?"

"I don't know," Helen said.

The woman stared. "You don't know? Then what are you here for?"

"My husband works here," Helen said.

"What kind of work?" the woman demanded.

"I don't know," Helen said.

"Crissake," the woman muttered. "You don't know what your own husband works at!"

"No," Helen said.

The woman stared a moment longer and stupefied by the mystery, she forgot to weep and the wind dried her tears. Then, with a long hopeless sigh, she plodded through the mud and down the lane, and Helen went into the house and shut the door. What should she have said? Perhaps at least, "My husband does some sort of war work," but no, even that would have been too much. Nothing whatever could be said. Stephen never said anything. Not one word passed between them of what he did now. Since that day in Chicago, that December day, now more than a year ago, he had not told her anything. Oh, he had explained to her very gently and kindly why he could not. There must be no difference between them, he said, no misunderstanding. The nation was in a fight for its life and everything personal must be put aside.

"That's all very well for you, Steve," she had cried, "but

what about me? Am I to spend my life waiting until you can talk to me again?"

She would never forget the haunted eyes he turned upon her. "You can talk to me. Please talk to me, Helen. Keep me in touch with life."

She had gone into his arms then and had clung to him desperately. "But my life is bound up in yours. There won't be anything left of me if we're not living it together."

He had held her, but he had not yielded. "I'm not my own master now," he told her.

They had never spoken again, not really, and the evil of such secrecy, the sinister evil of it, was that life between them flickered and was ready to die. The question now was, if there were no communication, none at all possibly for years, could love survive? Oh, she could chatter as any woman does about the day's small events, the gossip of women, the chitchat of children, but that was not communication with Stephen. He listened, half-smiling, his mind—his heart, for all she knew—in another world, where she had no part. And he had forgotten love. No, that desperate turning to her in the night, that brief encounter, was not love. Relief, perhaps, a moment's escape, but not the communion they had known of love. The war was destroying them from within. She was very glad she had no child; a fatherless child would be more than she could bear.

In this broken thinking she had let herself sink upon a pile of carpet not yet spread, and now she was roused by a young woman at the door, a pretty girl of a woman, holding a small child in her arms and with another clinging to her skirt. They were all young, these women, young wives of young men not twenty-five, and their children were babies.

"Why are they all so young?" she had asked Stephen.

"Scientists do their best work before thirty," he had told

her. "It's the first creative push that is the best, the most daring. It's fun to rebel when you're young, question and doubt the old and explore the new."

"Can you tell me where I am?" the girl was saying distractedly. "My husband hadn't time to come with me. He's the lieutenant colonel."

Helen rose at once. "Next door," she said. "Your house is next door. And I'm glad you've come. I was just sitting here feeling lonesome and needing someone to help."

"Oh," the girl-woman sighed. "Oh, thank you. Isn't everything awful?"

"Yes," Helen said, "perfectly awful, and there's not a thing we can do about it."

*   *   *

And yet it was impossible, as weeks passed into months, not to fell the atmosphere of shared responsibility. Even the women felt it, ignorant as they were of what was going on. Their men were eager and excited, something big was being done, everyone was important, and the General himself came to visit the new city into which daily more people poured until at last the population was seventy-five thousand. More schools were needed and built, more churches, stores, garages, a makeshift hospital, a little theater, a music club, a light opera company. They were all amateurs and as gay as excitement could make them. Excitement was the energy, a secret excitement, vicarious for the women. They drained it from their men, absorbed it through their nerves and senses. Voices were high, laughter was loud, tempers were brittle, talk was blunt and manners were bad. There was no time for good manners or for courtesy. Scandals were easy, men's urgencies were close to the skin, and wives were lonely. They were young, young, young, they were in

186

high spirits, the scientists more important than they had ever been before, the men of the hour, life-and-death men, and the General had a hard time controlling them. They were uncontrollable. They took out their riotous independence in bad language and intemperate attacks on the General, on one another, and the birth rate rose astronomically.

"Goddam, don't these scientists do anything but manufacture kids?" the General bellowed to Burton Hall one day.

Burton Hall, on his monthly visit, grinned. "They're young, and what else is there to do at night? What's that old Chinese proverb? Something about going to bed early to save candlelight and having twins? Be glad when they go to bed with their wives."

The General swore horribly under his breath. "From what I hear," he mumbled.

"Don't tell me," Burton Hall said irritably. "I don't want to know."

He was irritable because Jane Earl had unaccountably refused any longer to be his assistant and he had tried to replace her, had replaced her as far as work went, by a cool young married woman competent as the devil, maybe more competent than Jane in some ways, and so he couldn't dismiss her in good conscience, but she was no comfort to him, dammit, no comfort at all, and he needed comfort, nothing really physical, but the possibility of it. A woman had to be desirable if she was to be a comfort to a harassed man, even if he had no intention of ever going beyond that. Jane understood him and he could trust her never to let him go beyond the limit. He didn't have to be on guard with her. He was a little in love with her and that was delightful and relaxing, but it didn't mean anything upsetting to anybody, certainly not to Mollie. And then, listening to the grumbling voice of the General here at headquarters, it suddenly occurred to him to wonder if Mollie did have something to do with it. For it was soon afterwards that she wrote the letter—

The whole affair sprang to his memory as clearly as if somebody had etched it into his brain. Jane and the letter, of course! Jane saying in her clear low voice: "I want to resign, please, Burt."

Right in the middle of the most awful problems of getting four different works started and going, in four different parts of a huge country where the government wouldn't let him travel by air and he had to crawl around in trains that inched the miles along like caterpillars, while his soul and his brain raced ahead to where he ought to be, and as if that weren't annoyance enough he had bodyguards, he, Burton Hall, who had always been as impetuous and free as the wind now had plain-clothes men sleuthing around him everywhere he went because he was important. And then just as everything was going very well, the plant on top of the mesa in full swing under Bob Eaves, and the stuff being turned out like nobody's business, Jane had to resign.

"Resign from me?" he had bellowed at her that day. It was a nice day, too, a fine cold winter's day, and he had spent it with her climbing around the mountains above the valley of the Columbia River, in the midst of gorgeous scenery, and he was feeling like a million dollars. Maybe he had annoyed her, daring her to—

"Haven't we had a nice time?" he demanded. "And you know I don't mean half what I say. I respect you, Jane, I really do. And I wouldn't upset Mollie for anything. Can't a man and a woman be friends in a special sort of way?"

She sat down on a rock, and would he ever forget how she looked in that red suit of hers with the black fur against her white skin, and the wind blowing her black hair, her cheeks red and her eyes black as her hair? She had answered him calmly.

188

"I want to get back to my science, Burt. I've been away long enough. Somebody else can take my place with you. We're over the hump. It's a mere matter now of administration."

He was so frightened that his mouth went dry. "Nobody can take your place, Jane. You give me something nobody else does—a sort of—of energy that feeds my mind and my spirit. I don't want to be so corny as to call it inspiration, but that's what it is. You're a whetstone. You sharpen up all my processes. I'm a better man because of you."

She had continued to gaze out over the wintry landscape. "Thank you, Burt. That's wonderful to hear. We'll not stop being friends. But I'm asking you a favor. Let me go back to my own work. I'm thinking now beyond the war. I'm thinking of peace."

He had argued with her, he had besought her, he had accused her with anger and then with jealousy of being in love with someone. To everything she had answered with steadfast denial.

"You're a scientist, Burt. You ought to be able to understand that a scientist is not happy unless he's at work—his own work."

In his distress he had said exactly the wrong thing. "But you're a woman."

To this she had risen with resolution. "I'm a scientist, first of all. A woman can be something more than a woman, too. When will you ever know what we can be unless you know what we are? I must go, Burt."

And beyond that adamantine decision he had not prevailed.

"So, where do you want to go?" he had demanded when they reached the hotel that night and were about to part.

"I want to work on the mesa," she said. "I have some new ideas about plutonium—"

189

And then when he went home and left her there on the mesa installed in a laboratory and as forgetful of him, apparently, as though he did not exist—oh, he knew that world in which true scientists lived—he had gone home battered and bad-tempered and mean to everybody, to find the house empty and a letter there from Mollie. It was a love letter such as she had never written him, a love letter, no less, and which he could have sworn she was incapable of writing. But there it was, in her big even handwriting, on her big single sheets of paper.

"Sweetheart—"

She had not called him sweetheart since Tim was born and she became mother in his house.

"Do you remember—"

That was the way the letter began and the way it went on. She remembered everything, how he looked when she first saw him at college, a sophomore. She loved him at first sight and she had never told him until now. And word by word, line by line, she recalled their life together. He was amazed, he was shaken, and before he knew it he was sobbing and ashamed that he had not known her all these years. How had she hidden herself from him? Where had she escaped? Where was she now?

He read the letter again and again, sprawling in the big chair in his study, and getting up again and again to pace the floor and mutter, "Oh God, oh God," and wipe his eyes and read again. This was Mollie, his wife. Nothing was going to be the same again, nothing would be dull or common. He knew her now. And when she came home tonight, at six o'clock she said in the letter, because she was getting some families off to Tennessee, and their train went at five thirty so she ought to be home at six, he would sweep her off her feet, literally.

He felt his heart pound as the hand on the tall clock

crept to the hour. He went upstairs to the bathroom and washed his face and shaved and contemplated changing his shirt. Then he heard the front door open and close.

"Mollie!" he shouted.

"It's me," she said in her cheerful ordinary voice.

He tore downstairs then and took her in his arms. "That letter," he choked. "You needn't ever worry. You can't lose me."

"That's good," she said in her practical everyday voice. "I didn't really worry." She kissed him on the cheek, a pleasant usual kiss.

But he clung to her, he lifted her off her feet and he was crying again.

"Mollie, you're so wonderful. I never knew—"

"Put me down, Burt," she said. "I'm not any different than I ever was."

And to his amazement she was not. He put her down and their life went on as though the letter had never been written. She was here with him today in Tennessee, puttering around with the women and the children, like as not, advising on market prices and polio injections and hot school lunches and making a nuisance of herself to the administrators because the garbage collection was irregular and there ought to be another doctor in the community and certainly a couple more dentists. . . . If he hadn't kept the letter in the secret drawer of his desk, he wouldn't believe she had ever written it. But he had kept it.

*　　　*　　　*

In the midst of her employments Mollie Hall paused for an hour's talk with Helen Coast. The two women were not close friends, but they communicated essentials to one another of a sort which each perfectly understood and not for

191

anything would have explained. They sat together now on the couch in the living room that Helen had made into a pleasant if confined place, a tray with coffee and doughnuts on the table in front of them. They had discussed in detail the lives that were being led in the new community around them, and Mollie had given advice based on a similar community on the mesa at the other side of the country, and two others, one in the suburbs of Chicago and the other in Washington State. All the problems were the same, huge young communities, each working at top speed on the one immense project which must never be mentioned. In each community Mollie had her ally: Louise Starleigh, in the northwest, Beth Eaves on the mesa and here Helen herself. Through these henchwomen Mollie knew everything that went on among more than a quarter of a million people. She came and went as Burt's faithful shadow, stout and uncomplaining, providing an atmosphere of comfort whereever she went. Now there was a pause. Mollie waited for a certain question which might or might not be asked. It was asked.

"Did Jane Earl come with you?"

"She did not," Mollie said. She poured herself a third cup of coffee and took another doughnut. "She resigned—didn't you know? She wanted to go back to science."

"Where is she?"

"On the mesa."

"And Burt?"

"He has a new assistant, a very good one, not pretty and not a scientist. You didn't know about Jane?"

"Stephen doesn't tell me anything, of course," Helen said.

"Maybe he doesn't know. Maybe he hasn't asked," Mollie said in a reasonable tone.

"Maybe not," Helen agreed.

Mollie put down her cup and half the doughnut. "Gracious, what I'm doing to my figure! I must go, Helen. Well, you have done wonders, I'd say. So much depends on us women."

"Does it?"

Mollie laughed her rich comfortable laugh. "We know it, if nobody else does." She stood up and Helen stood up beside her. Suddenly Mollie leaned forward and kissed her cheek, for the first time.

"There," she said. "I'm not the kissing sort."

"Thank you," Helen said. "Neither am I." The two women clutched each other for an instant's embrace. "It's done me good."

She closed the door after Mollie then and stood leaning against it, reflecting. If Stephen said nothing about Jane, would it mean that he knew and did not tell? Could it possibly mean that he did not know because he did not care any more? The silence was too deep between them to be broken. If he did not speak, neither could she—oh, neither would she.

* * *

In the office of his laboratory Stephen in the same hours sat in deep talk with Burton Hall. The two men had not met for several months and the day had been spent in walking from building to building in detailed observation, ending with the new gas diffusion plant miles beyond the town. They returned now to the graphite reactor, to stand before it in mutual accord, regarding it lovingly and with awe. It had been at work for nearly six months, functioning almost perfectly. The twenty-four-foot cube of graphite was pierced by more than a thousand fuel channels, each holding aluminum-jacketed fuel slugs. Eight inches of graphite stood between each slug for moderating neutrons, and in addition to the fuel channels there were chambers for materials to be irradiated. It was possible to insert a thousand such targets at a time into the reactor and thirty-six different experiments could be carried on simultaneously.

"What a work horse," Burton Hall said fondly.

"When this war is over," Stephen said, "we'll be producing isotopes for research into the entire life of mankind. Biology, medicine, agriculture, industry—when do you figure this horrible holocaust will be over, Burt?"

"The day after our job is done, Steve."

"And that day?"

"Not set yet. The General is grim about it. Every decision he makes is based on time. If it delays the project a day, he says no."

Stephen was unrelenting toward the General. "Does he ever delay it himself? Oh, unwittingly of course, not knowing everything he ought to know."

Burton shrugged, grinned and waved his hands. "Some of the longhairs still think they could do the job better— and quicker. I don't know—anyway, we can't change now."

"I've heard we could have done it a year quicker without the military and industry."

"I don't know. It's this way now. We can't change it. . . . Are the fans working?"

Two huge fans drew atmospheric air into the reactor. "Perfectly," Stephen said.

"Rate?" Burton asked.

"One hundred thousand cubic feet per minute. There's an air space, as you know, at the front and back inside the concrete shielding. That's seven feet thick."

"Yeah, I know. I was in on the design."

The two men walked back to the office and sat down. Stephen closed the door.

"Where do you go from here?" he asked.

"Back to Chicago," Burton Hall replied. "I have a job to

do there with the engineers from Canaday-Farrell. They're wonderful fellows but they're not scientists and they have to be taught. . . . God, Steve, what am I saying? That's the truth about everybody except us scientists. They all have to be taught. And who'll teach 'em except us? Do you realize what we've done? We've flung open the gates of the universe, we're pushing the people through into a new world that scares them half to death. They'll bless or blame us. They've got to be taught—my, my, I never thought of it like that before. It's all got to be explained to them, or they'll kill themselves. It was that way when we first discovered electricity. People treated it like a toy, gave themselves electric shocks in parlor games, and suddenly the stuff flamed in their faces and killed 'em. And this atomic stuff is millions of times more powerful. Oh my, my, my—what would my father say? He'd say we've let loose hell-fire—maybe we have."

Burton Hall clutched his head in his hands and shut his eyes, overcome with the horror of what he suddenly imagined. He lifted his head and stared at Stephen with haggard eyes. "Ever read the Book of Revelation? I read it when I was a kid and had nightmares. The words are burned into my brain. 'I saw a sea of glass, mingled with fire.' 'Thunders and lightnings, a great earthquake such as was not since men were on the earth, so mighty an earthquake and so great that every island fled away and the mountains were not found.' 'And men blasphemed God.' "

He intoned the words in a strange heavy voice, loud as though he spoke them from a pulpit, and his green eyes glittered.

"Stop!" Stephen cried. "Stop it, Burt. It can't be that way—"

Late in the night he lay sleepless, remembering the scene. Burt's dazed look, his sudden shamed laugh. They had parted in mutual embarrassment. And suddenly, thinking of

195

Burt, he remembered that he had not seen Jane Earl. She had not come with him. Where was she, and what was she doing?

*   *   *

"The prisoners were marched in intense heat along the road to San Fernando, Pampanga, a distance of about seventy miles. They had all been on short rations for a considerable period before their capture and there was a high percentage of sick and wounded prisoners among them; nevertheless the sick and wounded were also forced to march with the others. Those who fell by the roadside and were unable to continue, and they were many in number, were shot or bayoneted. Others were taken from the ranks, beaten, tortured and killed. The march lasted nine days, the Japanese guard being relieved at five kilometer intervals by fresh guards who had been transported in American planes.

"For the first five days the prisoners received no food and never any water except what they were able to drink out of caribou wallows and ditches along the highway. Some food was thrown them by Filipinos, and occasionally they broke ranks and grouped themselves around a well or a wallow or ditch to slake their thirst. When this occurred, the Japanese opened fire on them. Throughout the march their escort maltreated them. They were beaten, bayoneted, and kicked with hobnailed boots. Dead bodies littered the side of the road.

"On the ninth day the prisoners received the welcome news that they would march no further. They were going to ride the rest of the way to Camp O'Donnell. Their relief on hearing the glad tidings was short-lived, however, for they were then crowded into very small Filipino railway coaches, a hundred men to each coach. So overcrowded were they, that there were many who, during the whole trip, never touched the floor. Hundreds fainted from lack of air, and many died of suffocation. It is not known how many died on the move from Bataan to Camp O'Donnell, but the evidence indicates that not less than eight thousand American and Filipino prisoners lost their lives during the journey."

Stephen Coast threw the pages down upon his desk. They were marked *Classified. To be destroyed.* Alone in his office he now destroyed them, tearing them into small pieces and dropping them into the wastebasket. Then he took up his receiver. The operator's blithe voice answered.

"Number, please!"

"Find Dr. Burton Hall, wherever he is." Stephen said.

"Have you any idea where he is, Dr. Coast?"

"Chicago, Columbia River, New Mexico—possibly Washington."

When Burton Hall's voice answered, faint and far, he was in none of those places.

"Hello, hello."

"Hello, Burt," Stephen said, "where are you?"

"I'm in Vermont, Steve, here in my shack by the lake. Doctor ordered a rest—a weekend, that's all. What you want?"

"I want a transfer," Stephen said.

"What for? Where to?" Burt demanded.

"To the mesa," Stephen said.

"What in—"

"Ever hear of conversion, Burt? Well, I'm converted."

"Converted?"

"Yes, you ought to know—the son of a preacher! Only I'm converted in reverse."

"Yeah?"

"Yes. . . . I want to kill."

There was a long silence. Then Burt's voice came full across the wires.

"All right, Steve. You're transferred."

That night when he told Helen he saw her look at him strangely, searching his soul.

"Why, Stephen?"

"I can't tell you," he said curtly.

"Is that classified, too—your motive for going to New Mexico?"

"Yes," he said. "We're leaving tomorrow."

❋   ❋   ❋

"That's how it was, Jane," he said.

A week had passed, seven days, and not until today had they found time to talk. Now, late in the afternoon, they walked along the path that led up the mountain range encircling the old crater. He climbed the rocky steps and paused to turn and look at her following him. "Oh, but it's good to have someone to talk to, someone who's safe and cleared—and knows what I'm talking about."

"It's good to see you, Stephen. I'd forgotten how good."

"You've had Burt," he said abruptly.

"Burt is not you."

She reached his level. They stood side by side and somehow their hands touched and clung and instantly parted. The touch was flame and fire. He felt the quiver of the blood in his veins. He wanted to speak and dared not, lest words he did not want to say should burst from him. He was in no mood to trust himself. Tense, angry, ignoring thought and conscience, he was in a mood which frightened him. He must not confuse this emotion with—with love. He was in love with his wife. No, he loved Helen and that was better than being in love. But he was dimly aware that emotion, however stirred, for whatever reason, could express itself in wild ways. He had once seen a bullfight in Mexico, when

198

he was on a summer's vacation in college, and with a girl who was no more than a casual companion for the afternoon, and suddenly, his whole being fastened upon the bloody battle between man and beast, he had been horrified and even frightened to find himself seized by lust. With difficulty he had controlled himself on the way home alone in the car with the girl, and with all the more difficulty because he divined in her the same urge toward him, and this without any love between them. Later, disgusted and ashamed, he had done a secret research on bullfighting and had discovered from the bald statistics that after witnessing a bullfight men sought their wives or prostitutes. . . . And this was true in war, too, for in those papers marked classified, which he had been careful to destroy, there were other pages, concerning the capture of Nanking. He had read them with guilty interest.

"Rape was the order of the day, and resistance by the victim or by members of her family who tried to protect her, meant almost certain death. Girls of tender years and old women, neither were spared. . . . During the first month of Japanese occupation approximately twenty thousand cases of rape occurred." The word was Japanese but it should be "Man" and his return to the beast. He stared straight into the sunset, his eyes narrowed, his mouth grim. "Jane, I want you to know that I had no thought that you were here when I asked Burt for a transfer."

"Would you not have come then?" she asked.

"I don't know." He hesitated and went on. "Yes, I would have come, because I want to work on the weapon. I feel compelled to work on it, but—"

He hesitated again and for so long that she spoke for him. "You needn't finish. I understand. You needn't be afraid of me. And I shan't be afraid of you. We're scientists first."

199

And with these words quietly spoken, she led the way down the mountain.

... That night at the dinner table in a house exactly like the one they had left in Tennessee he paused over an excellent beef stew to say something to Helen.

"I want you to know," he said, "that I don't intend to see Jane Earl alone while I am here."

She looked up alarmed, and her cheeks flushed. "Oh Steve, do you have to say that?"

"I just want you to know," he said doggedly.

She yearned to be mild, to be understanding, to laugh a little, anything not to be serious. But this was serious and she was so frightened that terror burned her tongue. "Why should you be afraid to see her alone?" she cried. "You must be in love with her."

He looked at her, knife and fork in hand, with honest trouble in his dark eyes, and said, "I'm not in love with her. I don't want to be in love with her. I don't want to be in love with anybody but you."

She flew from her chair and across the room and stood behind him where he could not see her face and put her arms about his neck and laid her cheek against his hair.

"Oh Steve," she whispered. "You break my heart—"

❊   ❊   ❊

"We can do it because we must do it," the General said.

He paused panting, on a ledge of the cliff above the Columbia River, flowing silver in the distance. The pounds were falling away from him, his figure was nearly trim, and might have seemed so had not Burton Hall stood on one side of him, big-boned and lean, while on the other was the slim elegance of Starleigh.

The men stood silent for a moment, regaining breath. It

200

was spring again, the spring of 1945, a fine day, mild in the valley but here on the mountain the air was laced with a snow-cooled wind. The new leaves of aspen trees were quivering, but the dark pines stood unmoved.

"Now that our engineers have caught the drift of your theories, Burt," Starleigh said, "it won't be hard. We've put all our power behind it, as you can see."

"I can indeed," Burton Hall said. "I feel like a fellow who has been running a relay race, and the relay has just stepped in."

The General barked, "Don't think you're going to quit, Burt, and don't forget I take responsibility for this development here. The Tennessee outfit is just too close to civilization for the big push. Too many people around, too easy to get to. That's why I decided on this wilderness. Seven hundred square miles—well, I don't count these two half-dead little towns. The area is half as big as the state of Rhode Island. Sure, we have sixty thousand people here now, but they're protected, ain't they? And don't you feel too proud, either, Starleigh. The United States Army engineers deserve some credit."

"Of course, General, of course," Starleigh agreed. In spite of the noonday sun and the steep climb he looked cool and neat.

"I'm sweating like a horse, Starleigh, and you look like a handsome icicle," Burton Hall grunted. "Don't forget, you two, that the scientists had something to do with all this." His arm swept the changed landscape.

The General grumbled. "Yeah, a lot of guesswork! Why, I'd ask 'em how in hell they'd expect some damned idea of theirs to work, and they'd say they didn't know if it would work, and we'd better build it and see! And try to hurry 'em! They can't hurry. 'In a few weeks—or months—or a

201

couple of years—we'll have the problem solved.' God, no wonder I'm losing my hair!"

Burton Hall grinned. "They were worried, you bet! They'd come to me and whisper in my ear—'We don't know what will happen to the graphite in the pile after it has been exposed to the neutrons for several months.'"

"What'd you tell 'em?" the General demanded.

"I said I didn't, either. The continual bombardment of the neutrons might change the structure of the graphite."

"Then what?" the General demanded.

"It would store up energy," Starleigh said quietly.

"And?" The General's red face paled.

"It would explode."

The General howled. "Burt, is he right?"

"We take the chance," Burt said. "We have to—there's no alternative."

Far below them the wide river flowed over the horizon to the sea.

"Oh, God," the General muttered. "What have we got ourselves into, with these scientists! Oh God, help me. I'm stuck in a job too big for any man. . . . Well, I can't get out of it. You're right, Burt. We gotta take all the chances. We gotta work together, we three fellows. I can see that. . . . Besides, here's this river, giving us unlimited cold water. It doesn't hurt to have a water-cooled plant instead of air-cooled. There's safety in variety. And the Yakima, joining the Columbia River yonder, gives us a flow of power."

Burton Hall let the General talk. His impatience of the big officer had yielded to respect, at first unwilling but now generously given. Garrulous and obstinate, nevertheless the man had achieved miracles. He was a good administrator, a stickler on small matters, vain and domineering, but he thought in concepts of huge size. Starleigh took size for granted. The contrast between the two men was even physical, the General an elephant and Starleigh a panther, sleek and slim. They were the doers of the world, he supposed, and the scientists were the thinkers, doing only enough to prove their experiments. He had been very right not to yield to Szigny and Weiner and Thompson and all the rest of the top brains when they had argued that the Project belonged to them, the conception theirs, the execution therefore their privilege. To this day Szigny still argued in rebellion, fomenting discontent in Weiner.

"Weiner would be all right, if that wild man would leave him be," the General had grumbled only yesterday. "He's pure brains, nothing else, and he don't think about anything else except his ideas. But Szigny runs around everywhere talking and arguing and messing things up for me. If I dared let him loose I'd get rid of him. But I don't dare. He's dangerous, a man like that, his brains busting out all the time with all sorts of notions. We can't get rid of him. He's more dangerous loose where I can't watch him than he is right under my eyes, however mad he makes me."

It was Weiner, and the small group of men who worked with him, who had first devised the water-cooled graphite pile, a bold new device, but Burt had learned to expect the bold and the new from Weiner, his magnificent kingly brain lodged in the fine big skull that sat above the incongruously slight frame. The design of the pile was simple, based on assumptions that could not be proved, but could only be used, assuming, for example, that the neutron multiplication factor would be larger than any experiment, so far, in the laboratories, and that they could use the cooling water and a sheath of protecting aluminum over the uranium slugs before they were inserted into the graphite pile. And then Weiner, after he had proved it on paper, had felt impelled to make experiments, only to discover that he could not find anywhere a tube of aluminum of the right length and thick-

203

ness, and not even Canaday-Farrell had been able to provide one—"Sorry we don't mass-produce that size of aluminum tube"—and so Weiner had made one himself for the trial experiment and Szigny had rushed to headquarters, shouting again that the scientists were best at production, after all.

"Oh, shut up," the General had growled, and breaking into a sweat of repressed rage he mopped his purple face.

Szigny, trained in the meticulous formalities of European courtesy, had frozen into wounded rage. Bowing from the waist, he had wheeled and marched from the hated presence of the military to collapse in tears upon Weiner's shoulder.

"Barbarians," he had muttered. "Why shall we save them?"

"Because they are all we have left of the free world," the gentle Weiner had replied, patting his compatriot's shoulder.

"They will destroy it themselves by stupidity," Szigny howled.

"That is why we must save them," Weiner said.

The quarrels, the quarrels, the wrangles, the endless jealousies astoundingly possible to these great men, to these powerful minds, these superlative human beings!

"I'm ground between the upper and nether millstones," Burt groaned to his Mollie.

"I'm glad I made fresh apple pie tonight," she said.

Weiner's design had worked, nevertheless, and Burton Hall submitted it to the engineers of Canaday-Farrell, giving Weiner all the credit. They examined the design and the experiment. Long aluminum tubes were embedded in the graphite moderator, and within the tubes were the cylindrical slugs of uranium smoothly coated with aluminum. The cooling water flowed through the tubes around the uranium slugs, and when the slugs were exposed long enough to the neutrons in the pile, they were pushed through the tubes, always by remote control, into a vat of deep water, the water a protection for those who worked with the violently radioactive material. The slugs were then taken to the chemical plant where the plutonium would be extracted. The modern alchemy!

"A fine intelligent piece of work," Starleigh had said. And himself, capably intelligent, had gone to Weiner to congratulate him. The exile had blushed like a woman praised.

"I have to thank the university at Budapest," he said. His delicate hands fluttered like startled birds. "My professors there made me to work very hard. My training was theoretical engineer, with so much mathematics, I think more than any American university perhaps, and in physics very thorough. Chemistry also."

"Many scientists in one," Starleigh had replied. "And I wish we knew how to do it here, instead of producing all these specialists. We need the synthesizing mind, eh, Dr. Hall?"

But Weiner was not finished. He went on hesitatingly, his face growing white as he talked. "I must thank the Nazis somewhat. They frightened me terribly. They have such good scientists, such great industries. We cannot think little of them. We must think very much of them, now that they are enemies of free men."

In the end, however, the Project still remained the work of many men, even of many companies. The aluminum tubes were resistant to welding, and aluminum had to be soldered to the uranium as a jacket. Three companies combined with the laboratory to find a cement hard enough to hold aluminum. There could not be one failure, for if one of the uranium slugs were exposed to water, it could stay the cooling flow and stop the reactor for days, perhaps, for repairs. Brains and brawn, both were needed, the directing brain, the executing hands, a symbolism, Burton Hall thought, as he watched the partnership, brains learning to respect the brawn, and brawn obedient to the brain. The secret of success was the unifying single purpose, now for war, but afterwards, could not the partnership continue for peace? From such thoughts he shook himself free, sometimes with impatience. The preacher father kept his hold upon the son's soul. And Burton Hall envied again the cool detachment of a tranquil Fermi, absorbed in pure science.

"Don't bother me with your conscientious scruples," Fermi had said. "After all, the thing is superb physics."

. . . "Well," the General said, "we've rested here quite a spell. It's not work."

They lingered, nevertheless. Far below them, on the banks of the rushing and powerful river, they gazed upon the atomic city they had founded. Three huge nuclear reactors were already built, each one as high as a five-story building. Vast and complex chemical processing plants were attached, each eight hundred feet long, where the uranium slugs were stripped of their aluminum jackets and chemical processes separated the plutonium. The new element, purified of radioactivity, was stored in small stainless spillproof vessels and put in a guarded vault. From thence it was secretly transported to the mesa. The radioactive uranium solution remaining was stored in enormous tanks, with which nobody knew what to do, but which the General insisted must be kept. The ribald scientists called them "the General's tanks." The General, always sensitive toward the scientists, whom he feared, hated and secretly admired, hearing all this by his private grapevine, had bristled with hideous oaths. "All the same," he snarled, "if I dumped the stuff into the river, there'd be a hullabaloo, the fish dead and stinkin'. You can't please these eggheads. That's my motto. . . ."

"Come on, fellers," he said now. "We gotta go down the mountain."

*   *   *

On the mesa the winter had passed in the strange incongruous mood of a feverish holiday. The company of men and women were isolated upon the magic mountain, walled around by barbed wire and cut off from the world by steep and dangerous roads. Within that citadel of science, they created their own world. They made music and built a theater, and when the dangerous work of a day was ended, they danced in impromptu parties and costumes, they played on the edge of love and death. The men were compelled into a brotherhood by secrecy and security rules and the women, left outside, maintained the sole approach they now had to the companionship of men. Beyond the routines of food and sleep, there remained only sex. Without comment or criticism, men saw their wives pair with other men in walks and ski trips and long evenings by some fireside while they were absorbed in the laboratories. They forgave the women whatever they did.

Thus Stephen Coast forgave his wife Helen. For he was fully conscious of his own guilt, as he called it, concerning Jane Earl. It was love, he acknowledged doggedly, though he allowed not the slightest sign of it to escape him, and not knowing that it did escape him every time he looked at her, or when she entered a room and he saw her and looked away, or when he sat in the audience at a lecture it was part of her duty to give each Tuesday evening to the newly arrived scientists, he could look at her while he listened. He knew the power of his gaze and he felt her resistance to it, her effort to look elsewhere, and at last the yielding when their eyes met. Week after week this was their encounter, while she avoided him steadily.

207

Nor could Helen be deceived. To his abstractions she was accustomed, but these were not the abstractions of the scientist. He was too conscious of her, he did not forget her as he used to do, and the playful chidings and teasings and laughter which had been a part of her communication with him now became impossible to her. She grew humorless and grave and polite, and one evening, impatient with this change in herself, she looked up from her book to inquire as he sat at his desk:

"Do you like the way I am now?"

He did not look up from his equations.

"How are you now?"

"Do you think a question is a fair answer?" she retorted. "But maybe it is. You see no change in me?"

He wheeled around then to contemplate her. "I do see a change. But I suppose we are both changed. We are surrounded with people, for one thing, and for another we are busy, I with the Project and you with all you do for these families. I admire you more than ever. I know that the peace and content with which my men work is because of you."

"What about love between you and me?" She put the question in a small clear voice.

"Everything I do is for you," he said, "and if that is not love—"

He saw her pleading eyes, the true violet, set in black lashes. She is more beautiful than ever, he thought. But what is it that can come between a man and woman to make beauty meaningless?

"I shall be glad when all this is over," he said aloud. "Then I'll build your house."

"When will it be over?" she asked.

"Not long now. A few more months—"

He broke off, wary of the forbidden, and turned again to his desk. It was true that it would not be long. The material

208

was beginning to come in from Tennessee and the Northwest. There would soon be enough for the first real test. With the secret indispensable men, the few centered about him, who were working on the bomb itself, he had now "the gadget," as they called it. That is, they had arrived at the critical size necessary for a sphere of the precious material to reach chain reaction. But a problem remained. The thing had to work. It had to be kept together long enough so that enough fissions could occur to make the explosion. A millionth of a second would be enough but—

He went over his papers again and again while Helen read on into the night and they did not speak. Two methods were possible. The first was simply a shot at a target enclosed in a tube, of which one end was blocked. The target was the uranium and so was the projectile. When the two masses met, they made explosion, a simple method, and the one upon which he had determined. The second had been suggested to him by a brilliant young scientist, an Englishman, Percy Hard.

"It's implosion, if you see what I mean," Percy had explained. "'Praps it's too late for this one, too complicated, and so on, if you see what I mean. It's just that—well, the explosion, guided, of course, focuses inward, if you see what I mean—like this . . . "

He had broken off to sketch what he meant, and the sketch now lay before Stephen on the desk. It was remarkably neat, the parts in proportion. Percy Hard was an artist and a musician. At the last concert he had played Tchaikovsky's Concerto No. 1 and with such brilliance and virtuosity that Helen had been overwhelmed. She had gone to the handsome young scientist afterwards with all her barriers down, as Stephen could see, her great eyes wet, words faltering upon her lips.

"I don't know when I have heard such music—I don't

know whether I'm glad or sorry that I gave up my own music."

Stephen put aside the brief memory and concentrated upon the sketch. In neat small letters Percy Hard had written:

> The curve-shaped high explosive may be called a lens. Thirty-six of these lenses surround the core of the bomb (hereafter called Fat Man), this core being fusible material. Their simultaneous explosion, its force directed inward, creates the necessary stimulus to set off the chain reaction and thus explosion.

Brilliant, brilliant, but very tricky, something to be tried, perhaps, for a second bomb, if the first one failed!

He fell into deep thought, and took up his pen to write a memorandum to his superior.

> BOB:
> In my opinion it is no longer a question of whether the gadget will work, but only of how well. My rough guess is that within four months we shall have finished the worst weapon and the most deadly ever created by man. It could destroy a whole city. I pray it never will. But the Big Boss should be told. . . . It will give him time to think. He needs it.
>
> STEVE

He sealed it and slipped it into his briefcase. Helen closed her book. "I'm going to bed. Shall you be long?"

"Another hour."

A moment later he heard her voice from the door.

"Steve—"

"Yes?"

"Do you mind if I take up music again—with Percy Hard?"

Did he mind? He waited a moment for self-explanation. "Of course not," he said. "I'd like to hear you play again. I've missed it—missed something, anyway."

"Thanks," she said briefly. He heard her footsteps on the stair, the moving about upstairs, and at last the windows thrown open.

*　　　*　　　*

"Steve," Jane Earl said the next morning.

He was checking a faulty light on the reactor with a young electrical engineer and he turned, startled at the ominous gentleness of her voice. She stood in the doorway in her laboratory coat, her hands in the pockets.

"May I see you immediately?" she asked.

"Of course." He threw a direction to the engineer and joined her. They walked down the corridor.

"I've discovered a rather terrifying possibility," she said. "I'd like you to check my figures."

"You're the theoretician, Jane," he said.

"So I may be wrong," she rejoined.

She was perturbed enough to silence him, her dark eyes unusually grave and her face pale. When they were in her laboratory she closed the door and unlocked the top drawer of her desk.

"You lock your desk," he said, amazed.

"Somehow I do," she said. "I wish I could trust everyone, but I can't. I don't trust Percy Hard, for example."

"You!" he exclaimed.

"He wants to know so much," she explained. "Yesterday for example, when I was working on this very thing, he was suddenly there, looking over my shoulder. Oh, he tried to make a joke of it—he'd been playing tennis, he said, and hadn't changed his shoes. . . . Don't let's talk about him. There's something else."

"Shall I look over your shoulder?"

"Yes." She ignored the mild joke and handed him a page of closely written figures. "What do you make of this?" He took the page and studied it carefully for five minutes, and then burst out in horror.

"Good God, Jane—"

"What shall we do?"

"We can't decide such a monstrous possibility—do you think Percy understood these figures?"

"I'm sure he didn't."

"He's a good theoretician, too."

"Yes, but what good would it do him to understand?"

"He might report somewhere that we'd struck a snag."

"It's not just our snag—it's a universal problem, facing the enemy as much as it does us. Steve—"

She leaned forward to whisper. "If the possibility is probable, it might stop us all—do you see?"

"Yes," he breathed. "But who is to decide?"

"We'll have to tell Burt."

"I suppose so," he said reluctantly. He considered and rejected reluctance. "Do you know where he is?"

"Still in Vermont."

"I thought it was to be a weekend."

"The doctor has made him stay longer."

"I didn't know. Shall I call him?"

"Yes, I'll get him."

He waited while she summoned the towns and cities across river and land to the small remote lake in Vermont where Burton Hall lay dozing in a hammock under a sugar maple tree. The telephone rang in the kitchen where Mollie was making a blueberry pie. She dusted the flour from her hands with her apron and answered it.

212

"In a minute, Jane—if it's important."

"Very important," Jane's voice said.

She walked with her solid footsteps to the hammock and looked down on Burt asleep. He looked peaked, she thought, and ten years older with all this going-on. And they wouldn't let him rest even here. The doctor said his blood pressure was too high.

"Burt!"

She made her voice gentle but he jumped half out of the hammock.

"Don't jump up fast like that—it's only Jane—"

"Here?"

"Just on the telephone."

"Oh." He sank back and closed his eyes for a moment. Then he dragged himself up and walked slowly across the shaggy lawn to the kitchen.

"Hello, Jane—"

"Burt, there is something Steve and I think you ought to know."

"Right away?"

"Yes. We'll take the night train."

"I'll meet you at the station. There's only one train a day here—around noon."

"Yes, Burt."

In the laboratory hundreds of miles from the Vermont lake Jane put down the receiver and looked at her watch.

"We have forty minutes."

"We must do it," Stephen said. They parted instantly and he raced home in his old car. There was a note from Helen on the kitchen table. *Percy and I are rehearsing at the community center. Lunch in the oven.*

He turned off the oven and scrawled a note beneath hers. *I have to see Burt. I'll call from Vermont.* He hesitated, then added these words: *I love you.* It had been a long time since he had remembered to say it.

* * *

"I can't take the responsibility alone," Burt said. He felt suddenly faint and he brought the car to a standstill by the lake. A quarter of a mile down the shore a boy stood on the grassy bank fishing. The day was clear and still, a fine day for fishing. The soft green mountains were edged with gold against the sky.

"Let me see those figures for myself, Jane."

She took them from her briefcase and handed them to him. "It's a bare possibility," she said, "so slight that I daresay I shouldn't have spoken of it. But no, I had to—the very idea that the intense heat of the explosion could set on fire the hydrogen in the oceans, or even in the air, that the earth could be vaporized—"

"Stop!" Burton Hall cried out. "I see it all—'A lake of fire, burning with brimstone, a sea of glass mingled with fire, and there fell a great star from heaven, burning as it were a lamp.' I can hear the voice of my Methodist father, foretelling the end of the world from the Book of Revelation. I used to laugh at him, God help me—and never dreamed I'd have anything to do with it."

He broke off abruptly. The sweat was running down his face and he snatched his handkerchief from his pocket and wiped it off. Somewhere in the woods a bird sang three notes, liquid and clear, and the boy fishing on the bank began cautiously to draw in his reel. The day was radiant and intolerably beautiful. Destruction was impossible, incredible.

"So I had to tell you," Jane said.

214

"I can't take the responsibility," Burton Hall said. "We will have to decide together, all of us—"

"The General?" Stephen asked.

"No." Burt said. "The scientists."

"But how?" Stephen persisted. "What will be the criterion? How much chance dare we take? You'll have to set the mark beyond which we cannot go."

Burton Hall did not reply. He opened the door of the car abruptly and got out. He strolled to the boy and stood watching as the line reeled in. At the end was a flapping trout, its sides gleaming silver.

"Good boy," he said. "Must weigh a couple of pounds."

"Yeah," the boy said, grinning.

Burton Hall strode back to the car and leaped in. "If there's so much as three-tenths of one chance in a million, I'll report it to the world and stop the whole works. Meanwhile, we keep on the job, you two. Now I'll take you back to the station." He stepped on the accelerator and they sped in silence through the fragrant woods.

Three months later, while the work went on, a hundred scientists handed in their report. There was less than three-tenths of one chance in a million that the earth could be vaporized. Burton Hall read the report and called Stephen and Jane to his office on the mesa.

"Take a look at this," he said. "It's the voice of God. . . . Go on, you fools, the voice says. See how far you can go. . . . He's not going to help us, we've got to help ourselves. So what can we do but go on?"

"Nothing," Stephen said.

Burton Hall turned to Jane. "You agree?"

She shrugged her shoulders. "The premise is wrong. Given the premise, I suppose there's nothing to do but go on. But everything is wrong from the very beginning. We ought not to be doing this for the reason we're doing it."

215

"Can't stop now," Burt grunted.

She looked from one man to the other. "Why can't we stop? How did you get us to this awful place?"

And looking at them she began suddenly to sob. "Oh, you're both good—so how did it ever happen?"

She ran out of the room and they did not go after her. Burt folded the report and slipped it into his drawer and locked it.

"We'll get back to work, Steve," he said.

* * *

A month later the accident occurred. Stephen had in his group of young men, the men still younger than himself, and all of them well under thirty, a devil-may-care physicist whose name was Dick Feldman, a careless experimentalist, a brilliant technician as well as a daring theoretician. Out of a hundred brilliant ideas he conceived, ninety-nine were useless but the last one was indispensable. Again and again Stephen had all but sent the boy home, or wherever he came from, the East Side of New York, probably, or South Philadelphia, and then Feldman had saved himself by an inspired flash of insight into a problem. Small, sallow, cynical, his black eyes feverishly humorous beneath his spiky crew cut, Feldman seemed to know when he had reached the final edge of exasperation in time to save himself. Now he had devised an experiment so simple and so significant in the measuring of chain reaction that he was safe for a while because no one else dared try it. Jane had given Stephen the first warning.

"I suppose you know what Dick Feldman is doing?" she inquired one day as they passed in a corridor.

"I do," he said, most unwillingly.

"If you don't stop the way he's doing it," she said, "he

216

will kill himself and anyone who happens to be near him."

"I'll speak to him," Stephen promised.

They had gone on then, each separately and in opposite directions, and he had delayed in keeping his promise, meaning every day to send for Dick and remind him that a scientist has no right to take risks with his life or provide risks for others, merely by carelessness in technique. Chances, of course, they must take, but not in recklessness. And then he forgot his promise, for the much more serious matter of Percy Hard came to his ears again. It began as a rumor to be disregarded, a rumor vague as a wisp of wind, brought to Stephen by a minor engineer, a man whom Percy employed occasionally to work out some tool he had designed.

"I don't say he's doing anything, Dr. Coast," the man said, sweating under his scanty mouse-brown hair. "I only say I don't know why he wants the tools he does. They don't look right to me. They look like something he sends things in."

"What things?" Stephen demanded.

"That I can't say," the man replied.

"Keep your eyes open, and let me know anything you see, from now on."

"Yes, sir. I don't want to get into trouble, you understand. All Englishmen have tempers, don't they? They're proud-like, specially these lords. I hear this one's a lord—is he?"

"You would get in more trouble if you didn't report anything suspicious," Stephen said curtly. "As to his being a lord, I've heard something about it. It doesn't cut any ice here."

"No, sir." The man backed away and out of the office.

Percy Hard! Stephen leaned his elbows on his desk and held his head. Helen made no concealments, he believed. She was practicing several hours a day for a community concert and he had taken to staying in his office here in the evenings because the small house was too noisy for work.

"Beautiful noise, of course," he told Helen in apology, "but I must have quiet. We are getting close to terrible things and I must be sure I'm right on every step. I live in a state of deathly concentration."

She had agreed instantly. "Of course. I understand. Don't give me a thought."

The words were spoken gaily and in her old mood, but they came back to him now with reverberations. Don't give her a thought? He had given no one a thought for weeks and months. The mechanism for the bomb was ready, waiting only for final shipments of material in sufficient quantity from the two plants. And Percy Hard had access to the plans. That was true. There was nothing he did not know. Washington had cleared him upon the guarantee of the British government and here on the mesa he had been accepted without doubt. The method of accomplishing the chemical separation of the plutonium was still a secret. The General had given orders not to discuss the method with the Canadian and British scientists and Percy Hard, he now remembered, had been angry about it.

"It's a waste of our time, if you see what I mean, Steve, especially as in England we are in fact working out a better method than yours, and we won't tell you, no fear. It's easy enough, actually, for any country to do it. The problem is production, if you see what I mean, and in production who can equal you Americans? Astounding, simply astonishing, what you've done in a short time. But isn't that your genius? After all, most of your basic ideas, in science at least, have come from foreigners, you know."

Stephen listened and considered. Percy Hard had a way of making him feel simple and naïve. What he said was true in an irritating way, and yet fundamentally not true, was it?

"I have no time for philosophical conversations," he had retorted.

"Constructive, though, you know."

"Yes, I'm sure they are, and I hope some time I'll have the leisure."

The tall and singularly graceful young man rose to his feet. "Ah yes, well—it's a difference in point of view, if you see what I mean. . . . By the way, your wife is a charming woman, and a very good musician, if I may say so. It's a wonderful relaxation, our musical evenings—too bad you miss them."

"She enjoys them," Stephen said, "and I am grateful to you. The women have a hard time of it here. They bear up wonderfully."

"Quite," Percy Hard had said, departing.

All the same, he could not imagine any Englishman betraying anything to the enemy. Besides, it was already evident that Fermi had been right about the Germans. There were rumors of defeat, if intelligence could be trusted. If Germany surrendered, the only enemy was Japan, and there was nothing to fear there, except continued and brutal warfare. Russia? The Russians were opportunists and therefore safe as allies. They would stay on the winning side.

He dismissed the rumors but later in the day, to shift responsibility somewhat, he dropped by the office of his superior.

"Bob, I have something to report to you—too vague to be a report, even, but—"

The weary, resolute man behind the desk listened, leaning back in his chair, his eyes bleary with lack of sleep and a cigarette hanging from his lip.

"I can't believe it, Steve, and I don't," he said at last. "Anyway, we're too near the end. And, as you say, the British are our allies. We can't afford to offend them."

He stabbed his cigarette on a flat stone he used for an ash

tray, and pinched his lower lip between his thumb and fore-finger.

"Look here, since you want me to take responsibility, I will. I'll have him watched, unobtrusively. You can forget it."

He touched a buzzer.

"Thanks, Steve," he said in abrupt dismissal. "But I still can't believe it. By the way, the final shipment has come in from Tennessee. Better get the fellows together in your office. I'll join you as soon as I can. We've got to decide where we can make the big test. The General is pressing me hard."

He nodded and Stephen left him. Half an hour later, as Stephen sat in conference with the scientists, waiting for Burton Hall, the telephone on his desk rang. He took up the receiver, still talking—

"We should be ready to make the first test within the next ten days—"

He stopped abruptly. Jane's voice—he had wondered where she was. He had missed her since the day at the lake, expected her here, and would not inquire when she did not come.

"Stephen?"

"Yes?"

"There's been an accident. A terrible one. Dick Feldman."

"Yes?"

"His hand slipped as he was showing one of the young scientists how to work his experiment. The two uranium slugs touched and made a critical mass."

"Good God!"

"Dick scattered the stuff with his hands to save the two men with him. He's badly hurt. The one in front is hurt, too. The third one broke and ran. Dick's in the hospital. I'll stay

220

with him. I wanted you to know why I'm not meeting with you—and where I'll be from now until the end."

"You mean—"

"There's no chance for Dick, of course. And he has no family."

She put up the receiver and he turned to the men.

"Feldman's had an accident. I'll have to get over to the hospital. It's that damnable experiment of his—the slugs in the globe. He kept the two halves apart by a screw driver or something. It slipped."

The men growled at each other.

"It was bound to happen—"

"I'd warned him a hundred times—"

"He's a blasted daredevil—"

"One of our best men, if he'd only had sense."

Stephen left them and hastened down the corridors and stepping into his car, raced for the hospital. The atmosphere there was tense and silent, the receptionist frightened.

"Yes, Dr. Coast. He's here in Room Twelve. Dr. Earl is with him. She came with him. They're taking tests. He doesn't feel too much yet, but they're afraid."

He left her talking and loped down the corridor to Room Twelve and opened the door. Jane was there beside the bed on which Dick Feldman lay. He looked cheerful, but pale.

"Hi, Steve," he said. "Come in. They're fixing me up. Keeping me busy."

Jane did not speak. She was examining a report from the laboratory and she looked up when Stephen came in and nodded without smiling.

"What are they doing to you, Dick?" Steve asked. He drew a small straight chair to the bed and sat down.

"Oh everything," Feldman said with bravado. "My hands are bothering me some. That's why they've packed them in ice. I grabbed the stuff—shouldn't have, I guess."

221

"Brave of you," Steve muttered.

"Instinct, pure instinct," Feldman said. He spoke in a high singing voice, lifted by fear and excitement. "I was hurrying too much, I guess. I had a date with a girl. We were going to have a picnic in the Indian pueblo village. She hadn't seen them. My vacation begins tomorrow and I was showing the fellows—"

He stopped and breathed hard.

"The pain is getting worse," Jane said.

"Yeah—in my hands," he mumbled.

He looked up at her and the sweat broke out on his forehead. "I feel sick," he whispered. "I feel very sick."

She reached for a pan on the table and he raised himself and vomited into it.

Jane glanced at Stephen. "Call the nurse. . . . I must talk with you, Steve. The gamma rays we can deal with but the neutron rays—"

Dick was retching again, and again he vomited. Stephen ran from the room to find the nurse.

*   *   *

"He's easier now," Jane said. She came out of the room with Stephen the next day and they walked down the corridor together.

"Has the doctor said anything?" he asked.

"We're still making tests, blood samples, of course, shots of penicillin, a blood transfusion."

"Whose blood?" Stephen demanded.

"Mine," she said, "but that doesn't matter. I was near and I have the right blood."

"Don't give another," he said sternly. "You're getting too thin as it is. I've noticed."

"I haven't. And I'll give another if it's necessary. He has

222

an unusual type. Not too easy to find. But there may not be time."

"You mean—"

"It's a matter of a few days, that's all."

"You mean—"

"Doomed, of course. The whole front of his body is burned. The pain in his arms is creeping up."

"What about the others?"

"The one that ran is all right. The other one—he'll lose his hair, on one side of his head anyway, and he won't have to shave for a few months. But medication will save him. Maybe he'll be sterile—I don't know."

"Does he have children?"

"Yes—two. Lucky for him and his wife. I must remember to inquire about his teeth."

"Teeth?"

"Yes. The fillings will be radioactive, if he has any, and they'll burn his gums."

"What can be done?"

"Pull them out."

"How do you know all this?"

"I've been studying the effects of radioactivity on rats, Steve. I'm terrified. And now Dick Feldman. . . . Do you know what'll happen to Dick?"

They were at the front door now, facing the summer landscape of the desert, and they stepped into the sunshine. Far up yonder, beyond the clouds, beyond atmosphere and darkness and space, the sun burned with eternal energy, the primeval energy which they were trying to harness and use —for what? It had always been there and always here, a part of the very earth beneath their feet. There was atomic energy enough in the gravel soil upon which they stood to make coal useless and oil a waste. Nothing new, this energy, but to know about it was new. And now leaping out of control it was destroying the body of a young man.

"Any hope for Feldman?" Stephen asked in a low voice.

"What hope?" she asked. "He will disintegrate. Great blisters will form and burst. The skin will slough away, gangrene will set in, the radioactive particles in his body will consume him. His temperature will rise, the white blood count will fall, and the very marrow in his bones will burn. And at last he will go out of his mind."

"You know it all," Stephen muttered.

"I shan't leave him," she said. "I shall stay with him until the end. There's no one else."

They clasped hands, and he put his other hand over hers. "I wish I could stay with you, Jane. But I can't. The big test is set. It's Zero. I have to go."

"I know."

Their eyes met and clung and they parted.

* * *

Through the next days she did not leave the hospital room except to eat quickly and to sleep a little so that she could keep awake. Hour by hour she lived with the dying boy. Doctors and nurses cared for the disintegrating body, scientists and officials came and went, but it was with his mind and soul that she lived and faced death. He talked to her endlessly after the bravado had passed. It broke suddenly when he asked her how badly his abdomen was burned— that and what was below.

"Pretty badly, Dick," she said.

"I feel hot all over," he said. "Inside all this ice I feel hot. Is it hot outside?"

"It's July," she said, "and it must be very hot on the desert.

Here on the mesa there's a dry wind, and the nights are always cool, as you know."

She had never been with a dying person before. Her parents were still living, retired to a small house on the seashore of New Jersey, as far away as another world. She had left them long ago, when she left India, two pleasant people who had given birth to a child they could never understand, her father brisk and practical, a pioneer in his way, literal-minded enough to think of India merely as a place where he had a job, and her mother a housewife. Genes of which they knew nothing had come together at random from their pioneering ancestors, generations ago, to produce a girl with the mind of a man, and how angry Jane had always been to be told that she had the mind of a man, as if only male children could inherit such genes! Her parents, recognizing what they had, half fearfully, had left her to herself, too early, she supposed, but what could they do with a child who did not want birthday parties, and a young woman who would not go out with men who bored her? She had ceased at last to return to them. Her very language was not theirs and it was useless to pretend, and finally impossible.

. . . "Tell me about your home," Dick said. It was late in the afternoon and the shadows of the mountains were already falling across the room. This was the hardest time, when night approached and the hours stretched into infinity before dawn.

"We lived in Almora, in India," Jane said. "The house was a big one, a bungalow encircled by verandas. There was a wall around the compound, but over the wall we could see the snow-capped mountains, part of the Himalayas."

"Tell me about your mother."

"My mother? She was rather quiet, very sweet. My father was the talkative one. He built bridges, and the first hydroelectric plant. He said that if India could only harness her rivers the people needn't starve. I think my mother hated India. She was homesick for her own country."

"I can't remember my mother," he said. He was restless now all the time, and yet he could not move without pain. He lay in a bed of ice, a pack of ice on his stomach, his face was red and his chest was burning scarlet. His blond hair was falling out. It was the third day.

"Where did you grow up?" Jane asked gently. She sat beside him, very close, and wished she could hold his hand. But his hands were hideously swollen, the skin peeling away, the blisters breaking into running pus. There was nowhere she could touch him.

"In an orphanage," he said. "It wasn't too bad. There was plenty to eat. We weren't kicked around."

"And how did you come to be a scientist?"

"There was a rich old fellow in the local church, I guess. He heard about me and put up the dough for my education. But he never talked to me or anything like that—just put up the dough. And instead of my going into the army they sent me out here from the college. There were a couple of us, but the other fellow was sent somewhere else. You're the only girl I've ever seen that was a scientist, though—a real one, not one of these kids that learn how to run a reactor panel. Takes 'em a year, they tell me, to run it right. . . . You think they're going to use the bomb?"

"No," she said. "No, I'm sure they're not. I couldn't bear it."

His mind wandered. "Yeah," he said heavily. "Yeah. I guess they will if they want to, though. Say, my chest pains me something terrible—"

Night and day she stayed with him, until the end, when his mind ran everywhere except that not once did he reveal a secret. Deeper than pain and the fear of death was the law

226

of secrecy. His voice meandered senselessly on. Sedatives were stopped, there was no firm spot now in that disintegrating burning body where a hypodermic could be thrust. She heard the cries of childhood, and again and again the loneliness of the boy and the man who had never known what it was to love or be loved. That much at least India had given her, the habit of love. Whether one understood or could not understand, one could still love, if the habit of love had been taught. But there had been no one to teach the child in the orphanage.

He died on the sixth day, just before dawn, and her vague and yearning pain was as near to love as he had ever received.

* * *

Stephen Coast drew up the collar of his coat and fastened its belt more tightly about him and stepped out of the car. The rain drove across the desert, and the wind was furious.

"Queer," the guard said, "mighty queer. I never saw a thunderstorm like this in July. It's supposed to be dry this time of year. Always has been, they say."

"Very queer," Stephen agreed.

He led the procession of scientists and high-ranking military men across the stretch of wet sand. In the darkness lightning ripped open the sky. A tall steel tower glittered for an instant and then disappeared again into the blackness of the night. There was no glimpse of star or moon. At the base of the tower he paused and turned to the men behind him. A guard in military uniform held out a microphone and he spoke into it.

"This is the point known as Zero. You will not stay here, of course. Nobody will stay here. I want you to see it, however. The component parts of the—gadget—were brought from the laboratory, a distance, as you know, of two hundred miles, to the base camp, ten miles from here. For the last four days we have been assembling the parts in an old ranch house near that base. There has been a delay because yesterday lightning struck the top of this tower and exploded a charge of TNT. Don't be alarmed. We have taken measures to prevent that from happening again. We have three observation posts all between five and six miles from this tower. At each of the three we have built wooden shelters encased in cement walls. They are further protected by earthen barricades. The one to the south is the control center. At the base camp an old reservoir will be your observation post. It is directed that when the moment of detonation arrives, just before the word Zero is called, you throw yourselves down and press your faces close to the ground. A fifth observation post is on a hill twenty miles away from here and there dark glasses will be protection enough. The test is set for four A.M. It is now midnight.

"Because of the weather there may be some delay. Please take your posts, nevertheless."

A strong spotlight from the tower fell upon the group of figures huddled in the windy rain, but the lightning was scarcely dimmed even by the acetylene glare, and thunder roared and rumbled through the clouds. He paused and turned to Burton Hall, standing next to him.

"Is there anything else? The General and Bob are at the south post now with the fellows who are to help."

Burton Hall hesitated. Then he stepped to the microphone. "There's one voice I miss here tonight. It's the voice of a man I never met or ever saw except upon the television screen. Somehow I like to say that I never even voted to make him President. I always seem to vote for the wrong man. You know who I mean. He died last April. But I feel he's here, looking down on us from somewhere. He had the courage to give us the go-ahead, the daring to spend the money.

Two billion dollars. It will be the wisest and most economical expenditure ever made in the history of the human race, or it will be the most fantastic loss. In the living spirit of that man I accept the gamble and the stakes. I predict success!"

He stood there, the rain dripping from the brim of his old felt hat, his broad shoulders gleaming in the wet raincoat, his height immense in the sharp shadows. . . . A dramatic figure, Stephen thought, half jealously, remembering Jane. He felt young and inadequate, certainly prosaic, and for some reason sad. What would success mean?

"We'll have to go, Burt," he said. "They're expecting you at the control station."

They climbed in the cars again, driving through the increasing rain to the posts assigned. Stephen himself was to remain at the tower beside the bomb, with the chief of the detachment of the military police of the base. But he had refused to detonate the bomb. Now that it was finished, a frighteningly small object in view of the unknown terrors which might result from it, he was deeply depressed. In the darkness of this night and of his own soul he found himself thinking only of Jane as he climbed the narrow winding steps to the chamber in the tower. The storm was still raging and even dawn was delayed, the sky black except for the receding lightning and the clouds low.

At half past three, the clouds began to shift and the telephone rang. He took the receiver and heard the General.

"Weather is improving, isn't it?"

"The clouds are moving," he said.

"Bob and I have been talking with the weatherman, here," the General went on, his voice strained and harsh. "He says the storm is about over. Fair weather was the prediction yesterday and he don't know where this storm came from. I reckon fair weather will take over again. Let's say we test at five thirty."

"We'll be ready," Stephen said.

"Twenty minutes beforehand you'll begin to tick off."

"Right," Stephen said.

"You'll be here at the control station by five."

"I'll be there," Stephen said.

At four o'clock he saw stars appearing fitfully between the clouds. The storm was over, a strange conflict between man and universe, he thought, his mind wandering over the immense dark landscape, and for the moment man had prevailed. The General was stubborn, obtuse perhaps, but not easily frightened. A storm was a storm to the unimaginative mind, and not a protest from the gods. The clouds were drifting now to the southeast, and in great patches of purple black sky a few stars shone. He stood in somber watchfulness near the oblong shape which held the future within its metal grasp. He was beyond fear now, or despair or even remorse, surrounded by darkness without and within, and in that darkness he saw only Jane's face.

If he survived this blast, he would return to her. He would tell her he loved her. After this desperate hour he would pretend no longer. He would face the truth about himself, with her.

"Five o'clock, sir," the officer said. "The car is waiting."

"Good heavens, you startled me," he muttered. "I'd forgotten where I was," and muttering he turned and strode across the chamber and down the narrow winding stairs to the desert, the others following.

The tower was alone then in the darkness before the dawn. The sky was almost clear now and above the black rim of the encircling mountains only the light on the tower shone out to dim the stars as they crossed the desert.

Burton Hall received them.

"The General has gone," he told them. "Army direction.

. . . Take your place at the microphone, Steve. We have only twenty minutes to go."

In the silence Stephen stepped to the microphone. The time was ten minutes past five. A pale light shone from behind the eastern mountains, a brightening of the sky that was almost unreal.

Behind the microphone he stood immovable in a marble calm which made him feel that he was dead. But he spoke, he announced the time every five minutes and then every minute, his eyes upon the watch. The watch—his mind trailed off. It was not his, not the one he had planned to use. Four weeks ago, wasn't it, he had asked Helen to send his watch to be cleaned and checked, not telling her why. And the jeweler in Albuquerque had delayed, "what with vacations and all, Mrs. Coast," and at the last minute Stephen had borrowed this watch from Burt. The minutes were endless.

"Three minutes."

"Two minutes." . . .

Now it was the last minute and he began to count off the seconds. "Forty-five seconds to go."

At this second someone closed the switch that started the mechanism into action, a complex piece of machinery that he had tested again and again during the last four days. . . . Was Feldman dead yet? Was Jane watching and counting the seconds with him? He had reached ten:

"Zero minus ten."

Nothing could be done now. It was out of human hands and the robot took over. He stepped back from the microphone. A streak of light shot upward in the sky and spread in a green flare, the landscape sprang into livid life. A second rocket and again that livid glow of light over the desert and mountains—

"Zero minus three!" In the momentary darkness he saw the

231

eastern sky brightening with the sunrise. Oh, heavenly light of rose and gold—

"Zero minus two—"

"Zero minus one."

He turned his back at this instant and saw the sky burst into blinding light. Miles away the mountains were black and then glittered into brilliant relief in the searing light. Color splashed over the landscape, yellow, purple, crimson, grey. Every fold in the mountain sprang into bold lines, every valley was revealed, every peak stood stark. Suddenly a roar shook the earth. He felt his ears split. As though a great hand struck him, he fell to the floor. For a moment he lay stunned, then he struggled to his feet. Across the room Burton Hall was on his hands and knees.

"Look," a man shouted. "Look—look—"

They looked. A cloud as vast as the desert itself was rising from the spot where the tower had stood, a rolling, boiling, surging, swelling cloud of many colors. It swallowed every other cloud and soared toward the zenith. In utter silence they stared at the monstrous moving shape they had unleashed. They stared and watched, speechless until the colors faded and the mass was grey. They watched while the winds tore at it and pulled it to pieces and scattered it around the globe. Then Burton Hall spoke.

"The tower is gone."

Stephen turned. Burt was looking through the telescope.

"It doesn't exist any more," Burt said.

Stephen snatched the telescope and searched the desert ten miles away. The tower had vaporized and beneath it the desert was melted to a sea of green glass, shining in the sunlight.

"We've done it," Burt was screaming. "We've done it— we've done it."

He threw his arm about Stephen's shoulders and began to sob and to laugh.

"A new heaven," he sobbed. "A new heaven and a new earth—man, it's revelation!"

"A new age," Stephen said somberly. "But is it heaven?"

IV

THE THUNDERSTORM had cooled the air. The intolerable dry heat of weeks without rain was gone. A soft damp wind blew into the open windows. Jane woke in her bedroom in the little adobe house at the foot of the mesa and lay for a moment remembering the day. She had gone to bed late last night, unable to sleep. Zero night! She should have been there with Steve and Burt, and the rest of the men. A big chance missed, Burt said—

"Woman, you're no scientist if you can miss Zero!"

He had muttered the words at her between closed teeth only day before yesterday when they were measuring the rising heat of the new reactor—Maniac, he had named it. He always gave the monsters names, Maniac, Anidac, Ruminac, and his favorite, a plain dingy early reactor he called affectionately, George. And there was one little reactor, stripped of everything except its essential shape, that he named Godiva.

She had reflected for an instant before answering. "I can't go, Burt. It's the day of Dick Feldman's funeral and there's

237

nobody but me. You won't miss me. Besides, I'm not sure I want to see the big show."

"Let the dead bury the dead," he had retorted. "That's out of the Bible," he had added hastily, catching her shocked glance, and had continued to urge. "You're a scientist first, aren't you? At least that's what you're always telling me when I make a little mild pass in your direction!"

To this she had made no answer. Who could know what she was? She did not know herself. Her confusion was absolute. It had never occurred to her years ago in Almora that her young delight in mathematics would lead her to this mesa, rimmed by the mountains of an ancient volcano. Irony that the catastrophe of that explosion long ago should now be matched by modern man!

She sat up in bed, suddenly restless. She ought to be on the mesa this very moment. They would know by now whether Zero had been a success, a secret, of course, but no secrets were hidden from her—a lonely situation for a woman, she thought, to be the solitary one of her kind admitted to the secrets of men. She should be proud and was not. The responsibility was hideous. . . . Perhaps the storm had delayed the test. Perhaps it had failed, perhaps—anything! Oh, stop thinking—

She got out of bed quickly, bathed and brushed her hair and, as she was accustomed to do when she was alone, she wrapped an Indian sari of green silk expertly about her slim freshly washed body. Nothing was quite as comfortable as a sari, a length of material soft and yet firmly clinging. It had been the costume of her childhood and was still a habit so pleasant that when she wore it tension slipped away.

The morning was glorious after the storm. The desert was watered again. She found herself singing under her breath, happy in spite of herself. Were there always two levels of life for a woman? At any rate, there was this pleasant level of a house, however small, a little kitchen, a stone terrace. She'd have her breakfast on the terrace. She put the kettle on to boil and was in the process of squeezing oranges when she heard Stephen's voice at the door. She stood, unbelieving. How could it be Stephen, at this hour, today?

"Jane!"

She flew to open the door and there he stood, haggard and storm-stained.

"Why are you here?" he demanded. "Why have you left the mesa?"

"I haven't," she said with indignation. "How dare you think I could?"

He stalked into the room and took off his coat. "You've left the mesa. I've been there."

"I've left the women's dormitory, if that's what you mean," she retorted. "I couldn't go back to it. After Dick's funeral I had to be alone. And I saw this little house for rent. It was only two days ago—it seems weeks. An artist's house— he's gone East to arrange an exhibition. So I simply stepped in—got my clothes, of course."

"My God," he whispered. "It's too simple. You're in a house. As if it had been—arranged!"

He sat down upon the kitchen stool and stared at her.

"What do you mean?" she demanded. "Arranged for what?"

"For what I've come to say."

"Have you had breakfast?"

"No. I haven't eaten for two days—couldn't. . . . Don't you know what happened?"

"No. I sent word to the lab I wouldn't be there for three days."

"Don't you want to know?"

"Only one thing—was it a success?"

"Stupendous."

239

"Don't tell me more—not now. Go and wash. I'll make your breakfast. The bathroom is that door."

He got up and dragged himself across the floor and she watched him. Something had happened to him, something more than success. . . . So it had been a success! She wished it could have failed. It would give them more time—more time for what? More time—oh, stop thinking!

She made a pitcher of fresh orange juice and set two places at the table on the terrace. The sun was already high but this was the west side of the house, and the terrace opened upon a small desert garden, sand-floored for cactus plants and a round pool. The air was still cool, but within an hour she would close the house against the daytime heat. Then she'd go back to the mesa to work. Toast, eggs and bacon, a jar of English marmalade, and the kettle suddenly boiled and shrieked. She lifted it hastily aside, startled by its insistence. What man had invented a shrieking teakettle for woman's annoyance? She was still not used to this American way of doing things. Her Indian childhood had been cushioned by many servants, soft-voiced, silent-footed— which reminded her that she herself was barefoot, and the artist had warned her about poisonous spiders and even a tarantula.

"I'm used to creatures," she had told him. "I grew up in India."

His sunburned face had suddenly lighted. "India? I've always wanted to see India."

"It's not what you think," she said. "Well, yes, perhaps it's what you think, what most people think, but it's everything else, too. You don't just go to India. You go to everything—poverty and riches, misery and joy, evil and good, the greatest beauty and the most awful ugliness."

She glanced about the terrace and saw no spiders or tarantulas and the stones were cool to her feet. And Stephen came out, looking clean even in his dust-stained shirt. She liked a man to look scrubbed and she smiled at him.

"That's better. Sit down. I'm starved. Don't talk."

He sighed, relaxed and sat down. She poured orange juice into a tall green glass and sat down opposite him.

"May I ask what that is you have on?" he inquired.

She laughed. "That much you may ask. It's a sari. I wear it when I'm home. This house is suddenly home. It was the moment I stepped into it. I feel as if I'd been here always, maybe because the village houses in India are adobe too, not like this one though, with electric things."

"I like a sari on you, it looks comfortable."

"Yes."

They did not talk for a few minutes, and he ate voraciously. She poured coffee, one cup, two cups, and finally a third, three eggs for him, strips of thick bacon, broiled crisp, and toast and the bittersweet English marmalade. He sighed at last and leaned back.

"I disgrace myself."

"I'm so glad."

He pushed aside plates and cup. "Now I talk."

She put her hands over her ears. "No, please. I'll hear it all this morning up on the mesa. You'll make a report. The newspapers will print a small notice, 'Successful test in the Nevada desert.' And the world has changed. Has everybody?"

"This talk is just for you . . . and it's true the world has changed for me, anyway."

Her hands dropped and their eyes met. He felt for his pipe and lit it. "And don't interrupt me, if you please, Jane. After I've had my say, you can have yours. I only beg you to understand that this is nothing sudden. I've come to it—yes, you may say I've come to the final point in a flash, but it was long in preparing. Zero! A big flash at the end, but four years in the preparation. Well, it's the same thing. . . ."

She was smitten to stillness, as frightened as a doe in the wood. He did not look at her. No, he turned away from her and gazed at the round pool, now illumined by sunshine creeping over the low roof of the house.

"I suppose," he said, "that being a scientist I shall have to go at this in a scientific way. Maybe the preparation for Zero began years ago when I met Helen—and fell in love. Yes, I fell in love, but being a damned scientist, I stood aside from myself in love. I conducted a research, let's say. Question, given a scientist, a pure theoretician, how much human companionship does he need? Should he marry a scientist? Some of us do, most of us don't. I went to the men I knew best and not mentioning myself in love, I asked them —there were seven, I remember—whether they were satisfied with the women they had married. Six of them had married women, not scientists."

"Oh, don't."

He glanced at her. "Don't what?"

"Don't say 'women, not scientists.'"

He put up his hand. "I'm coming to that. I couldn't learn everything at once, could I? I had to make the experiment. . . . Well, of the six, four were loyal to their women. They were happy—they said. The women looked after the children and the house, kept things going, freed the scientists of responsibility and so forth. God!—"

He broke off suddenly and stared at her.

"What, Steve?"

"It occurs to me only now. I didn't ask the women how they felt—I forgot them! And I thought I was doing a good job of research!"

She smiled over hidden heartbreak. "That's all right,

Steve. I wouldn't expect you to remember the women. Go on, please."

"The other two of the six weren't sure. They could imagine—I remember one of them—he's here now, and I won't mention his name—but he said there were times when he thought it would be wonderful to be able to talk with his wife—about everything, that is. He said it even affected his —his sexual life—inhibited him sometimes because there was so much of his life he couldn't explain to her. Then she'd get upset. I know now what he meant. I didn't then."

"Steve, what about the seventh man?"

"I'm coming to that. . . ."

He knocked the ash out of his pipe and filled it again slowly, thoughtfully. "The seventh man told me he couldn't think of marrying only a woman, because he wasn't only a man. He'd married both scientist and woman. The right woman, of course, but also the scientist."

"Madame Curie," Jane said.

"Something like that," Stephen agreed. "Only I've an idea she married the right man first as well as the scientist."

"Of course," Jane said with a touch of indignation that made him look at her and laugh. The look was dangerous. Jane got up to fill the coffeepot again.

"I'm not sure I want you to go on," she said unsteadily, her back to him.

"I'm going on," he said firmly. "Because in that Zero flash, when heaven and earth fused into one great reality— they say that when a man is about to die he sees in a flash the whole reality of his life—well, that's what happened to me. I saw only you. I've come straight back to you. I haven't been to the house or to Helen. They told me at the office where you were. I got in the car and drove like hell—to you."

He lit a match and his hands trembled. "Everything I've been subduing and denying and refusing in myself all these

243

months—years—since I first saw you, was released in that great flash. I can't explain it. Maybe part of it was the tension of the job. I don't know. But I'm here. The tension is over. I know what I want. Complete companionship. You."

She leaned her head in her hands, elbows on the table, and could not answer. Deep silence fell between them, a communing silence. She broke it at last, not looking at him.

"We're not children."

"Not children," he agreed.

"I have no ties, but you—"

"Not to Burton Hall?"

"No . . . not in the way you mean."

"I have a hunch he's in love with you. Maybe the same thing happened to him that's happened to me."

"Let's not talk about him."

"All right."

"But you have ties, Steve. . . . I like Helen. She loves you. I'm not competing. I don't have to. I'm a scientist—not just a woman. I have something of my own. She hasn't."

He got up abruptly and paced the terrace, length by length. "I'm not sure. She and Percy Hard—"

"Don't. She's your wife."

"I haven't been much of a husband. She's always wanted a house—children. Now she doesn't talk about either. She's deep in her music again—with Percy Hard."

"Are you sure?"

"Yes. . . . And—I don't care. Maybe nothing matters now."

He stopped beside her. "Why are you thinking only of her? Why don't you think of me?"

"Oh Steve—you're a scientist, you have something of your own, too."

"You don't count her music?"

"No. She gave it up when she married you, didn't she?"

"I suppose so."

"Then it isn't something of her own—not really. If it had been she wouldn't have given it up. That's the trouble with women—so few of us have anything of our own."

"Don't philosophize, for God's sake—not at this moment. Jane—kiss me. Kiss me—" He pulled her to her feet.

"Oh, Steve—"

He was irresistible. And it had been so long since she had wanted to kiss a man. His arms were around her, and his mouth was upon hers, sweetly at first, warmly, and then with sudden power and passion. She quivered with response —impossible not to respond, oh joyful to want to respond and so to be able—

He drew away at last and pressed her head against his breast and held her close, his cheek on her hair.

"Now," he said. "Now, do you understand?"

"Yes." She whispered the word against his heart.

"Then it's settled. I'll tell Helen."

She drew away from him. "Oh no, Steve—"

"But I must, Jane. How can I live in the house and not tell her? I can't pretend."

She wrung her hands. "Oh don't tell her. It's too quick."

"But my darling, aren't you sure?"

"Yes, yes, I'm sure. I'm sure I love you. It's not that."

"Then what—"

"There's so much more than love—"

"There isn't."

"Oh yes, there is."

She tried to smile at him but tears hung on her eyelashes. "Give me time, Steve. Remember I didn't see the flash. . . . I wasn't at Zero. . . ."

He looked at her for a moment. "Very well. I'll give you time. But I'll never change—never."

He caught up his jacket from the chair and stalked out of the house.

"Oh," she moaned softly and alone. "Oh—oh—what shall I do? What shall I do now?"

She stood looking into the desert garden. Then she ran to her bedroom, loosening the sari as she went. She let it drop on the floor and lie there and she reached for her clothes, her everyday clothes, the neat little girdle, white and clean, elastic and yet firmly restraining, the white bra, the white slip, the blue skirt and shirt, the nylon stockings and the white shoes. Her work coat hung in the lab on the back of the door, and to the lab she was going. Back, back to work, blessed work, where she had only to think about cosmic force and not about this blinding blaze in her own heart.

* * *

"Well," Helen said. "What's the matter with you?"

The words were pleasantly spoken but they were as cold as night on the mesa.

"I'm tired—I guess." Stephen said. "I shouldn't have—"

"You slept all afternoon."

"It's not the same as night sleep."

She got out of bed and put on her nightgown. Then she went to the small dressing table and turned on the light and began to brush her hair. He watched her from the bed, her face in the mirror. He was not in the least deceived by her seeming absorption or by her silence. She brushed her hair and curled the ends over her fingers as though it were morning. Then she creamed her face, examined it carefully in the mirror and wiped the cream off again with a pink tissue.

"I think I'll not come back to bed," she said in the same pleasant voice.

"It's only two o'clock," he said.

"Two o'clock or ten o'clock, what does it matter to me?"

He threw back the covers and fastened the strings of his pajamas about his waist.

"You don't seem to understand what I've been through."

"Put it that I don't understand you," she said. She was filing her fingernails, slowly and carefully. She had to keep them short now for the piano. The community concert had been a great success but she had not mentioned it to Stephen because he had forgotten to ask. Percy said, "We ought to tour, you and I, darling. We'd be a sensation. Too bad I'm a scientist, if you know what I mean."

"Too bad," she had agreed. "You're a wonderful musician."

"So I've been told, but it's lovely to have you say it."

"All right," Stephen said. "You don't understand me." He was suddenly cold and he reached for the jacket of his pajamas.

"I submit that no one can understand a scientist," she said. She was ready now for the fingernail polish, a pinkish silver.

He did not reply to this. Instead he walked to the window, wide and low and very modern, and pulled up the venetian blind. Over the crest of the old dead volcano the moon shone crooked and bleakly clear.

She glanced at his back sharply. "Or have you found someone who does understand?"

He did not reply. He had to control himself, give Jane time. He must not betray her. But irritation at least was uncontrollable.

"Perhaps it's you who have found someone who can understand you," he said.

"Oh, if it's the game of *tu quoque*," she said.

"Isn't it *tu quoque?*"

"If you mean Percy—"

"Of course I mean Percy."

"Sit down," she said. "Let's have it. I'll complain and then you complain. Fair? And I promise I won't lose my temper."

247

She turned on all the lights and he drew the blind. These houses were beehives, cell by cell, and the females in them had nothing to do but gossip.

She arranged the articles on the toilet table carefully. "Do you know that you haven't made love to me for a whole month?"

"I hate being kept on a calendar," he mumbled.

She paused and then replied reasonably. "I know you better than you think. I know you as you once were. You're warm, not cold. So am I warm. We made a wonderful pair in bed, didn't we? And you were a scientist then, too. Mad about cosmic rays nine tenths of the time, but oh, the tenth that was left was worth waiting for. Now it just—isn't, any more."

"This Project hasn't been cosmic rays. It's been a thousand times more exacting. The pressure has been—killing."

"I'm aware of that—I've taken it into consideration. But the years, Steve—the years out of our lives, four years, no house, no children. Am I ever to have children?"

"I thought you didn't want them."

She yielded suddenly. She came over to him and dropped on the floor and leaned her forehead against his knees. "But I *want* to want them. I hate living in a world where I'm afraid to bear a child. Oh Steve, talk to me!"

"I can't—not yet."

He bit the words off. Let her think what she would. They might mean the Project. She didn't know how far the Project had gone, or when it would end. Nobody knew, for that matter. The question now was, would the bomb be used? He had not faced it himself. He couldn't, not until Jane let him speak. The whole universe was in confusion, the outer cosmos and the inner cosmos within himself, reciprocal confusion.

"When?" she asked.

248

"I don't know," he said.

"Then I'll tell you everything," she said.

He did not answer and she looked up at him and reached half timidly for his hand. "May I tell you everything?"

He restrained himself from pulling his hand away. "If you wish."

"Steve, maybe I'm in love with Percy—a little."

He was ashamed at the rush of joy to his heart. Obscene joy—

"I thought so."

"Do you mind?" she asked wistfully.

"I want you to be happy."

She stroked his hand and laid her cheek against it. "But only a little—because I'm so lonely."

He pulled his hand away now. "How can you be only a little in love? You are or you aren't."

"I couldn't be at all if you and I—if you and I were—the way we used to be."

"Nothing is the way it used to be," he said harshly. He was beginning to feel sorry for her.

"It isn't just that," she said. She got up restlessly and sat down on the edge of the bed. "It's—I don't know how to tell you."

"Are you trying to tell me you've slept with Percy Hard?"

If she had, how to tell her he didn't care!

She burst into laughter and mingled sobs. "Oh Stephen —how can you! As if—oh God, is that what you've been thinking? Oh darling, really have you been thinking—"

She was on his knees, her arms about him. "Oh, hold me, Stevie—oh no, no, I haven't done that."

He would have been a beast not to put his arms about her.

"Anyway, there's something else about Percy—I couldn't

love him. . . . Did it ever occur to you that he isn't just—
that he's—"

"What?" he demanded.

"Not to be trusted?"

They looked at each other and he put her off his lap.
He got to his feet and paced back and forth. "Yes," he said.
"It has occurred to me."

Thank God, he was thinking, there's something bigger
than ourselves to talk about.

"He has tried to make love to me," Helen was saying,
"and I won't say I wasn't tempted—temporarily."

"He's very charming," Stephen agreed.

"You don't care!"

"I want you to be happy," he said again.

She went back to the mirror and sat with her back to
him, and toyed with a small perfume bottle . . .

. . . "Darling," Percy had said. "Don't you see what fun
we'd have? We're almost through here on this desert. I'm
due back in England in another fortnight. . . . I do want
to see the big bang."

"Is there to be a big bang?" she had asked.

"Of course," he said carelessly. "Why else are we here?"

"Should you mention it?" she had asked.

"To you," he had retorted.

"Stephen doesn't tell me anything—"

Percy had flung out instant contempt. "You Americans
make such a fetish of secrecy! I know a chap here who
works in two departments, hush-hush, with the consequence that he can't even talk to himself!"

He made high thin laughter and she did not smile. He
threw her a glance and went on. "That chap Feldman—did
you know why they isolated him completely? Hustled him
off to the hospital, actually, and his doctors and nurses had

250

to be cleared, and that woman scientist—what's—her—name—"

"Jane Earl," Helen said.

"Yes, well, she stayed with him night and day to see that he didn't babble any secrets."

"How did you know?"

"I hung about, just to be friendly, you know. Poor chap—"

He met her eyes and suddenly began to make passionate love to her.

"Sweet! Don't look at me like that. I don't care about any one or anything except you—"

She had let herself be swept into his arms, responding against her will, body clamorous against mind and conscience. . . . Stephen should never let the weeks pass. He ought to know her by now—

At the last moment she had resisted. "Percy, no!"

"When, darling?"

"Not yet—"

"When—when?"

"I don't know."

When she didn't know herself, how could she tell Stephen?

He was yawning. "Anything else, Helen?"

"No," she said, "not yet."

"I believe I can sleep," he said, and drew the covers.

*   *   *

Burton Hall, halfway back to the mesa, was seized by a strange and unexpected remorse. After the glorious success of Zero, he had bade his fellow scientists good-bye and had congratulated the General and his henchmen.

"See you on the mesa," he sang. "The next job presses hard upon us."

251

Everyone knew what the next job was. Germany had surrendered suddenly in May and sooner than could have been expected. And the month before that the Big Boss, the man tenderly loved by so many and bitterly hated by a few, had died even more suddenly. Burton Hall had been on the train that April afternoon, on his way back from Washington, when the news spread over the nation from a small town in Georgia.

"The President is dead!"

No need to ask what President or where. There was only one in the world. The small energetic man who had stepped into his place was still unknown, untried. Burt had gone back to Washington at once and had met the small man and had worried a good deal. Though the sprightly good nature of the erect and dapper figure was evident enough, in spite of temporary gloom, it hardly seemed possible that he could fill the big empty shoes in the White House.

"I'll have to rely on all of you," the small man said. "I'm scared to death and I might as well admit it. You'll find it out. I'm sticking close to my Secretary of War. I reckon he's as good a guide as any."

Yes, the Secretary was a good guide. Burt had listened to him, too.

. . . "Gentlemen, it is our responsibility to recommend action that may turn the course of civilization. Our great task is to bring the war to a prompt and successful conclusion. Our new weapon puts into our hands overwhelming power. It is our obligation to use this power with the best wisdom we can command, remembering how our use of this weapon will appear in the long view of history."

And then the generals had taken over, and the Secretary of War, who was no general, had taken Burton Hall aside.

"Burt, after this is all over, you scientists have got to see that atomic power is in the hands of civilians. If I'm dead,

Burt, and I'm so old I may very well follow the Big Boss over yonder, then you scientists will have to see to it."

"We'll see to it," Burt had promised.

It was this promise that now stuck in his breast like a dagger. The General had already worked out the strategy for the use of the gadget. Call it the bomb. That's what the gadget was, and from now on he was going to say bomb, at least to himself, so that he would remember his promise.

And at this moment, for reasons he could not divine in himself, Burt turned abruptly northward, away from the mesa, and driving across desert and plain he went to Arizona, to a certain camp, where behind barbed wire, Yasuo Matsugi was imprisoned as an enemy alien. Twenty years he had lived in the country of his adoption, painting his vague and lovely pictures, his technique the inimitable combining of ancient Japanese and modern American art. The pictures hung on the walls of museums and in the homes and galleries of great collectors. Yet when the moment came, the moment decided upon not by artists or even civilians but by military men in a panic of ignorance and fear, he was herded into the concentration camps with terrified little men and women, restaurant keepers and truck gardeners and household servants, whose sons were now fighting for the United States on Italian soil, fighting for the life, liberty and happiness denied to their slant-eyed parents.

These remorseful thoughts milled around in his many-chambered brain while he drove across the desert and stopped exhausted at the gates of the Arizona camp for enemy aliens.

The guard came out of his little house and yawned before he asked who it was in the dirty Chevrolet sedan.

"I'm Burton Hall," the occupant barked, "and I'm alone. I want to see an old friend, Yasuo Matsugi."

"Card, please," the sleeper said.

253

Burton Hall fumbled for his wallet, a damned nuisance made necessary because wherever he went he had to say who he was and why he was there. If he could not give his own name he had three other names, approved by the General, which he was legally allowed to use under the peculiar circumstances of war and secrecy. None of his names meant anything to this slumberous youth.

"Okay. How long you want to stay?"

"An hour."

"Okay. He's in seventeen."

He went in and counting the barracks he arrived at seventeen. There, since it was already dusk, he inquired and found that Yasuo was inside, and he waited until the slender stooping figure came to the door, both hands outstretched.

"Dr. Hall—you come to see me here!"

"Yasuo, I keep thinking about you. How are you?"

"Come in—come in—"

He was drawn into the long room, to the end, where curtained by an army blanket, Yasuo the artist had made himself a narrow place in which to live. There were no pictures, but upon a shelf stood a collection of sculptured shapes which Burt could not at first divine.

"What are these, Yasuo?"

Yasuo laughed softly. "They are my work. The days are long here and I don't sleep very good. So I make something—"

He lifted from its pedestal a birdlike form, a heron standing on a flat stone. "This is root of sage. Nothing here in this desert but sage. So I get some sage. The soldiers are nice and good. They interest, and get me sage roots. I carve and make. So I am not too sad."

"They're beautiful," Burt said and was ashamed.

"Oh, not only I myself," Yasuo said cheerfully. "Many people make something. It is very ugly to live here without mak-

254

ing. Some people plant flower seeds. You see outside? Some very nice flowers. Some people get vegetable seeds. We all make something except the lazy bad ones. But they are not too many. Mostly are good. Sit down, please, on the cot. I am sorry I have no tea. I can't help."

Burt sat down and was face to face with the benign and gentle man he had known for so many years. Yasuo beamed on him without embarrassment. And why should Yasuo be embarrassed, Burt inquired of himself. The embarrassment was all on the other side. He had come here with some vague notion of telling Yasuo not to allow his spirit to be further crushed by another devastation that might fall some day soon. He wanted to say to Yasuo, "Let's not get mixed up about anything. You and I are exactly the same men we have always been. I see that now. I know you have nothing to do with those fiends over yonder in the jungles of Asia. You and I are here."

But he said nothing of the sort. It was too complicated. He sat for half an hour, all but speechless while Yasuo chatted amiably about his life and spoke hopefully of the day when he could be free to paint again. That he could not paint was his chief sorrow.

"I cannot," he told Burt sadly.

"You mean you haven't the brushes, the colors—"

Yasuo shook his head that was badly in need of a haircut. "No, I cannot here." He pointed a delicate forefinger at his heart.

"I understand, Yasuo. . . . I guess we all feel the same way. We can't express what we feel. I'd better be going. Let me know—"

He shook Yasuo's hands, both of them, and went away.

And what good it did me or him, he thought the next day, after a wretchedly uncomfortable night in a dirty motel, I'll never know. But I had to go and now I've gone. Maybe it

255

would have been better if I hadn't gone. It makes my job harder. There's probably a lot of good old innocents like Yasuo over yonder in Japan.

He mourned in this fashion during the journey back to the mesa and two days later, inquiring by telephone after Jane Earl, he discovered that she no longer lived there, and came only to work in the morning. He called her at the adobe house the same evening.

"What on earth are you doing down there in the desert?"

"Living," she said, "just living."

"Didn't things suit you up here?"

"I wanted a house of my own."

"A house!" he repeated, incredulous. "Are you alone?"

"Of course I'm alone."

"Then I'm coming to see you. Now. Are you cooking dinner?"

"Yes, but only for one."

"Make it for two."

He snatched his ancient felt hat and threw directions over his shoulder to Rosie. "Tell Mrs. Hall I'm going to eat with Jane. She can get me there if she has to."

Rosie pursed her lips. "Yes, Dr. Hall." There was a lot of talk on the mesa about Jane Earl going off to live by herself. A lot of talk—

*   *   *

"Good dinner, Janie," he said, and wiped his mouth. "I didn't know you were a good cook."

"I'm not really," she said. "I'm only pretending."

"Yeah? So who comes to see you here, dark eyes?"

She leaned her elbows on the table and considered the face opposite. She loved this big careless man, oh, not in the least in love, but simple love. He's such a human being, she

256

thought, and I trust him. I have no one else so nearly like a father.

"How old are you, Jane?" Burt asked suddenly.

"I'm twenty-seven."

"Were you only twenty-two when you became a nun here?"

She laughed. "Yes. I was twenty-one when I went to Fermi."

"Ah yes, Fermi. He's back in Chicago—lost interest as soon as the gadget was made. He's working ahead a hundred years or so."

"Yes. He wants me to go back to him."

"You going?"

"I don't know. It depends on how useful I can be here now that the job is done."

"Not done by a long shot. The whole question is how it's to be used."

"Used! You're not thinking of using it!"

"War has to be stopped, doesn't it?"

"But Burt—"

"Hush, Janie—let me talk. You listen. I can't even talk to Mollie now. It would scare her to death."

"Let's go into the other room. . . . Leave the table as it is."

She led the way, her face very grave, into the small living room. The evening was cool and she lit the sagebrush roots in the fireplace. He stretched himself on an old red velvet sofa that the artist had brought there to the desert from his Victorian home on Long Island, and she sat down in the big armchair that matched it.

"Don't talk, Janie—"

"No, Burt."

"Just listen, eh? Until I'm through—"

"Yes."

She composed herself and gazed into the fire, and he folded his hands and closed his eyes as though he were dead.

"Here's the situation, straight from the battlefields in Asia and in Washington, D.C. The Germans, Janie, never even approached us in the making of the bomb. Fermi was right. We didn't know it, of course, and we had to proceed on the supposition that he might be wrong. Their failure was in production. They had the idea of fission but they never thought of plutonium. Three years ago, mind you, they gave up even the idea of uranium. Production again. The separation of the uranium isotopes was simply beyond them. But they were dreaming up a reactor. As late as last January they were still dreaming it up. Then Hitler told them to lay off anything that wouldn't produce a weapon in six months. He was like all these improvisers. If you can't get a thing done right away they get impatient and turn to something else. Of course they might have made more headway with that heavy water in Norway. But the British knew about that and bombed it in 1942. We bombed it again a year later and the Nazis decided to carry the stuff to Germany—three thousand gallons of it in one ship, but the Norwegians and British sank that ship. The real weakness was that the Germans never got together the way we have. Production again. The scientists and the military didn't work together over there—and in industry not at all. So there wasn't any production. I know—I know. We all get mad at old Bubble-guts here, and there've been times when I wanted to cut Starleigh's dainty throat. But we've worked together, nevertheless, and I respect 'em. I think they respect me. We've made a team in spite of Szigny crabbing to Weiner about us—all that bunch! Bless them, we couldn't do without them, either. You realize that the whole idea of the atomic bomb came from Europe? Suppose the longhairs had stayed over there, eh, Janie? Makes my blood drip ice into my heart! Bless their old stubborn independent brains! All we've done, really and truly, is to use their ideas. That's our genius—production. . . ."

He sighed without opening his eyes and unfolded his hands. "So what are we going to do with the bomb, tall girl? Drop it, maybe—"

"Oh no, Burt!"

"Listen, I'm not through. The argument is to end the war. To drop or not to drop—which way will save the most lives? That is the question. There's only Japan now as enemy. Surrender she must. How can we win with the least destruction? Honey, the date's been set for invasion—November the first of this year of our Lord, 1945. I wonder if our Lord knows! Our men are to land on Kyushu, the lovely isle of Kyushu. I was there once for a few days—a seashore like none in the world, and a backdrop of mountains, a lot of fisherfolk, in peaceful villages, and the little children pattering around in their kimonos like dolls."

"Oh don't, Burt—please don't." She hid her face in her hands.

His voice went on, inexorable. "I've been over it all with the military bigwigs. The figures are graven on my brain. It's conservatively estimated—conservatively, mind you—that half a million Americans must die if we invade. And two and a half million Japanese. They're proud and they're not afraid to die. They live on the edge of death always—tidal waves and earthquakes, and they've been taught for generations that sweet it is and right to die for one's country. Their secret weapon—the only one they have—are the kamikaze, the suicide bombers. And so they won't surrender. Their military men won't let 'em. Even if we blockaded the islands and sank their fleet, millions would starve before they'd surrender. We have to shock them, show them such a terrible new destruction that they give up as one must give

259

up to destruction from heaven . . . 'What is man that thou
are mindful of him?' "

"I can't listen any more," she whispered.

He gave a great sigh and rose slowly, a behemoth, to his
feet. "No, I guess you can't. I can't hardly talk any more.
But what are you going to do when a whole nation goes to
war? We've already had to kill the little people by the thousands because the men at the top are so smart. Their weapons aren't made as ours are, in great factories. They're made
by little people in their homes, little machine shops, the men
and women working away like gnomes in the streets of the
city, making parts of something they don't know about and
couldn't understand if they did. But the men at the top take
those little parts and put them together in great weapons
that kill our men and sink our ships. So we've already had to
kill the little people, the husbands and wives, the little children, the old people living with their families. We have to
kill them. If we don't it means our boys dying in the jungles
and on the islands."

She got up abruptly and put more sage root on the fire.
"If we use the bomb, it will be the beginning of the end—
we of all the peoples on the earth—"

"Maybe because we of all the peoples of the earth—"

"No," she said, "no—no—no."

He looked at her closely.

"I'd better go," he said. "I won't talk any more. Good
night, my darling child."

He leaned over and kissed her on the forehead. "Know
how old I am? I'm fifty years old this month. What made me
ever dream you might want to sleep with me some day? I'm
beat up—a beat-up old character."

He went off muttering, and she went to the telephone, and
dialed.

"Stephen," she cried. "Oh, Stephen—where are you? I must see you right away."

From some far distance she could not encompass she heard his reply. "Jane, I cannot come. The General is waiting."

She did not answer. She could not speak.

"Jane, do you hear me? Jane, are you there?"

She put up the receiver quietly and stared across the room. "No," she said aloud. "No, Stephen—I am not here."

*   *   *

Burt pulled himself slowly out of the abyss. He was in the big bed here at home. How had he got here? He had been on a train, asleep. Mollie was sitting there in the rocking chair knitting or crocheting something.

"How'd I get here, Mollie?" he croaked.

"Be quiet, Burt." She got up and came to the bedside and put her big cool hand on his forehead. "You've scared the life out of me."

"I didn't—sleep here last night."

"You've been here in this bed for a week," she said. "Now lie still. I'm going to get you some soup."

"Soup? Get me a beefsteak," he snarled.

"Soup," she said firmly and disappeared.

He lay blinking at the ceiling. His right side felt dead. Where had he been? Talking to Jane. She'd been upset. About the bomb. They'd been talking about the bomb. . . . And now he was here in his bed. Something had happened to him. He waited for his mind to recall. Mollie came in with the bowl of soup on a tray.

"Something has happened to me," he said. His speech was almost clear. He could hear the words in his own voice, slightly slurred but understandable.

"I'll say something happened," Mollie said, making cheer. "Hit me like a b-bomb." That word was not easy. Beginning and ending—

"When they carried you in I thought you were dead," she said. "You were on the train when it hit you."

"What was I doing on the train?"

She shook her head, set down the tray and prepared to administer soup. "How should I know what you were doing? Do I ever know?"

He grinned. "You going to force me to eat that slop?"

"I certainly am," she said, "and don't you dare make a fuss. I've had all the worry I can take."

He laughed at her fondly. God, she was a comfortable sort of woman, never asking questions, always here. Best of all, she didn't hide anything. She really didn't care what he was doing, so long as he wasn't running around with some other woman.

He grumbled from excess of love, "I hate a bossy woman."

"Hate me," she said amiably, "but drink this soup."

He drank it, spoonful by spoonful. More than love pervaded his being. Relief crept into his heart like a spreading light. He was sick. He was sick in bed, maybe a stroke. A stroke was serious. He'd have to stay in bed a month, even two. He had a perfectly honorable reason for not being over there on that island when the bomb was dropped. Stephen would have to take his place. If he believed in God, he'd say that God was good. Hell, he'd say it even if he didn't believe.

＊　　　＊　　　＊

"Jane, take a holiday," Stephen said. "Your job is done, so far as the gadget is concerned. The thing is out of our hands now."

262

She had come early to her laboratory this July morning, too restless to sleep. She was beginning to wonder if that breakfast hour with Stephen had ever taken place. It was as vague as a dream and they had not been alone again; her fault, perhaps, for she had asked for time. But time had passed, five days, six days, and he made no effort to seek her out. Burt's illness, of course, had been a catastrophe. Stephen had to take over everything without notice. Yet need this mean total silence between them for six days? Unable to endure, she had gone to his office this morning for instruction, and now he suggested a holiday.

"Where would I go? What would I do?" she asked blankly.

He sat back looking, she observed, exhausted and harassed. She sat down and looked across the desk at him. "Steve, how can I help you? That's what I want to do."

"I don't know—honestly I don't," he said. "I have to find out what's happening, for one thing. I have a hunch that a number of things are going on at the same time that nobody but Burt knows about. I'm going to see him day after tomorrow—for half an hour. That's all the doctors will allow. Maybe after that—"

He made no movement toward her, there was no recognition in his eyes as he looked at her. She was wildly wounded for a moment and then she dealt with herself ruthlessly. She knew that look, she of all women. Of course he was not thinking of her. He was thinking only of what he had to do, of his responsibility. I ought to be ashamed, she thought. I am ashamed. I'm behaving like any—housewife. And I'm not a housewife. I'm a scientist.

She rose, graceful and restrained. "You'll let me know if I can be of any use, won't you, Steve? Meanwhile I'll not take a holiday. I'll be in my lab as usual. I shall be working on some isotopes. Wonderful if we don't have to work on the war job any more!"

"It's merely a matter of production now—getting another one made—hopefully two, in case of a dud." He was searching among the papers on his desk. "That, and co-ordination. Thanks, Jane."

She slipped away and he scarcely noticed it. A vague memory somewhere, he'd have to renew it when all this was over. Jane understood, he could count on that. Meanwhile he'd have to tell Burt that there was something to this business of Percy Hard. There certainly was something. Helen wouldn't believe it, but the bank reported a large sum of money deposited to Percy Hard's account from abroad, a very large sum. They had investigated and had found that he had no personal wealth. The family was good, but wealth had been squandered in the last generation. The estate in England was hopelessly entangled, the great house closed even before the war, and now being used as a convalescent home for wounded British soldiers.

Stephen had listened to all this only yesterday from the rotund and sober-faced president of the bank, brought to his office by the Army security officer assigned to investigate Percy Hard.

"I shall have to report it," he said. "Of course I am worried. Meanwhile watch the withdrawals—checks made out and to whom."

"He always makes them out to himself. That means he deals in cash, and cash is hard to trace," the banker said.

"I'll see that your requests get to the right desk," Stephen said. "If you don't mind, I have a very pressing—"

The banker interrupted. "I've said what I've come to say."

He barely remembered the incident now. What he had to face was the strange and terrifying assembling of certain facts which until now he had supposed were isolated and having little or nothing to do with the mesa. For example, the Air Force group, training harmlessly, he had supposed, for a year and more in the flats of Utah, had been sent, he now discovered, some three months ago to the island of Tinian, where it had remained in total idleness ever since. That small spot in the Marianas, six thousand miles from San Francisco, was, he had supposed, merely an advance base for the flights of the B-29s. Two days ago, reading the secret orders which Burt had turned over to him, he found that component parts of the bomb were to be sent by cruiser to that island, and additional parts were scheduled to be flown in by B-29s. Certain of the scientists, of whom he had not been one, were due to appear on the island. They were scientists whom he knew well, who had worked here on the mesa, and were in fact still here, not knowing their destination. He had their orders in the locked vault. It was still not too late to countermand them. He had two weeks in which to work.

He took the receiver from the desk telephone and gave the code number for the direct line to the General's office. Through three voices, a secretary and two aides, he reached and heard the heavy voice of authority.

"Yeah?"

"This is Stephen Coast, General."

"Oh hello, Steve. What's on your mind?"

"I should like to have a conference with you not later than tomorrow morning, General. I'd like to bring three of my fellow scientists with me."

"Is it urgent?"

"Very urgent."

"All right. Ten o'clock."

"May I ask that no one else be present?"

The General gave a snort of amusement. "Think I can take on four of you? All right. I reckon I can, at that."

He ended the conversation by hanging up his receiver. Stephen heard the empty silence for an instant and then grimly put back his own instrument. Eaves, Thompson, Jane, and himself. Jane? No. . . . Not now. He could not admit her to his thought even for an instant. He must work alone.

＊　　　＊　　　＊

"What are you fellows ganging up on me about?" The General was in an amiable mood. Everything was going like clockwork, his clock and his work. Too bad about Burt Hall, but maybe just as well—one more scientist out of the way. There was no use in any scientist now, so far as he could see—oh, a couple or so to put the thing together, of course, at the last minute. He'd be worried enough at that, what with the parts being shipped separately and the risk that one ship would be lost and the whole Project wrecked. The delays, the pigheadedness, the way the scientists had to have everything exactly so, was enough to drive a man insane. Temperamental as women, touchy and vain and irritable! He never wanted to see another scientist as long as he lived. Szigny was running around like an old hen trying to cook up trouble. Now that the bomb was made he didn't want it used. And who had been the one that stirred up all the atomic fuss? Why, Szigny! He reminded the fellow of it, and Szigny had clenched his fists.

"There is much difference between being ready for the Nazis who might have made the bomb first and using it on the Japanese who we know very well don't have the weapon. Also, the Air Force has it computed that the B-29s can do the job. The incendiaries and the TNTs are equal, every two or three days, to one A-bomb." When he said that, and how in hell did Szigny get his information, the General had bellowed at him.

"Don't talk to me about the Air Force! I'm the Army!"

Szigny had swelled up like a mad rooster then and he'd

gone off cursing in his own language that no sensible person could understand anyway. And here were these scientists sitting in front of him again.

"Thought you said there'd be four of you," he growled.

"On second thought, I believe three will be enough, General," Stephen said.

He was very pale and his lips were dry.

"You look sick," the General announced, staring at him.

"I am," Stephen said frankly. "I am sick at the possibility I hear—that we intend to drop the bomb."

"What did we make it for?" the General demanded.

"For defense, not to kill thousands of people! I beg you, General, to realize what it will mean in the public opinion of the world if we drop it on human beings. The peoples of the world will suspect us, hate us, fear us."

"And the time may come, General," Thompson drawled, "when for our own safety we'll want to outlaw the use of the weapon by international agreement. How will it look then if we've been the first to use it?"

Bob Eaves, slender, nervous, with a new tic in his right eyelid, lit a cigarette. "We're in a weak position now that the Germans have surrendered, don't you think, General? The Asians will say we waited until the Germans were out of the war so we wouldn't have to use it on white people."

The General grunted. "If I bothered about people and what they'd say, I never would have got anywhere. I've been assigned a duty and I'm doing my duty. That's all I know about and all I want to know about."

At the end of a half hour Stephen glanced significantly at his fellows. We're getting nowhere, the glance said. As though he had spoken they rose, and with a few brief words of parting, left. In silence they returned to their own building across the graveled street and locked themselves into Stephen's office.

"We'll have to take this to Washington," Stephen said.

"To the Secretary of War," Thompson said. His ears were scarlet with anger.

"At least we can insist that the thing be used only on a concentration of troops or war buildings."

"We'll insist that it not be used at all," Stephen said grimly. "And we'll leave immediately."

       *   *   *

In Washington a famous General was talking. "You are all civilians. I will not persuade you. Last spring I was against the use of the bomb, but now—I must declare my views changed. I do not believe, on the evidence of the recent months, that the Japanese will surrender as a result of conventional air attacks and naval operations. I believe that the only way to save American lives—and lives of Japanese citizens—is to bring the war to a quick conclusion."

He was old and tired and he had seen many men killed. At seventy, remembering the battlefields of two wars, he wanted to see no more. Anything to get the boys home again and safe, before he died of weariness! He had never wanted to be a soldier, and decades ago on his father's pleasant southern estate he had feared in his secret heart that the winning of a scholarship to West Point would force him into the business of killing and ordering men to be killed. But at eighteen, when he finished preparatory school, and had the choice of going to the University of Virginia or to West Point, it seemed more romantic, or more honorable, he'd rather say, to put on the uniform. He'd been a handsome young man, and how much the exclamation of a pretty girl had influenced him to the decision he did not know. Her name was Amy, and though he had been in love with her he hadn't married her. When he came home in his sophomore year she had married a rich fellow from New York and he'd never seen her again.

He hadn't wanted to come here this morning, or listen to the arguments of these scientists. Why had they made the bomb in the first place, if they thought it was wicked? He was tired, very tired, and he felt faint.

"If we drop the thing on a city," the old General went on, "my guess is that not more than twenty thousand people will be killed. Most of them will take to cover."

The Secretary of War was old, too, and he was a civilian "We must remember that Japan is not just a place on a map. It is a country of kindly and industrious people. That they have been misled by their military leaders does not change the fact of their humanity. I was in Kyoto once—"

He paused to remember. His mouth trembled slightly.

"It is a lovely place. I can only think of one word to describe it. There is a tenderness in the air. You'll think me sentimental. But it's very beautiful. The homes, so beautiful, even the quite poor ones with little gardens and a twisted tree or a rock—and the great houses and museums of beauty. Temples, set with moss gardens—I've never seen their like elsewhere in the world. I forbid the bombing of that city. It lies in a cup, encircled by mountains. The people would be annihilated—reduced to ash. All beauty gone—"

They were silent for a moment. Then the quavering voice of the old General began again.

"From the consideration of our own nation's safety alone, it might be better not to use the bomb. If we can keep it secret we'll be in a stronger military position—later. There may be another enemy that'll be harder to conquer than the Japanese."

Bob Eaves spoke with nervous energy. "We can't keep it secret, sir. Every nation is working on atomic energy. Sooner or later someone will use the explosion."

"But if we have it and use it," the old General argued, "it will be an incentive to others to develop it, will it not? Yet I know we must take all the risks. We must use the bomb and use it quickly."

His erect and slender figure was that of a young man in the handsome uniform with the gold epaulets and the service stripes and the five stars on the sleeve. But his white head trembled with a slight palsy. The Secretary noticed it and was alarmed. "Let's adjourn, gentlemen. And, General, don't feel you need to stay with us. We have your opinion, and it is very valuable."

"Thank you, Mr. Secretary," the old General said. He rose and bowed with stately formality and withdrew. A moment later he passed the window in his limousine, the Negro chauffeur in a dark purple uniform and cap.

In a private dining room fifteen minutes later the Secretary let his soup grow cold. "While we eat, gentlemen, I would like to have you put before me any ideas you may have for not using the weapon. I have asked some members of my staff to meet with us, and two officers from the Pentagon. They are here." He introduced them.

"We could give warning," Thompson began.

He was interrupted by an officer. "And let the Japanese air force attack us? No, sir!"

The aging Secretary spoke slowly and with grave reluctance, a small thin man in his old grey suit, his face worn, his eyes sad. He turned to Stephen.

"As I understand it, Coast, the bomb is still far from perfected. The enemy might attack while you're putting the thing together if it's not kept secret, and that would mean failure. You only have one, isn't that true?"

"Yes," Stephen said. "As yet—"

"It might even make the Japanese get into production themselves and then we'd be the first ones bombed."

"Yes," Stephen said. "That is possible."

The argument went on through two hours at the table and for three hours more at the Secretary's office afterwards. No one could devise a means of warning the enemy so seriously that war could be stopped.

"And war must be stopped," Stephen insisted. "Whatever happens we must stop this brutal massacre that is going on day after day. Merely to add another frightful weapon is no solution."

At the end of the afternoon, the Secretary was exhausted. He had grown old at his task. Years before he had foreseen this present war and his was the solitary voice that had spoken against aggression in Asia when the Japanese seized Manchuria. Had they listened to me, he thought—but nobody listened to anybody any more.

"There is no use in continuing," he said dryly from behind his desk. "We agree upon what we wish to see done but we can find no way of achieving it. We must throw the problem back to you scientists. After all, perhaps it is your problem. You have made the bomb. You must teach us how to use it."

Bob Eaves broke in with young alacrity. "I cannot accept that, Mr. Secretary. Our responsibility as scientists is to pursue knowledge wherever it may lead. We can't be responsible for how the rest of you use what we discover. We can tell you what will happen if you do this or that, we can explain the total destruction that the bomb will produce if you use it. But you must choose to use it—or not."

"Help us," the Secretary said. "Go home and talk among yourselves. Put your superb brains at the service of humanity. For once be our advisers. I shall expect your report in ten days."

*   *   *

271

"It is an international crime," Szigny argued passionately. "Please—read what I am writing."

He was talking to Jane in her house on a Sunday morning. He was talking everywhere, in Chicago, in New York, in Tennessee and Washington. And while he talked he laid before her on the table in her small living room sheets of parchment paper. Upon the pages he had written his appeal to humanity.

Jane read it in silence. "The nation which sets the precedent of using these newly liberated forces for the purposes of destruction must bear the responsibility of opening the door to an era of devastation on an unimaginable scale—"

She read through to the end and saw the list of names appended. The most distinguished names in science were there —no, not all. Burton Hall's name was not there, nor Bob Eaves, nor Thompson, nor—

"I don't see Stephen Coast's name," she said.

Szigny groaned and pulled his long curly hair, grizzled as a ram's coat. "Ah, I did go to him. I went many times. He says he cannot sign until he thinks of alternatives. Are there alternatives to death, I ask him? To which he does not speak."

She did not reply and Szigny sat watching her anxiously. What would she do? A young scientist and a woman, perhaps her name was not important, but she was respected very much. And if she helped him, she could help very much. A delicate face, and beautiful, but he had not thought of a woman for a long time—not since his beloved wife was murdered because she was a Jew in Berlin, the greatest center of science in the world.

"I will not press you to sign your name," he said. "Let it be as your conscience speaks. And your heart. I think, with a woman, it is the same."

"I will sign," Jane said firmly. She took the pen he offered

272

her and signed her name in bold black letters. Stephen would see it there.

"Thank you, thank you." He rose as he spoke and bent over her hand and kissed it.

"Speak where you can, when you can," he urged.

"I will," she promised.

That afternoon, remembering, she spoke to Stanton, the biophysicist whom Stephen had brought here to the mesa. She was amazed when the blond young man turned on her. He was mild and harmless, she would have said, working on a new project not related to war, and Stephen was assuaging his own conscience, she divined shrewdly, by planning projects for after the war. Stanton was experimenting on the edge of life, at the tremulous line where non-animate crystal becomes living cells in the tobacco mosaic, the delicate unknown area where matter merges into living tissue. It was Stephen's area of interest, his obsession with the unity of everything, Einstein's obsession as well, but Einstein was aging and the task was now beyond even that magnificent brain. Stephen was still young enough—not yet thirty. But nobody here on the mesa was over thirty, except Burton Hall, and Burt was here no more. Only the youthful brain, fiercely athirst with curiosity, could pursue the creative search with the pure concentration necessary. I'm wasting my own brain, she thought. I'm letting my emotions eat up the energy of my brain. I'm in love with Stephen and I'm desperately afraid of the bomb. Yes, and I'm angry.

"Stan," she had said to the snub-nosed young scientist. "Have you seen the appeal that Szigny is making?"

He turned on her with fury. "Who hasn't seen it? We have all seen it. The fellows were talking about it last night at my place—a bunch of us. We sent the women off to the concert—chamber music with Percy Hard. None of us will sign it. Aren't those fellows fighting over there in the islands and jungles Americans, too? If we can save the life of one of them, I say drop the bomb. I have a brother on Iwo Jima. If he gets killed because we don't end the war, then I'll be his murderer. No, I won't sign."

"I have signed," Jane said quietly.

He threw her a look of contempt. "You would," he said. "You're a woman."

She did not answer. She met his look fully and he turned away first. Then she took off her white coat and went to find Stephen.

❊   ❊   ❊

"Come in," he said. "I'm sorry I had to keep you waiting. I've been on the telephone twenty-four hours a day, it seems, since I got back from Washington, eight days ago."

She sat down in silence on the chair across the desk from him and he glanced at her.

"Jane, you're not ill?"

"No," she said.

"You're very pale."

"I feel strange," she told him, "as though I were a stranger here and you strange to me."

He winced and pulled his right ear ruefully. "I know. We're in a queer period—waiting for so many things, waiting to know—"

"I haven't waited," she said quietly. "I wanted to tell you. I have signed Szigny's protest."

He lifted dark eyebrows at her. "Oh? I'm sorry you did that."

She leaned forward on the desk. "Stephen! You're sorry? I never thought to hear you say that you're sorry I protest the dropping of the bomb."

"What I mean is—why didn't you talk it over with me? It's what I'm working on now—getting opinions from every-

274

where—from all the scientists—Chicago, Tennessee, here on the mesa. I put five different approaches to them, from not using it at all to using it without warning. Eighty-seven per cent have voted for using it without warning."

"No!"

"Yes."

"But what will other countries think of us?"

"I've had polls taken in Canada, Britain and France. They are overwhelmingly in favor of using it at once—three times as many opinions for its use, as against. And the Little Boss in Washington says that he and his joint staff have talked it over, and they approve unanimously."

Her eyes were burning like dark stars. "Then I'm glad I signed—a thousand times I'm glad I signed. After watching Dick Feldman die, could I have argued for death?"

"I wish it were as simple as signing a paper," he said doggedly.

"Stephen." Her voice was a whisper. "Are you not going to protest?"

He breathed a gust of a sigh. "I'm taking no part in it. The majority decides."

She yearned toward him, she longed to touch his hand. He was still human, he was the man she loved. But she could not so much as put out her hand to him. Her hand was cold and his would be cold. Where would she ever find warmth again, human warmth, the warmth of desire and passion?

"Oh, Stephen," she cried. "What are you? I thought you were a man. Are you letting others decide for you?"

He looked at her with haggard eyes, encircled with shadows. "I have made my own decision."

"You have decided not to decide," she said scornfully, "so that you won't be responsible. That's it. You don't want to be responsible. Well, I want to be responsible! I want to be responsible for fighting, with all my strength and body and brain, against the thing we have made. I would have cut off my right hand before I'd have helped make it, if I'd ever thought we could use it. Steve, what will the rest of the world think of us if we use it? We're Americans! They'll never forgive us. In India the children on the streets loved me because I was American, not British. When I was a girl my schoolmates loved me because my country had once been a colony, too, and we'd fought ourselves free. My first physics professor was an Anglo-Indian. We had long talks after class. He told me he wished the white half of him could have been American. Steve, if we drop the bomb we'll destroy ourselves, everywhere in the world. People won't believe in us any more."

"As if I hadn't enough to harass me—" He paused and then went on. "Percy Hard is being returned to England."

"No!"

"Yes. We've been working on it for the last five days. The General has found the proof. Percy is in communication with the Russians."

"Oh no, Stephen! For what reason?"

"A twisted conscience. He thinks that the only safety is to have everyone know all the secrets about the atom. He's been feeding stuff to them."

"How?"

"Through a couple of technical fellows he's influenced."

"Bribed?"

"No, curiously, it's all been done through the conscience. Much more dangerous! I know how a conscience can sit in judgment, suggesting, compelling, like an alter ego. I'll have to tell Helen. . . . I don't know how far her feelings are—concerned."

"You must think of her first," Jane said.

Agony and then relief rushed out of her heart and pervaded her being. He was not thinking of her and this was agony. But if he was not thinking of her, then she was free. She was free of love. Oh, she loved him but he could no longer compel her.

As though he divined her withdrawal he spoke with sudden sharpness.

"As soon as I can, I shall tell Helen about you and me."

"Oh no," she said softly. "That would be too cruel. What would she have left? I could never bear it."

"What do you mean—*never?*"

"Just—never."

"Jane, you can't."

"Yes, I can, Stephen. I must. I don't want to love you. I know that now. It's the mesa, I think. It's forced us together in an unnatural sort of way. We've got used to—to companionship and we've let ourselves think it was love—haven't we?"

"Jane, I tell you I'm coming back as soon as I can tell Helen."

His eyes were pleading with hers. "Believe me—believe me—"

"I know you want me to believe you," she said, "but I know you too well, Stephen. You won't be able to come back. You have a conscience, too. You're quite right. You must think of Helen first.

He got to his feet. "I may have to think of her first, but afterwards—"

She shook her head and he stared at her with bitter eyes. "It's a little late for all this."

She returned look for look. "You never did love me!"

"I love you desperately," he said. "And I beg you to leave me alone."

He meant it. She saw that he meant it. He loved her and he wished her gone. What was there to say? She turned and left him, alone as he wished to be.

And when she was gone he pressed his lips together and proceeded firmly to do what must be done as quickly as possible now that Percy was gone. If the Russians had the secret then the bomb must be used immediately. The scientists had agreed in majority. He was relieved of the guilt of decision. This morning the General's aide, the Colonel next in command, had come to him.

"Steve, they want to know in Washington about the polls. What do the men think?"

"I'll write it out."

While the Colonel waited he wrote it out and handed it to him and he had gone away. Then Jane had come in, Jane whom he knew he loved and yet even love was a listless thing in his heart, dwarfed by the monstrous object he had helped to create. What meaning had love, if the world were destroyed? Love could not save so much as a single life, even his own. And she had looked so beautiful, pale with sadness, and her eyes great and dark and unutterably lonely. He longed to be single-minded, as she was, sure of what she thought was right—the impractical right, the non-existent absolute. His scientist mind combined, he supposed, with the compromise that was part of the Quaker faith in which he had been reared. Long ago he had cast aside that faith, but its habits remained. "The sense of the meeting . . ."— how often he had heard his father say those words after the long gatherings when tight-lipped men and women sat defying each other, waiting, in bitter disagreement, always repressed, for the first sign of yielding, so that there could be a sense of the meeting! Let the majority decide this fearful question now. He would not take sides.

And at this moment, when he sat alone, his hands clenching and unclenching and sweat starting from his temples, he heard a knock on the door. It might be Jane back again, and in that instant he knew that he never wanted her to go. He

278

did not want to be alone. He leaped across the room and flung open the door. The Colonel stood there.

"Come in," he said, his voice faint with disappointment.

The Colonel came in briskly and closed the door behind him. "Sorry to bother you again, but Washington wants to know what you think."

"What I think?" Stephen echoed.

He sank down on the window sill, and felt the sunlight, crystalline in the pure desert air, hot on his back.

"Washington wants to know what you think, you alone," the Colonel repeated.

"What I think," Stephen said helplessly. "I've been thinking for four years. My father was a Quaker. He didn't believe in war. I wonder why he didn't do something about it —I don't remember that he did anything about it, nothing really decisive—no prevention of an active sort."

"Do you feel all right?" the Colonel asked.

Stephen got to his feet. He put thumb and finger to his lower lip and gazed at the patch of sunlight on the floor.

"Yes, I feel all right," he said hesitating. "Yes."

But he felt far from all right. A clutch in the pit of his stomach, a mist of dizziness crept through his brain. Jane shouldn't have left him alone, no matter what he said. She should have known.

He sat down at his desk and took up his pen, and tried to steady the trembling of his hand and wrote these words: *I vote with the majority . . .*

He paused and added another line uncertainly: *although I deplore the necessity. I pray that it may not be used more than once, so long as the world stands.* He signed his name, blotted the page carefully. Through his brain a thought flashed in a line of fire—but once may be enough to end the world. He folded the sheet, slipped it into an envelope, gave it to the Colonel and the Colonel left the room immediately.

Alone again he sat for a long moment, behind his desk, his hands outspread upon it. That which he had helped to discover, the thing he had made, the secret of creative energy, the source of life in the universe, he had given away to death. In terror and self-doubt he seized the telephone and dialed for Jane in the adobe house. She would be there now, at this hour of sunset. When she left him, that is where she would go for refuge. He listened. The telephone rang again and again. There was no answer. She was not there.

So where could he go and what was there left for him to do? He sat rigid in thought. How could he undo what he had done? How could all the scientists undo what they had done, the scientists and the military men and the statesmen, those who had put their hands to the making of the bomb and their minds to the decision of using it? He must get to Washington without delay.

❊   ❊   ❊

An hour later he was throwing things into his suitcase and rushing to catch a plane against all orders because a train would be too slow. Helen called upstairs from the kitchen where she was making him a sandwich to put in his pocket and eat when he could.

"Steve, Dr. Szigny is here. He says he's got to see you."

"Tell him to come up here."

And in a moment there Szigny was, panting and short-winded as usual, his wild hair flying about his head.

"I catch you," he cried. "I catch you just right. You go to Washington? Listen, Stefan! Here is something you must know first. I have just come away from Washington. I have seen pictures of Japanese cities—photo-reconnaissance—never mind how I have seen them. The destruction is hell there.

280

Our B-29 planes have destroyed like—like hell-fire, strictly. Japan's navy is nearly all destroyed. No ships left for use. Blockade, both surface and underwater, and she must surrender. The people will demand it. The rulers cannot contain them. So Americans need not to invade. We need not to use the bomb. Speak so to the President, Stefan. Tell him it is too late. Japan will surrender. I swear it. Japan is already on her knees. Oh yes, yes, a very proud people, yes, but a little honor to them, a little forgiveness, in words only I mean, as for example not to say unconditional. Just to say surrender, only. That gives some honor, no? It is worth it for ending the war, no?"

He was pleading with terrible earnestness, the ready sweat pouring down his face, and he was not to be resisted.

"I can try, Szigny. I will try," Stephen said.

*   *   *

"The Little Boss knows all that, Steve," the Secretary of War said. He was deeply troubled, dejected, sad. He had lost weight, and his collar was too big for his scrawny neck. As soon as the war ended, he had promised his frightened old wife this morning, he would go to the hospital and see why he had such a pain in his right side.

"How long will that be?" she had demanded.

"Only a few days now, Sarah."

"He knows and still he gives the order to drop the bomb!" Stephen exclaimed.

"It's in the works now," the old man sighed. "We can't go back. We can only mitigate."

"Mitigate! How does one mitigate a holocaust?"

"We'll warn them," the Secretary said. "The Little Boss is all for warning them. I have to say that for him. Surrender will make invasion unnecessary—and the bomb too."

281

"Is he asking for unconditional surrender?"

"Yes, he will not accept anything else. He doesn't think the American people will accept anything else. In fact—" he hesitated and then went on. "We've already had feelers from Japan—but they won't accept unconditional surrender."

"So we insist upon it?"

"Yes. . . . But I must say in our defense that the terms we propose are honorable. They will keep their sovereignty."

"And the alternative, if they won't accept?"

"Utter destruction," the Secretary said.

The silence of destruction fell between them. "Then they must be warned, and warned not once but many times!"

"Yes. There will be a preliminary bombing by our planes. Then we will send the offer."

"The people must know," Stephen said. "We can drop millions of leaflets."

"There isn't time."

"There must be time. I'll see to it myself—"

The Secretary looked up at the tall young man and warmth crept in his faded blue eyes. "I'll advance the money —there isn't time for appropriations!"

"Thank you, sir," Stephen said. "And now if you'll forgive me for rushing away—"

"Rush," the Secretary said, "run, hurry, do what you can. Let me know how to help."

"Thanks," Stephen said again.

❈   ❈   ❈

The demand for surrender was broadcast and published on the twenty-sixth day of July. Stephen in the Secretary's office waited for the reply. It came, cold and formal. "The Japanese government cannot receive the ignominious offer."

"Drop the leaflets," the Secretary ordered.

On the next day thousands of leaflets fell like a summer snow upon the cities of Japan.

"Can they read?" Stephen exclaimed. It was an afterthought. What if the people could not read?

"They can read," the Secretary said. "Japan has the highest literacy of any country in the world."

The leaflets warned of bombing first by conventional planes.

On the twenty-eighth day six cities were bombed.

Still there was no word to Washington. Day after day Stephen sat out the hours.

On the fifth day of August, a steaming summer's day in Washington, hot clouds pressing low over the city, there was still no reply. The Secretary ordered special warnings and millions more of leaflets. The day passed and there was no reply. At midnight the weary old man turned to the tight-lipped young scientist. Neither of them had left the room for forty-eight hours.

"Stephen," he said softly. "We've done all that we can. Go back to your laboratory."

❋   ❋   ❋

Over the city in Japan the plane floated like a butterfly above an open flower. It hovered like a fish hawk above a silver pond in the morning when the goldfish swarm to the surface to catch the light of the sun. It was a midsummer morning, the day's business just begun. Men walking to their offices, women riding in rikshas to the market, children ready to march to their classes, heard the roar of the wings above them. They lifted their faces and saw a plane in the sky, a single plane. They were reassured. One plane. What damage could it do? Enemy planes came in hundreds to do their work. This was one—a reconnaissance plane? People smiled at each other in relief and went their way.

Unnoticed, a silver thing fell out of the plane and twisted downward, a small thing in the sky, not bigger than a toy, a glittering dot, a piece torn from the sun. It was in fact a piece of the sun, a globe of fire, one third of a mile in diameter, with a temperature in the center of one hundred million degrees Fahrenheit, compressed into a small metal container. Suddenly the container burst. The air around it was forced away by the enormous pressure and out of the fierce violence winds arose at hundreds of miles an hour, even a thousand, in great waves. The mighty push, the violent blast, set aflame everything within its reach, wood, cloth, thatched roofs, great works of art, and human flesh, blood, bone and brain. And following were the unseen rays of radiation. Of three hundred thousand people in the city a third were dead in one instant, and of those remaining most were burned, crippled and scarred for life, the deep returning scars boiling up out of their renewed flesh.

*   *   *

"How did it feel to drop the bomb?" a newspaper reporter asked the young American bombardier in Tokyo.

How had it felt? He lit a cigarette. It had been a fine day, the sky cloudless, the sunrise magnificent, a golden semicircle of flame on the ocean horizon. The morning flight from Tinian had been swift and straight and the target city appeared as plain upon the earth as upon a map, a big city, the suburbs sprawling to the sea. By the shore ships waited to carry troops away, fifty thousand of them, to jungle battlefields. At quarter past eight he had touched the button and released the bomb—that shape, neat, shining, compact with death. Then the pilot had banked the plane sharply and they sped toward Tokyo.

So bright was the sun that the explosion, a minute later, seemed not so bright as the test had been upon the desert. But the same huge red ball took shape, it swelled into the upper air, the city burst into smoke and fire, and the column of grey-white cloud, streaked with purple, spread into the massive mushroom. Beneath it the city was hid, flame and all, by smoke and dust.

And when they were safely away, his comrade, his friend, the man who had assembled the bomb, showed him a pistol, hidden under his jacket.

"What did you bring that along for?" he had demanded.

His friend had grinned. "Think I'd be taken alive if the bomb didn't work? Well, take another think—"

"How'd it feel?" the young officer repeated that night in Tokyo. He drew hard on his cigarette and blew out a ring of smoke. "Like any other bomb—that's how."

But in the dead city a living man crawled out of a cellar. He stood for one second and stared around him. He was in a desert, a smoking desert of death and destruction. He gave a wild cry, a howl of despair, and he lifted his arms and cried to heaven.

"This—this is beyond human endurance!"

*   ❁   ❁

A great silence fell upon the earth. It was deepest in the city upon the mesa. Yes, it was a city, a new city, founded and built upon the creation of the bomb. Now its work was finished. The morning newspapers, the radio commentators, the telegraph wires, the cables under the oceans, all had announced the mission fulfilled. One city, and one more, had been destroyed, and the great silence spread everywhere in the world.

And this morning of all mornings, in the silence, by the strange coincidence of life, Jane received a letter in the mail. It waited for her there in her box in the office. She had come to the laboratory this morning because there was nothing else for her to do, and in the silence she had spoken to no one, and no one had come near her. Stephen had left the mesa two days ago, without telling her where he was going. She guessed that he could not bear to be here when the bomb was dropped. Helen had gone with him. They were together. She was not jealous. She felt nothing. The silence was in her, too. Something was over, something was ended.

And at this moment between end and beginning, here was the letter. She knew the moment she saw the familiar Indian stamp that it was from Raman, in Almora. Between them there remained only the intuitive communication which they accepted as their total relationship. It had been a full year since he had written her. He had not even answered her last letter, written in an agony of loneliness after he had acknowledged his love for her and his decision not to allow her to return to India or to him.

"I have repudiated my English blood," he had written a year ago. "I have chosen India, and to choose India means to live the Indian life. We do not divorce our wives, we Hindus. And Lakshmi is innocent. She is a good wife. Shall I send her away because I love you? Is this worthy of me?"

It was a cruel letter gently written and she had replied to it with love and fury. Now, after a year, the old instinct between them since she had been a schoolgirl and he, her teacher, sprang alive when she saw his handwriting. Of all days in her life this was the day she most needed to hear from him, and he spoke.

She went to her laboratory and closed the door and for

286

a few minutes sat with the letter unopened in her hand, remembering him, drawing back to herself the tall figure, the sad beautiful face, the dark and candid eyes. Then she opened the letter and in the world silence she began to read.

My dear Child:

That was the fiction between them, that he was her teacher-father and she was his child.

You will think this a strange letter to receive upon this day. I write it to you, because you are the only American I know. Have you a voice? Since you are a scientist at least you are near other scientists, and perhaps you can borrow their voices. My facts are that American scientists are preparing a new weapon. You may ask me how it is that I know this. I know because I have two Russian students in my classes, sent to me from Moscow, for what purpose I do not know. We have more than a few Russian students throughout India and they are not usual young men. They are here with some mission, I am sure of it. They know many things that usual students do not know. For example, about this new weapon, they have the information. How did they get it? They have it of course from spies. But what spies? It is not my concern to know these things. My concern is simply that if you are making a new weapon—but no, how can you, my little child, make a weapon? I remember you as gentle and intelligent and wise, and also beautiful. Nevertheless you are working among men. If there is a new weapon, I implore you to keep it from being used. It will be a weapon against yourselves, against your country. You will not be forgiven for this new weapon. Yes, yes, I also know something about this

287

weapon. My students have told me. They have told a few significant people, for they know that after the war is ended, India will be independent, and they hope that we will follow Russia.

My child, the strength of this new Russia is that she knows what she wants. She wishes to change the pattern of life in every country, in the whole world. Therefore you must work also in your country. First, never allow the weapon to be used. It will be said that you refrained from its use while Germany was in the war and saved it for use against Japan. But if it is used and you cannot prevent it, then beg your government to keep your forces in Europe. Do not withdraw quickly and leave empty spaces for Russian armies to occupy. And this I tell you. Russia will join with China, first with Chiang and then with Mao. Do these names mean something to you, my child? If not, then study about them at once. A new age begins—a fearful new age. From the moment the weapon is used, if it is used, everything will be obsolescent. . . . My child, come back then to India. Here you will be safe.

She forgot instantly all his warnings. She saw only the invitation—come back to India, and there she would be safe. The landscapes of her childhood appeared again in memory, the valleys and plains of Almora, green and fruitful, the snow-crowned mountains, the mild and loving people. She longed to be there, safe as Raman said, near him if not with him. Alas, she was no longer a child. How could she escape being what she was? Here or in India she was a woman. She let the letter drop from her hands and she bent her head down upon her folded arms on the laboratory table and wept.

*   *   *

288

"So—what's next?" Helen inquired.

Stephen had left the house early that morning and they had not met until evening. In the silence of the day he had remained in his office, talking gravely with the scientists as they came and lingered. The facts were all in now, by special communication from Washington. The bomb had been completely successful. There was nothing more for them to do. The scientists without exception did not speak of the bomb. They talked of what they would do next. They were in haste to be gone, to go back to their classrooms and offices, their jobs with big industries. In a few days, a few weeks, the mesa would be deserted, the buildings empty, the life gone. There must be new life, new work, new plans.

"What are you doing, Steve?"

They put the question to him again and again, and he answered it simply by saying that he did not know. Now he did not reply at once to Helen's question. It was impossible to tell from her voice what her mood was.

"I'm tired to death," he said at last. "I'm too tired to think now what I want to do."

"You're tired because you hate yourself," she said. "I know because that's why I'm tired. I hate myself."

"I can't take any fireworks tonight."

"I shouldn't think you could," she retorted, "not after the fireworks you've let loose over yonder."

He did not answer. He began to climb the steps slowly like an old man, and she let him get halfway. Then without pity she stopped him.

"Before you go any further—Percy Hard is what you think he is."

He wheeled around.

"What—"

"Yes, he told me. He's leaving, ostensibly for England, but actually—for parts unknown."

"He told you?"

"He asked me to go with him."

"Good God—"

"He's probably gone. He knows I'm telling you. I promised I wouldn't, until he was gone. I thought he would kill me. His hands are horribly strong—all that piano practicing. I don't think I'll ever touch the piano again."

"Come upstairs and tell me—"

She followed him upstairs to their bedroom and he closed the door. "Now, tell me everything. Sit down—"

She sat down, and under her vivid speech the scene unfolded before his eyes.

"While you and your scientists have been busy at your private life there's been another sort of life going on. You can't lock a lot of people up on a mesa like this without having things go on. In some ways it's been a big holiday —hasn't it? All you brain brothers—haven't you had a good time, Steve? Always somebody smart enough to understand what you were talking about! Why, I heard a man say one day it was like heaven. He'd been working in a big business laboratory, lonely among people who didn't understand what he was doing, and here he was working with all of you at the same thing, a big job, your brains working together. It must have been wonderful. Even Percy said it was wonderful. But he had his music, too—he wasn't pure and simple the way you are. I guess that's why he could do what he did do. He hates Americans—did you know? Thinks we're crude and that he'd rather have the Russians. The Russians respect their intellectuals, he says. He says their scientists get huge salaries and all sorts of honors, much better than English. What's he got to be loyal to? That's the way it began—"

"And you listened."

She nodded. "Because he had an ethic, too—you'll not

290

believe it, but he does. He thinks the science should be shared with everybody—even the atomic stuff. He says it's the only safety. If everybody knows, nobody will use it. That's what he says. Maybe there's sense to it. Anyway there's no sense to what we've done."

He looked at her. "Why do you hate yourself?"

Her eyes swam in sudden tears. "Oh, I don't know, Steve. It's not Percy, but he's mixed me all up, somehow. I don't know what's right any more."

"Neither do I," he said.

"Do you feel guilty?"

"Yes, and no. We had to do it, didn't we?"

"I don't know."

They looked at each other across a desert. He needed help and he was not able to help her. In such a moment it was useless to offer the emptiness of a caress. A kiss was mere gesture. And yet she was touching and more beautiful than he had ever seen her. The slight bravado, the air of independence, the surface hardness, which she had made a habit of in recent years, had dropped away. She was quivering and naked before his eyes. Her flushed face, eyes soft with tears, hair awry, revealed a woman he had not seen here on the mesa.

"I wish I knew how to help you," he said abruptly. "Perhaps then I could help myself. We'll have to wait. Everything has to wait."

He left her there alone.

*　　*　　*

She was still alone an hour later when she heard the doorbell ring.

She had been recovering, moment by moment, not from heartbreak but restored by the necessity of small things to

291

be done, her parakeet restless with hunger, a vase of faded flowers. Percy had sent her the flowers and now she wanted to throw them away. Where was Percy and how much had he meant to her? The very memory of him was entangled in the music they had made together, music the enchantment.

As long as her heart beat she would never forget the last hour with him. He played Tchaikovsky again, always Tchaikovsky, and she had listened, torn to fragments, memories and feelings and impulses mingled and flying around the world. She had lied to Stephen. It was Percy who had confused her, his kisses, his expert seeking hands and her too ready response. There was something evil in her, maybe, something that Stephen's goodness could never satisfy. Percy had evil in him, too. They both knew it. When he laughed at Stephen—"Saint Stephen," he called him, she laughed, too, and hated herself. . . . And when he had dashed into this very room—was it only two days ago?—she had all but yielded to him.

"Helen, come away with me—"

"Away? Where? What's wrong?"

"I'm going back to England—"

"Now?"

"Within the hour. Special plane. You could meet me in New York, sweet—"

His hands were on her, stroking her cheeks, her neck, down to her breasts— It had taken all her strength to wrench herself away.

"Percy, do they—are you—"

"Am I accused? Yes, darling, and proud of it, if you know what I mean."

She was suddenly afraid of the fanatical light in his pale eyes—

"Oh no, Percy!"

At that minute they had heard the knock on the door.

"They've come for me, sweet! Telephone me—"

He had thrust a bit of paper into her hands, and in an instant was gone. She watched him from the window, walking between two officers, and in the same instant she tore the paper to shreds. . . . The ache in her heart was still here, but she could bear it.

She paused before the mirror on the chimney piece and made her hair tidy and then opened the door. Jane Earl stood there, a slender figure in a blue cotton dress, dark hair pulled back and knotted.

"Oh, it's you," Helen said, taken aback. "Stephen has just gone out."

"I haven't come to see him," Jane said. "I've come to see you."

"Then come in."

They faced each other across the narrow room.

"I don't know how to begin," Jane said. "Perhaps I don't know why I have come. I want to see another woman, talk with a woman, and I thought of you. I know very few women. My work has kept me isolated."

"I envy you," Helen said.

They were fumbling for honesty, for communication, across the barriers between women.

"You really think I am to be envied?" Jane asked.

It was a wistful question, asked in self-doubt, and Helen was touched. "It must be wonderful to work with men, especially with scientists. Oh, that sounds banal—I don't know how to say what I want to say. I feel as if it had been a long time since I've said anything worth saying. While Stephen has been working day and night on this Project, I've just been playing about. I know it, but what else has there been for me to do? Don't interrupt me, please. I know I've helped the families and been baby-sitter for mothers who wanted to shop and I've comforted Project-widows and all that. But you know what I mean. You must know. You've been in the center, with the men. They've told you everything—haven't they? You've known their secrets. Yes, I do envy you. I'm jealous of you—not just with Stephen—though that's been bad enough. But I've been jealous of your very life."

To this outburst Jane listened with painful interest. "I've never heard a woman really talk before. I do know what you mean. I've never lived your life, but I know. And I've envied you, too. I've wanted to marry, have children—"

Helen interrupted. "That's another thing—I'd wanted children, and then suddenly I was afraid to have them. What sort of world is this that the men are making behind our backs? I don't know. It isn't the world I was born into. Have I the right to bring children here when I don't know what faces them? Why can't I ask Stephen? We don't talk. But you know everything. Would you want children? Do you?"

"I dream of them," Jane said. "But they're no more than a dream. I've never loved a man enough to give up my work."

"Could you love any man enough?"

They were no longer themselves alone. They were asking the huge questions of sex.

"I don't know," Jane said. She was thoughtful. "I suppose that—well, Madame Curie has always been my ideal woman. She was a great scientist, and she married a scientist, they worked together, they lived together. Together they made the complete being, she knowing all of him, he all of her. They shared laboratory and children. I suppose it can't happen very often."

"As often as there's a Madame Curie," Helen said.

"So why doesn't Madame Curie happen more often?" Jane asked.

They were not asking each of the other now. Their minds were communing in common question.

"We're afraid," Helen said.

"Afraid of what?"

"Of men." Helen said. "Afraid of their disapproval. Oh, don't look at me like that—I don't mean Stephen. He's goodness—pure and simple."

She stopped, her blue eyes enlightened by sudden awareness. She bit her red lower lip, and still meeting Jane's inquiring gaze, she forced herself to go on. "I suppose—that you and Stephen could have—could be two such people. I don't know if I am brave enough."

"I am certainly not brave enough," Jane said.

She got to her feet and went to the window and looked out into the morning. The air was pellucid, the day windless. A scintillating brightness shone over the desert. "And please believe me—I didn't come here for—for such a thing to be said to me."

Her gentleness infused Helen with courage. "If I thought Stephen would be happier with—with you, I'd accept it. Maybe not at once, but with a little time, I could—"

"He's your whole life, isn't he?"

"I think so," Helen said. "I don't quite know."

"He's not my whole life," Jane said quietly. "I don't think any man could be my whole life. I can see a whole life with—with a man but it would be a life we'd make together, two scientists, one of them a man, the other a woman. We'd make a life, complete, a fourth-dimensional life!"

She turned and flashed a smile across the room. "I don't understand the fourth dimension," Helen retorted, "and so I can't very well live it. No, I mean what I said, Jane. I mean it seriously."

Jane sat down again. "And I am just as serious. In cold fact, I can make a life as a scientist, and I shan't marry unless I find a man, or a man finds me, with whom I can achieve the fourth dimension, let us say. But that doesn't mean I can allow you to—to contemplate any such sacrifice as you suggest."

"Suppose it's no sacrifice—"

Their eyes met. Jane shook her head. "I'm going to India," she said.

*   *   *

Burton Hall was on his feet again with a cane, but walking. He was uneasy, conscious of atmosphere about Mollie that he did not understand. He had not told her about the bomb because honestly he didn't know the day or the hour or the place. Well, he hadn't wanted to know. It was not his business. He was a sick man. The doctor had told him to avoid strain. So the first thing he knew was when he saw it in the newspapers yesterday. Hiroshima, Nagasaki. War over.

He glanced at Mollie across the breakfast table this morning, the morning after. The newspaper had the whole story now, and he had read it and so had she. For the first time in their life together he saw her read the front page instead of turning to the woman's page. And she said not one word. She pursed her lips into a hard line and her round and rosy face was suddenly pale.

"Well, anyway the war is over," he said with false cheer.

Still she said nothing. She poured her coffee and buttered her toast and did not look at him, although usually she was full of chatter especially on a nice bright morning. He ate in silence, stealing a look at her now and then across the bowl of roses in the middle of the table. At last he could bear no more of this silence.

"You sick?" he demanded sharply. "Or has the cat got your tongue?"

"I'm sick," she said.

"Looks like it—you eating all that buttered toast and jam and swilling down your coffee!"

"I'm sick," she repeated. "I'm so sick I could walk out of this house and never come back." Her voice ended in a squeak and she wiped her eyes.

He pushed back his chair and flung his napkin on the floor. "All right," he said grimly. "Let's have it. Spit it all out at once."

But she would not spit it out at all. Instead her round blue eyes swam in tears and her face flushed. She swallowed hard.

"I suppose you think I did it," he growled.

She burst out. "You shouldn't have had anything to do with it! It was a nasty sneaky thing to do—I don't care if we are at war. You shouldn't have done it. What'll happen now? Nobody will trust us any more. I won't trust you, either. Hiding from me what you are doing all the time up on that mesa, and down there in Tennessee—"

He shrieked in outrage, "Hiding? I told you everything."

"I didn't know what you were talking about."

"Is it my fault you're stupid?"

"I trusted you, Burt—"

"Listen, a lot of American boys would have been killed. Think of Tim—and Peter. You want them killed? You want them shot down in jungles, starved and beaten in prison camps—"

"We've killed a hundred thousand people all at once. The paper says so."

"Then you do want your own sons—"

"I don't want any of it—none of it at all. And I wish I'd

297

never had any children. It's not decent to have children in a—a world like this. If I'd known—"

They were screaming at each other, and he heard these incredible words from her, the mother of his sons, the mother of men, the mother. That was Mollie, all mother, and she did not want her own children. No more children if she'd known? Now she knew. It struck him in a blast that millions of women were saying these words, young women, women with babies, girls not yet married.

"Mollie, do you know what you're saying?"

She nodded, sobbing.

"Mollie, you must understand—why, look, woman, it's here in the paper, too. The war is over! Tim will come home safe, alive. Peter won't have to go to war. Maybe there'll never be another war. Maybe it's stopped forever, the death, the sorrow, the waste."

But the unreasonable woman would not give over her weeping. She sobbed until he was frightened and angrily he stumped over to her, leaning upon his cane, and still angry he smoothed her hair, and forced his handkerchief into her hands, a clean linen handkerchief that he'd put into his pocket this morning when he changed his tie. She took it but instead of wiping her eyes she buried her face in it and wept aloud.

He stumped back to his seat then and sat staring at her. She was inconsolable. For the first time in his life he couldn't comfort her.

"Mollie, stop it," he commanded.

But she did not stop it. She continued to sob, unabated, and he was furious with her obstinacy. He was horrified and yet fascinated by her weeping, childlike, unabashed, unconcealed. Her eyelids swelled, her small round nose grew red and she did not care.

"I swear you must carry a tank of tears in you somewhere,"

298

he went on irritably. "I never saw a grown woman who could cry the way that you do." He stumped out of the room and to his own study. But he could not bear his own loneliness. In less than an hour he was looking for her, shouting through the house—

"Mollie, damn you, where are you?"

A faint voice answered from far off.

"I'm cleaning the attic!"

Up the stairs he stumped, panting, to find her sitting in dust and cobwebs. He began immediately.

"Mollie, do I have to go all over the arguments again?"

She looked at him with tear-washed eyes as clear as a child's. "I don't have to agree with you, Burt, and I don't. You used that bomb, all of you, because it was something you'd made and you couldn't bear not to use it. So you argued yourself into righteousness but that doesn't make you righteous. . . . I wish I knew what Jane thinks of it. I'd like to talk to her."

"Well, you can't. She's resigned. She's going to India."

She was shocked. "India! That means she can't bear what you've done, either."

"She's a fool," Burt growled. "What can she do in India? She'll make a grave in some village or other and bury herself. She's a scientist, a genius, but she can't take it because she's a woman."

"You can't, either," Mollie said. "Don't think you're fooling me, Burt. You hate yourself."

He blustered. "No, I don't. I—I—I—"

"You hate yourself," she maintained. "And you don't know what to do with yourself now. You're trying to think up some sort of good work. You won't go to India, but you'll— you'll—"

They argued for hours there in the attic, she weeping again and again until her face looked like a steamed pudding,

299

and yet, she was as impervious to his arguments and his reasons as she had been when they began this morning. Neither of them ate any luncheon. They did not answer the telephone. It was enough to bring on another attack and he reminded her of this several times and she ignored him. With her habitual simple and unerring instinct devoid of reason, she pierced him straight to the heart. He collapsed finally into a broken chair and put his hands over his face and groaned.

"I'm sick. I'm really sick. I still say we had to do it. But I want to get out of the whole damned business. . . . What else could I have done? But I yield to this extent—I ought not to have let myself be put in that position. The glory of science compelled me to devise superlative means to murder—what's that but sin against the Holy Christ? The unforgivable sin—"

She stopped him firmly. "Burt, don't you get to maundering, like your father. There's no use punishing yourself for what you've already done. You've got to think what you want to do now. What do you want to do?"

He lifted his head. "Mollie," he said brokenly. "I've always wondered whether you're stupid. Now I know you're not."

"Of course I am," she said.

Her tears dried and her voice resumed the energy of its usual cheerfulness. This meant that she had reduced him and that she knew it. She put back the strands of her disordered hair and continued, "You're too old to go climbing up mountains and sweating in jungles to learn some more about cosmic rays. And I'm getting too old to follow you around. You ought to find some nice job teaching or something, in a nice college. Let the young people do the hard work."

"By golly," he said in honest admiration. "How did you know? That's exactly what I want to do." He rose and put

300

out his arms inviting her to rise to his embrace. "You know me better than I know myself," he said.

"Of course I do," she said, and came into his arms. "What else have I had to think about all these years?"

They embraced, he patted her plump buttocks, and they went downstairs. The calm of his house was restored. She would powder her ravaged face and then go to the kitchen and find comfort in baking an apple pie. And in the quiet he would plan the rest of his life. . . .

He returned to his study and to peaceful reflection. A good fight with Mollie was restoration. He could think about his next job . . . the scientists.

They were leaving the mesa like rats fleeing from the proverbial ship. A ship was not a bad metaphor in that dry and desert sea. And industry would take over completely the great works in the northwest and in Tennessee. The reactors would now begin to irradiate the isotopes of peace. But beneath and above all else was his promise not to allow the creative essence hidden in the nucleus of the atoms to remain in the hands of the generals. It must be put in the hands of civilians, men—and women, too, he supposed, when he thought of Jane—whose purpose was to create life and not death. He'd get his scientists together, they would descend upon Washington and make such a disturbance that the nation would hear and heed. Then when the hubbub was over he'd retire to a certain small college he knew, a religious place, founded by a father of the church, and he'd spend the rest of his life there, teaching and training men and women to be fit to use the divine energy.

Here in his shabby study, alone with such thoughts, he laughed silently and deeply. How clever of God to hide the dynamo of creation in a thing so small that the eye of a human being could not see it! And how diabolically clever of that human being to devise ways of enlarging his vision and stretching his sight so that he caught at least the shadow of the reality and with his monstrous imagination guessed the truth! Adam, Adam! The Garden of Eden was happy ignorance and now it was lost forever. He had eaten of the fruit of the Tree of Knowledge, and there had been no Eve, either, to hand him the rosy apple. He had only himself to blame.

✻   ✻   ✻

Raman rose early by habit and he was now sprinkling his laboratory and his house with water from the holy Ganges. The morning was cool and sunny, and his brown and handsome face was as calm as his soul. The house was quiet, his children grown and gone, and his wife was a thin wisp of a woman who did not rise from her bed until late afternoon. He was proud of his children, his son a trusted secretary of the Viceroy in New Delhi, and his daughter a governor in one of the provinces. Sita had gone into politics as so many young Indian women did nowadays, but she had also married and had children. She was lucky to be living in India, he reflected, where there were plenty of ayahs to take care of the children. Pity about western women, tied to their household tasks! His dear Jane had never married.

"Beloved child," he had said last night when they sat on the veranda in the moonlight, "why do you not marry?"

"I should have to give up my work if I had children," she said.

"You might marry a rich man," he suggested.

"I'd only marry a scientist," she said, "and he'd never be rich." And then with a glance from her dark eyes to his, she had added, "The real reason is that I do not wish to be married."

Her Hindi was perfect. She had forgotten nothing. And with her smooth dark hair and brunette skin she might have

302

been his daughter, except that he never thought of her as a daughter. She was his pupil, his charge, his dear concern. He was vastly proud of her brilliant brain. He had turned from marriage talk to talk of the atomic energy.

"Yes, yes," he had said impatiently. "But it is very unfortunate that your countrymen should have made the divine fire into a weapon to destroy other men. The thing is done and now we must forget it and consider the future. What do they plan?"

"Nothing for the moment," she replied. "We need first to recover from success. You should have seen the men hasten from the mesa, Babu. Suddenly they thought of many things they wished to do—anything to get away. They returned to their classrooms and to their laboratories in big industries, which they had been eager to leave. Yes, they were happy on the mesa. They had reveled in one another's company— great company, Babu. I reveled in it, too. To be able to speak to one's peers every day! We had scientists there who had worked alone in industrial research doing what they were told to do instead of what they wanted to do—making discoveries to sell. And suddenly they were taken away from such loneliness to live only with scientists."

"Great joy," he agreed. "I feel that joy when you and I talk together."

When they had parted for the night they did not touch hands. Instead each had made the gesture of reverence to the other, palm to palm. . . . He had not slept well, nevertheless. The truth remained alive in his heart that he had never loved any woman as he loved Jane. He did not deny or contend. He had learned to live with truth. But his flesh still stirred. He might have married her long ago, but he would not take advantage of her young love, not even on that last night of her graduation from the school where he had been her teacher. She had sobbed against his breast, and he would never forget the warmth of her in his arms. His determination had held, nevertheless. Long ago he had chosen his place. He had given himself to India.

"But I'll live here," she had sobbed. "I love India, too."

"I will not allow you to live here," he had told her. "You belong to your own country. You must leave me."

He had found the strength for these words. Knowing already the incomparable quality of her mind, he could not accept such sacrifice, even for love.

Nor had he regretted his decision. Here was his home, the familiar rooms fresh and consecrated again to his work and to the gods. He had eaten early this morning, and now he sat down upon the high stool in his laboratory, facing the snow-capped mountains beyond the green valleys of Almora. Before him on the table was the instrument, infinitely delicate, with which he measured through an electrical charge the sensitive areas of a carrot, impaled by a steel knife. He watched the waves of shock move in wavering lines upon a sheet of paper beneath the needle trembling across the page. He was interrupted.

"Of what use is it to know that a carrot also suffers, Babu?"

Jane's voice, over his shoulder! He turned and smiled. She was barefoot and he had not heard her enter, but she was here, smiling, in a pale yellow sari, silver bracelets on her wrists.

"You look rested," he said.

"I am rested," she replied.

"To answer your question," he went on, "one may say truly that it only adds to the sum of suffering in the world to know that this golden vegetable also knows pain when impaled. To me, however, the importance is the proof that all life is one. Carrot or man, we suffer. Pain is our common possession. . . . Have you had your breakfast? I told the servants to take it to your room."

"I have eaten."

He touched a button on his machine and shut off the electricity.

"Don't stop your work, Babu."

"I can work all the other days of my life," he said, "and why should I work the few days you are here?"

"Is it to be only a few days, Babu?"

"Not more," he said with decision. "This is not the place for you to work. I cannot allow it. You must return to the centers of science, far from here. You must return to your own country."

She sighed. "Oh Babu, when I have only just come, less than a month ago, you are sending me away again. Am I not to stay a year or two?"

"No," he said. He led the way through a corridor to a cool marble-floored room, furnished only in bright satin cushions. They sat down, she at his feet.

"Let me stay with you," she murmured.

"I will not allow you to stay with me," he said cheerfully. "We have what there is between us, wherever you are. You cannot return to your childhood."

A scent of dust and water rose from the flower beds beyond the verandas. The gardener was watering the flowers and the grass. A child laughed somewhere loudly and a woman called. Peace was the atmosphere, an exquisite peace, restoring the soul.

"This is not reality," he went on. "It is not the center of the world. Some day, perhaps, but not in this age. The center is in your country, not mine."

"Why will you not acknowledge yourself?" she inquired. "You are half English."

"That is why I send you away," he said. "I cannot let you

305

live too near me. I must enjoin you to leave me. I am still too young to be safe. When I am old and blind you may come back and live here in my house."

She laughed, half sighing. "Babu—if you only knew—there is a man on the other side of the sea who said those same words to me—"

"Tell me about him."

She told him about Stephen, hiding nothing. He listened, intent upon her look and word. "You love this man?"

"I think so."

"But he is married?"

"Yes."

"Then you are fortunate."

"Fortunate, Babu? I am miserable. First to love you and now to love him!"

"You are very fortunate. You are saved alive by this love. You love, but you are forbidden by life to yield."

He put up a long narrow hand to silence her. "You are one of those who would be destroyed by love. So would I be destroyed. Do you think I could dare to love you as I have longed to love? You would destroy me. We are the ones who must live alone."

This was his theme now that she was here. He returned to it again and again, whatever they talked about, and she knew that with his inimitable and habitual skill he was teaching her, enlightening her mind, toughening her will, compelling her to return to her own work.

. . . "It would be sad," he began on another day, "very sad, my child, if you were to lose the immense joy of progressive knowledge. Were you to stay here with me, you would learn something, yes. I am a biophysicist and I make my own small experiments. But I, too, need connection with the greater centers of energy. For example, when you return to your own place, I shall wish to experiment with radiation,

306

by your help. How do we know what this new energy will do to plants and their seeds? It is the energy of the sun which enables the plants to fulfill their function to feed mankind. Who understands photosynthesis? I cannot hope to work with a reactor here in India for years to come. We have not reached that era. But you are already living in the future and I can reach out to you—"

She knew what he was doing. He was enticing her, a spiritual seduction, delicate and infinitely powerful. He was daring her to be a great scientist but with complete faith, using their love as the propellent.

. . . "Now," he began on yet another day. "There is this matter of living human tissue. I do not work with human flesh and bone and blood but see how it is here about us, everywhere corrupted."

They were walking down the street and the beggers showed their sores and their knotted joints. A leper stood and sunned himself by a wall. Before the leper Raman paused, cane in hand, and pointed at the rotted flesh of the man's thigh, at his white and protruding bones.

"Could you help this fellow if you stayed? No, you can fulfill nothing here. You must use the new energy that you have helped to discover. It may be that this flesh can be healed again. You have no right to deny the possibility."

. . . When a score of days had passed she yielded suddenly. "I know what you are doing, Babu. You are breathing the breath of life into my nostrils, as a god breathes. You are saying something to me. I hear your words, but what is your meaning?"

It was evening and they sat in the garden in white wicker chairs. Raman's childlike wife had drifted away to her own rooms, leaving them together. She was a graceful friend, humbly knowing that there was something between these two that she could not understand. Raman was teacher and

Jane was pupil. It was a holy bond, good and not to be broken. From beyond the wall a strain of music wound into the air, repeated again and again in a clutch of melody.

Raman lifted his head and gazed into the sky and Jane saw his profile, clear and beautiful in the twilight. She loved him but she was not in love with him any more. In his own delicate and definite fashion he had made such love impossible, not by rejection but by recognizing it, and acknowledging it without passion. My beloved, he called her, but without passion.

"There are many ways of expiation for sin," he said, "and the best of all, the only true one, is to live. You feel you have sinned, a huge collective sin, I know, but for yourself you can expiate it. I wish you to return to your work. You will leave me tomorrow."

"I must obey you," she said. "But will you allow letters, Babu?"

"Until we die," he said.

＊　　　＊　　　＊

Yasuo Matsugi was free again. He packed his small goods and wandered out of the gate now freely open in the tangled barbed-wire fence. He refused all offers of help from the relocation centers and, laden with boxes and bags, he set off on foot to the tin-roofed railroad station. He was going to Chicago where he would rent a small apartment and begin to paint. And he would find his friend Burton Hall.

On an October morning, therefore, Burton Hall found Yasuo upon his doorstep.

"My God, Yasuo—come in," he bellowed.

He dragged the slender Japanese into the house and slammed the door. "You're staying here," he announced. "You stay in our guest room until you find a place to live.

And we'll talk for hours—I want to explain everything to you. I'm dead beat from having a fight of my own in Washington but I've won. The Little Boss is setting up a civilian agency to handle the hot stuff. . . . Oh, the big boys in the Pentagon will have their two cents' worth, but they won't have all the say-so. Mollie, Yasuo is here! Put some rice on the stove for dinner. Sit down, feller. I'll go and find her."

Yasuo sat down on the edge of a chair and waited while Burt tramped to the kitchen. He was back in a moment.

"She isn't here—must have gone to the grocery or something. She'll be back. Come into my study."

He limped ahead of Yasuo and the two men sat down in the shabby old room. Burt's eyes filled with the tears that came too easily to his eyes nowadays. "Gosh, I'm glad it's over. We're still friends, eh, Yasuo?"

"I come to you first," Yasuo said simply.

"You going to start painting right away?"

Yasuo hesitated. "I don't know what I do first. Sometimes I think I go back to Japan for a little while, not to stay. I want to see how is Japan now. If it is different I better to know. Else I get mixed up in my pictures."

"I wish you wouldn't go," Burt said.

"Why not to go?" Yasuo asked, surprised.

"I don't know. Yeah, I do know. I don't want your heart broken."

"Maybe we both better to go," Yasuo suggested.

"I? What for?"

"To see what," Yasuo said quietly. "Then you know. I know as artist, you know as scientist. So we both know."

Burt got to his feet and went limping up and down the room. "I never thought of going over there. Maybe you're right. I wonder what Steve would think of it?" Maybe he'll want to go along."

Impulsive always, he took up the telephone and called

his office. "I want to talk to Steve Coast. No, I don't know where he is now—still on the mesa, I reckon. I haven't heard different. . . . Well, call me back."

In fifteen minutes he was called back and heard Steve's voice from the distance. "Hi, Steve, Yasuo and I are going to Japan. Right away. You want to come?"

He listened and Yasuo waited. Then he put up the receiver. "He doesn't want to come. Says he's through. He's taken a job with Canaday-Farrell. . . . Okay, Yasuo, it's you and me together. We'll fly. Wait till Mollie hears this—"

When she came in with the groceries half an hour later, he was dashed to find that she approved.

"I think you ought to go over there, Burt. You just ought to see what you all have done. You oughtn't to run away from the results."

"My God," he breathed. "Here I'd got myself all hepped up to have a fight with you—"

She swept on, ignoring him. "And I'm glad that Yasuo is going with you. You must make him wear a sweater under his coat, Yasuo. He gets cold easy now and he forgets everything when he's interested."

"I tell him," Yasuo said.

"And now," she said, "you two men clear out of my kitchen. I'm going to stir up a cake for Yasuo."

＊　　　＊　　　＊

The great airplane soared in a wide curve above the city of Tokyo and settled down on the runway. It had been impossible to hide the arrival of Burton Hall and Yasuo Matsugi. Scientist and artist, they were news, and when they walked down the airfield, a swarm of newspapermen followed. An American official met them and muttered while he shook hands.

"Don't talk here. I have a press conference arranged at the hotel. They're out for blood. I hope you have your arguments."

"Do we have our arguments, Yasuo?" Burt inquired. He was in high mood, embattled, daring, defying a creeping exhaustion.

"We don't have to argument," Yasuo said. "We just here to see what is happening next after what happening before."

An hour later, nevertheless, in a sumptuous private suite at the Imperial Hotel, Burt felt the need of every argument. The room was crowded with keen spectacled young Japanese, among them a few pale faces, an Englishman for the London papers, an Italian and a Frenchman—no American yet. He sprawled carelessly in a big round-bottomed chair while Yasuo sat erect by the table, his hands folded.

The American officer introduced them and Burt grinned.

"So fire away," he said amiably.

The faces confronting him did not smile back. They were serious, observing, inquiring. A young man spoke, his pencil poised above his notebook.

"Dr. Hall, why did America make the bomb?"

Oh Lord help me, Burt groaned inside his soul. How can I take this? Why did I ever come?

Aloud he was belligerent. "I'll ask you another question by the way of answer. Why did you bomb Pearl Harbor?"

"We did not," the young man said promptly. "It was only military men. But you are scientist. Scientist is noble man, like philosopher."

How explain to this young intellectual that philosophy will not save a nation in time of war?

"You are a journalist, are you not? Then why didn't you stop your military men?"

Bewilderment spread over the bleak young face. "Oh

311

hell," Burt said. "What's the use of pot-and-kettle talk? The war's over. And we want to be friends."

"It is impossible forever," the young man said.

Burt leaped out of his chair roaring. "Impossible? Not unless you make it so—" The argument was on. It lasted four hours.

*   *   *

"Is it impossible, Yasuo?" Burt asked.

"You better forget that simple young man talk," Yasuo replied cheerfully.

They stood on the flank of the mountain above Nagasaki and looked down upon the ruins of what had been Yasuo Matsugi's home city. He had wept for a while when they came upon the rubble of what had been his childhood home and the tears had left silvery streaks upon his brown cheeks. Burt had wept a little, too, reluctantly, refusing to believe that there could have been alternatives. Or if there were, they had been buried long ago in the ignorance, the careless obliviousness between peoples. It was all too late now. New houses would be built, new children born, and what had been done was not to be undone. The two men stood, both exhausted, upon a rocky spur of the pine-covered slope. They had been to Hiroshima. They knew all there was to be known, they had seen the people about whom newspapermen had made reports and newscasters had talked on radio and television, and they wanted to go home.

"You think it will all be forgotten some day, Yasuo?"

"Never forgotten," Yasuo said. "How can you forget or I forget? We remember. But we don't think. We have to work. I paint, you teach. No use to stay here. We can't build. We are too old. We only do our own work. Never mind anything more, ever."

"I guess you're right," Burt said.

312

Their journey had been too swift, too crowded. He had refused other interviews and all invitations. He wanted to see, to understand, and go home. How it had all happened he found it more difficult than ever to explain. While it was being done, the great brotherhood of scientists working with the General and with Starleigh, it had been a sacred duty and obligation. He knew it had been that. But he could not understand how it had become duty and obligation. These Japanese were wonderful people. If he'd known them before it all became so sacred and necessary, he could never have made the bomb. It would not have been necessary and certainly not sacred.

"I guess I'm tired," he told Yasuo.

"I am being tired, too," Yasuo said.

They walked down the mountain, Burt following Yasuo along the narrow stone-paved path that wound between the spurs of the mountain. Down in the valley again, down by the seashore, they stepped into the small military plane detailed to take them to Tokyo and the great Constellation that would carry them back to America. They slept a good deal over the Pacific Ocean, and neither of them had appetite for the good food nor indeed, Burt thought, wryly, for the pretty girls who served it. The fire in him was dying. He supposed he ought to be glad, but he wasn't. From now on he would be an old man. He had planned to stop at the big observatory to commune with the stars once more, but he decided against it. The stars could wait. He'd meet them face to face and soon enough one of these days, maybe—that is, if there was anything to those notions his father had given him. A new heaven and a new earth? He'd believe it when he saw it.

He wanted to get home, he wanted to see Mollie. And he dreamed of a comfortable classroom, young faces lifted to learn and to listen and the morning sun shining through the windows.

*   *   *

Stephen lifted the stiff body from the kennel and laid it tenderly on the basement floor. Scrap was dead. Sometime during the night the old dog's heart had ceased to beat. Well, he had died at home, and beside him was the feeding bowl, still warm. At least he had eaten warm bread and milk at the end.

Steve went to the foot of the stairs.

"Helen, Scrap died in his sleep last night."

"Oh no, Steve—"

She came hurrying down the wooden steps. "Oh poor Scrap—" She stooped and stroked the stiff white coat. "Why, he seemed all right yesterday—"

"He was old," Steve said. "I guess it was his time. Lucky dog at that—to live out his time."

"Now, Steve—"

"No, I'm not going to talk about it, Helen, or think about it. . . . The plans for the house came today from the architect's office."

"You didn't tell me!"

"I was going to—shall we bury him?"

"Yes—out under the poplar where he liked to sleep, don't you think?"

"Yes. Is there a box?"

He reached for the spade and Helen found a wooden box she had kept for kindling. It was long and narrow and Steve lifted Scrap into it. They walked to the poplar tree in the back yard.

"You needn't stay," he said, digging.

"I want to," she said.

They were sad, a little, but not very sad. They would

314

never be as sad again as they had been a year ago when two cities they had never seen were leveled to ash and rubble. Nothing would ever be as sad. Nor would they ever be as gay as they had been before. They had recovered. Stephen was earning more money than he ever had before, and he had more freedom for research than he had imagined possible in a great industry. His employers respected him, were even awed by his extraordinary achievements on the mesa.

"Just let your brain go to work, Steve," Starleigh said.

Yes, Canaday-Farrell were good employers. He had a fine job, an assured position, and he did not allow himself to think that what he was doing now had any relation with what had happened on the mesa. He heard from Jane occasionally. She was working in photosynthesis. Wise, he wrote her, biology was the coming science. The improvement of life, the creation of new life, was the next area. They'd gone about as far as they could in physics, for a while at least. The space-travel people, the military men and all the rest of them had to catch up with theory now. This missile business—last time he'd been in Washington he found the youngsters, all bright as silver buttons, talking a new language of their own making. "Azusa system," "bootstrapping," "zip fuels—"

"Wait a minute," he said, "what's all this talk? What's Azusa system?"

They had laughed. "Apparatus that measures velocity and position during flight."

"And bootstrapping?"

"Feeding back some of the engine output to drive it faster and increase speed—"

"Seen this?" a yellow-haired boy of twenty-two demanded. "This" was an easily detached cable powering a missile on its vertical stand. "Umbilical cord," the kid

315

grinned, "and zip fuel is a high energy fuel, based on boron—"

"Oh yes," their chief had said proudly. "They make their own talk, these fellows. God knows what they'll be saying when they come back from space travel. Yeah, no doubt of it. Space travel's the coming thing. It'll keep us too busy to think about wars, maybe. I'll say this for the big blast you men made in the desert—it's sent us ahead a thousand years."

"I don't know if it was worth it," Stephen had said.

"One never knows," the man had agreed cheerfully. "Gotta take it as it comes—"

He went back to Chicago and talked to Burt about what he had seen. Burt was just back from Japan but he hadn't talked much about what he'd seen there.

"No use talking," he had said. "We're already obsolete, Steve. We've worked for four years, all of us, on the Project. We succeeded. We made the bomb and it ended the war. But it's what we used to call it—a gadget. A mere gadget. And we're old hat. The kids aren't thinking about us any more or even about the bomb. Oh, the military fellows will play around with it, but they're old hat, too, though it takes them a long time to know it. Maybe never—

"But these kids! We found the divine fire for them and they grabbed it away from us. They're riding into space on the wings of power. . . . Lord, lord." He scratched his head and put his feet on a chair. "It makes me think of my father. How my mind goes back! I'm getting old, Steve. I've grown old since the big days on the mesa. My dad was fond of roaring the Old Testament at me. He liked it a lot better than the New. He said he could set his teeth in it. I remember a sermon he preached out of Job—where God asks Job kind of sarcastically why he should think himself so high and mighty that he couldn't endure a little of the suffering common to humanity.

316

" 'Hast thou,' God asked, 'hast thou commanded the morning?'

"Well, it put Job in his place, I reckon. He was meek and lowly by the time God had finished with him. I know how he felt—kind of like the way I feel. But I don't know about these kids nowadays. I have a hunch that when the first one goes soaring off into space and driving for the moon with the energy that you and I and all those longhairs had something to do with, Steve, he'll yell back to the rest of us here on the little old earth:

" 'Yeah, man, I do command the morning!' "

EPILOGUE

Nuclear Power Liberated; The Creation
of Plutonium, 1943–1944

Hail, miracle, which in these dreadful years
We built, drawn on by hopes, and goaded on by fears.
Hail, man-made star! God help us who aspire
To fan spent embers left from cosmic fire!

For this phlogiston's weight was vainly tried
And Newton linked the whirling earth and moon.
How many minds at Nature's secrets pried
Through the dim hours before this glorious noon?

Hail, resurrected metal, which we thought had gone,
Æons before, in the galactic dawn!
Our eyes can see, our very hands can feel
A ghost incarnate, a primordial steel!

Spawner of elements! Triumph making pale
The dreams of alchemists! But, shall we fail
To use with wisdom worthy of our skill
This transcendental power for good or ill?

—S. K. ALLISON
Physicist